the
truth
about
love

the
truth
about
love

SHEILA ATHENS

Text copyright © 2014 Sheila Athens

Published by Montlake Romance, Seattle

www.apub.com

ISBN-13: 9781477825624
ISBN-10: 1477825622

Cover design by Eileen Carey

Library of Congress Control Number: 2014907967

Printed in the United States of America

To Linda Sue (Houchen) Hammer, who taught me about all the good in the world and for passing on her love of books.

To Lena Diaz and Valerie Bowman for believing in me.

To my husband and sons. Thanks for giving me the luxury of quiet time to write. You all are my rock. And, boys—I hope this shows you that any goal is worth pursuing if it is important to you.

CHAPTER ONE

W ho *is* Big Red anyway?" Landon angled his chin toward the tall strawberry blonde standing with her volleyball teammates on the other side of the sports bar.

Boomer laughed as he swung his arm across the back of the booth. "You mean the girl who just kicked your ass?"

"She must have played in college somewhere." No girl had ever gone toe-to-toe with Landon at the net like she had. Hell, no *guy* had ever done that.

He took a pull from his longneck beer and studied her. She had to be six feet tall. Maybe even six one. And she wore it proudly—an athlete whose height had served her well. Worn orange kneepads hung at her ankles like badges of honor from victories of the past.

"You think she played at Florida State?" Boomer asked.

Landon shook his head. "I'd have met her at an athletic banquet or something." After all, Tallahassee had been *his* town for the last five years. He'd pretty much owned it since earning the starting quarterback position his sophomore year. And even though he'd been out of college for two years now, this town worshiped its football players in perpetuity.

Yes, he'd definitely have noticed her.

"And someone would have recruited her onto their team a long time ago," Boomer said.

Landon nodded in agreement as he watched her across the bar. She tugged at the bottom of her bright red shirt—a jersey that had undoubtedly belonged to a smaller player the previous season. Landon's gaze slid from the fabric pulled tight over her breasts to the hint of skin that peeked out above the waistband of her shorts.

Ricardo slid into the booth seat beside him, jarring his attention back to their table.

"You up for some hoops on Saturday?" his friend asked before breaking into a sarcastic grin. "Or are you going to practice your spikes instead?"

Ricardo and Boomer bumped fists, a little too happy that Landon may have met his athletic match.

He drilled them both with a glare. "Can't. I'm helping Imelda move."

"Imelda?"

"The lady who sweeps the gym. She's moving to a new apartment."

"Since when are you tight with the cleaning crew?"

"I talk to her sometimes. Her husband had back surgery last week and she was telling me how they had to get a new place." Landon paused before he took another swig of beer. "I told her you two would help."

Boomer grunted and looked toward Ricardo. "He didn't really tell her that. He's just pissed 'cause the tall girl made him look bad."

Ricardo chuckled. "Let's hope she doesn't play rec football in the fall. I'd hate for her to make him look bad there, too."

"My place," Landon said. "Saturday morning at nine o'clock." He pushed Ricardo over toward the edge of the booth. "Now let me out."

Ricardo complied. "Where are you going?"

Landon inclined his head to indicate the group across the room. "To talk to the competition."

He watched her as he ordered a couple of beers at the scarred wooden bar. She stood near the rest of her team, talking with a couple of the girls and the stocky guy with the knee brace. Like everyone else on their teams, she'd come straight from the gym. He liked the camaraderie. Reminded him how most of the players used to hang out together during his football days.

He paid the bartender and headed Red's way with the beers, trying to remember the last time he'd found a girl this interesting.

"Trying to forget your loss?" one of her teammates teased as Landon approached their group with two bottles in his hands.

"A peace offering," he said. "For the new girl." The redhead's eyebrows rose as he handed her the beer, the same brand he'd seen her drinking from across the room.

"You didn't buy me a drink when *I* was new," the stocky guy said. "But I guess I'm not your type."

The team hooted with laughter as they scooted away and gave him some space. He clinked the neck of his bottle against the one he'd just handed her. "Good game tonight."

"Thanks. They should have warned me the other team had some height." She grinned. He'd noticed her great smile from across the court earlier, but it was even better now that it was focused only on him.

"I'm Landon." He offered a handshake. "Landon Vista."

"Sounds like a subdivision," she teased as she placed her hand in his. "Gina Blanchard."

She had a firm grip, but with a softness that made him want to hold it longer. Her eyes locked on his long enough for him to know that she, too, was intrigued.

He liked her confidence. The way she stood her ground. "You've played a game or two of volleyball before."

"University of Tennessee." She slid her hand away, her fingertips lingering on his. "And you played football at FSU."

Ahhh, so she did know who he was. He normally disliked his regional celebrity and the people who'd fawned over him during his playing days. And since that time, those pitying looks that implied he should have done more with his football talent. But in this case, the notoriety seemed to be working in his favor.

"You a Seminoles fan?" The garnet and gold of the Florida State Seminoles blanketed this college town, which pretty much made him a hero to the local fans, whether he liked it or not.

Her ponytail floated in a gentle swish behind her as she shook her head. "Just here for the summer. An internship at a local non-profit. For law school."

Stacked *and* smart. "We come here after every game. Kind of a tradition."

She looked around the dimly lit bar where patrons in their twenties and early thirties moved from table to table greeting friends. "It's cool how everybody knows each other."

"Some grew up in Tallahassee," he said. "Some came for college and never left." He'd always liked the small-town feel of the place. "Seminole blood gets in your veins."

"That must make you a pretty important guy around here." She gave him a teasing grin as she raised the beer to her lips.

"Yeah, I used to be a real player. 'Til some girl started blocking all my shots in volleyball."

She laughed. "My mom used to tell me to take it easy on the boys on the playground."

The chorus of a country song bellowed from the jukebox. Several people in the crowd joined in. Landon moved closer to talk over the music. She was tall, but he still had three or four inches on her. A chubby man with a pool cue passed behind her, pressing her toward Landon. Her breast grazed his arm.

He tried to ignore the frisson of awareness that sizzled between them. That one touch gave him the urge to pull her closer. To see if her skin felt as soft as it looked. "Doesn't seem like you listened very well," he said.

"At least not in volleyball." She gave him a flirtatious smile. "But it doesn't seem to have scared you off."

He chuckled. He liked a woman who would challenge him. A woman whose brains were as attractive as her body.

"And what did your mom teach you growing up?" she asked.

He sucked in a breath. A jagged memory, like a shard of broken glass, lanced through his brain. The picture of a country store flashed through his mind—his mother's body bent over the counter, her white thrift-store tennis shoes soaked in blood. That picture he couldn't shake, no matter how many years had passed. He groped for something else to talk about. Luckily, the crowd started to sing along with "Sweet Home Alabama," which gave him an opportunity to change the subject.

"It's kind of noisy in here." He glanced through the windows toward the outside deck. "You want to go out on the patio?" At least heading out there would give him a few seconds to think of a different topic of conversation.

She nodded and made her way through the boisterous crowd to the door to the deck. The thick humidity weighed them down the second they stepped outside.

The moonlight glinted off her hair as she settled her hips against the porch's railing and faced him. The few loose tendrils that framed her face danced from the soft breeze of the ceiling fan.

"So what does the famous Landon Vista do now that he's not playing football?" she asked.

He cocked his head to look at her. He liked her teasing tone. Her playfulness. "You guys at Tennessee probably hated me."

"You were the guy my father cursed at while we watched the game on TV." She tucked a strand of hair behind her ear. He wished he could do it for her. "I saw you play in person a couple of times."

"Yeah? How'd I do?"

"I think we won once and you won once."

He nodded, though he knew the score of every game he'd played during his college career. He'd never lost to her alma mater. "You guys were always tough to beat."

"So what do you do now that football is over?"

"I work in Senator Byers's office."

Her eyebrows rose. She started to say something, then stopped herself.

He laughed. "What's that look supposed to mean?"

"My boss has done battle with Senator Byers since he got elected to office. She pretty much thinks he's the Antichrist."

"Because he fights for tougher sentencing laws?"

"Because he doesn't understand the notion of innocent until proven guilty. He just wants to lock them all away."

"No—he just wants criminals to have long sentences. So they won't commit more crimes." *Shit.* How did this conversation go in such a random direction? He didn't want to be talking politics with a girl who . . . looked like that. Sure, he wanted to do a lot of things with her, but this wasn't one of them. "Where is your internship, anyway?"

"At a nonprofit called Morgan's Ladder." She tugged at the bottom of her shirt. "We help wrongly convicted prisoners get out of prison—"

"Using DNA evidence." His work for the tough-on-crime senator meant he'd come across Morgan's Ladder a few times before. He thought of Cyrus Alexander, the man Landon had seen running from the country store the day his mother had been murdered. The day his life had changed forever. Thank God Cyrus Alexander would never get out of prison.

"Maybe not what you bargained for when you bought the new girl a beer, huh?" she asked.

Not even close.

She smiled. "I do have some other redeeming qualities."

There was that playfulness again. He definitely liked the playfulness. "And what might those be?"

"I bake the second-best lasagna anyone's ever eaten."

"Only second best? That's disappointing." He took a step toward her, enjoying the closeness. Glad they were the only ones on the quiet patio. The beat of a raucous country song from inside the bar thrummed at the windows, but seemed miles away.

"My mother bakes the best, but I use her recipe."

"And what else?"

"Hmmmm . . . let's see." Her gaze fell briefly as she thought, then rose again, her eyes bright. Her forefinger rested briefly on his chest with a playful poke. Her light touch burned him with anticipation. "I'm pretty sure I can still do a backflip off the diving board."

"Seems like a useful skill for an attorney." He stepped toward her as she relaxed back onto the railing behind her.

She laughed—a light, airy sound that floated into the Spanish moss hanging from the trees on the other side of the railing.

"And what else?" He wanted to keep her talking. Maybe she'd never have to leave if the conversation didn't end.

She gave a sultry smile. "I'm a really good kisser." Her voice had dropped to a husky whisper.

"Oh, yeah?" His hands rose to the railing behind her, framing her hips. "How do you know?"

"Mickey Taylor told me." Her chin slanted to a cocky angle. "He was my boyfriend freshman year of high school. I had to break up with him when I got to be four inches taller than he was. Tall girls feel gigantic when they date guys who are shorter than they are."

"I'm six foot four," he said, nudging closer to her. He was almost always the biggest guy in the room.

She leaned forward and whispered playfully. "Then you would be taller than I am."

"So Mickey said you were a good kisser?"

She hesitated, then nodded slowly. An invitation.

His gaze rose to hers. "Maybe you should prove it."

~

Gina's skin prickled in the humid air as Landon's lips grazed hers. Once. Twice.

"Is this okay?" His voice was barely a whisper.

"Yes," she said, bathing in the warmth of his breath. His lips settled on hers, soft and gentle. His tongue flicked against her lips— flirty, but not too aggressive. God, what was she doing? The last time she'd kissed a guy without going out on a date first was during Truth or Dare in Megan Crane's basement when she was thirteen years old.

But this felt so good. There was no way she could stop herself. Her body had been on alert since she'd first seen him in the gym tonight—his shoulders, arms, and calves sculpted with muscle, but not bulked up like some overmeaty weightlifter or football lineman. When he'd raised the bottom of his shirt to wipe the sweat off his forehead, she'd gotten a glimpse of his lean, flat belly. That sexy little trail of dark hair that disappeared into the waistband of his nylon shorts had made her warm all over.

And now here he was kissing her. Touching her. Making her want to get even closer to him.

She rose from where she leaned on the railing. His well-muscled body invited her to press against it, to thrill over its hard planes. She opened her lips, welcoming him in. A masculine groan echoed in his chest. His hand rose to her jaw. His fingertips swept across her skin. His touch was so gentle. So unexpected for a man who'd made a name for himself being mauled by oversize linemen. For the first time in ages, she felt wanted.

In the periphery of her brain, the door from the bar swung open. She pulled away from him, suddenly aware of another presence on the patio. His hands fell to her hips and held her still, as if he didn't want to let her go.

"Hey, Landon. We're up on the pool table," a male voice said from the doorway, but Gina's brain didn't register anything other than a blur standing at the door. Her senses danced around her—Landon's scent, his dark, curly hair, those distinctive olive-green eyes.

"Find someone else to play," he said, his gaze not leaving hers.

"It's those guys from last week," the male voice said. "They've been talking smack all night about how they're going to beat us."

"Not tonight." Still, his attention didn't leave her.

"You're really going to walk away from a rematch?" the male voice said from the doorway.

Landon's shoulders dropped. "You'll still be here when I finish the game?" he asked her.

She shook her head. "I told my friend . . ." She quickly thought of ways to change the commitment she'd made to her teammate.

"Then Saturday night. Can I see you then?"

Her heart hammered in her chest. "I'd like that."

He pulled his cell phone from his pocket. "What's your number?"

She reached for the phone and enjoyed the surprised look on his face as she gently slid it from his hand. She punched in her name and number, then handed it back to him.

He grinned and nodded. "Saturday night."

"Thanks for the beer," she called as he headed toward the door to go back inside the bar.

He smiled as he turned to look at her. "No problem."

"And sorry you had to lose tonight."

He chuckled, a low, husky sound that echoed through the night air. "I don't consider tonight a loss at all."

∼

Gina smiled as she read the text that popped up on her phone.

Is it Saturday night yet?

She glanced toward Suzanne's doorway to see if her boss could see her. Only she and Suzanne worked for the small nonprofit full time. Gina didn't want to get caught goofing off during her second week on the job.

And last night's texting marathon with Landon Vista had shown her that the two of them could go back and forth for hours as they got to know each other.

She smiled as she typed her response. *Does the senator know you're texting the opposition during work hours?*

I don't want to talk about work.

Good. Because neither did she. Talking about her job would lead to questions—what she did all day, how she'd come to work at Morgan's Ladder. She wasn't sure how to tell someone she'd put an innocent boy in jail. That the grief of her brother's death had been compounded by her own unforgivable mistake. That she'd come to Tallahassee this summer to begin making up for what she'd done to Nick Varnadore. *I don't want my boss to catch me goofing off,* she typed.

Tell her you're texting this really hot guy you met last night.

Gina smiled as memories of their kiss washed over her. She glanced toward her boss's office again, wondering what Suzanne would say if she knew Gina had major lust for a guy who worked for Suzanne's opponent.

But how could she not lust after him? That dark stubble on his jawline. Curls the color of onyx, cut just the right length to be a little unruly. A little wild. *Have you decided what we're going to do Saturday night?*

I've been asking around about the best place for Thai.

A warmth blossomed in her chest. Thai food. She'd said she loved it. He'd texted back that he hated it. Only one of the many back-and-forth volleys they'd exchanged as she lay in bed a couple of hours after their kiss at the Twilight Pub. *I thought you hated Thai food.*

You convinced me to give it another try.

She typed her response. *Or you're sucking up to me?*

Why would I do that?

She laughed under her breath. To get her in bed? Wasn't that what all guys wanted from girls they took out on dates? But in this case, the feeling was mutual.

Except she didn't sleep with guys on the first date. Or the fifth. Or the tenth. The intimacy of sex was something she reserved for those who'd shown her that she meant something to them. Who'd shown her they were as interested in the rest of her life as they were in her body. Christopher's betrayal had proven she was right to feel that way.

But this was Landon Vista. A man who epitomized everything masculine in the world. Just the closeness on the patio last night had tempted her to break all her major rules.

Her phone vibrated, dragging her back from her daydream. *Gtg. Conference call.*

And a follow-up text. *Saturday night. Thai food.*

Yes. He was definitely sucking up.

And she was perfectly fine with that.

~

Landon walked past the opaque-glass wall of the conference room on his way to get a second cup of coffee. Gina's kiss last night had left him awake until three in the morning. He'd lain in the dark after they'd texted for a couple of hours, his mind ping-ponging between memories of her soft curves and what he might look forward to with her on Saturday night.

Scott Meredith, the senator's chief of staff, jumped from his chair as Landon passed the meeting room. Scott held the door open and waved Landon over. "Can you come in here a minute?"

Landon looked around. Was Scott talking to him? Rarely did he get to go into the high-level strategy sessions in the boardroom. He'd long ago realized he was a pawn in a football-crazy town—someone the senator invited to parties when potential donors were being wooed. But he wanted to be one of the guys who set the strategy. Who decided which bills would be written and endorsed. He'd been crunching numbers on important issues—crime statistics, recidivism rates, success factors in turning juvenile delinquent facilities around—but as much as he loved statistics and analytics, he was tired of being a behind-the-scenes numbers guy. He wanted to make a difference. It's why he'd come to work here and why he stayed—that hope of making this a better place for people to live.

He set his cup on the narrow decorative table in the hallway and walked into the cherry wood–lined room.

"Sit down, son," Senator Byers said, looking even more serious than usual.

A stranger in a dark suit watched as Landon pulled out one of the rolling leather chairs. Scott introduced him as a prosecutor from Pascaloosa County.

"I assume you recognize the name Cyrus Alexander," the senator said.

Landon swallowed and looked from one face to the next. His breathing grew shallow as his body went on alert, waiting for what might come next. "I know who he is." His answer was barely audible.

Scott handed him a chilled bottle of water. He set it on the heavy, custom-made coaster in front of him.

The senator continued. "There's a group called Morgan's Ladder that works to—"

"I know who they are"—he stared at his hands where they gripped the edge of the table—"sir." *They get people like Cyrus Alexander out of prison.*

"They've been digging into the case," the prosecutor said. "Planning to do a DNA test. Talking about getting him out of prison."

"The prosecutor's office thought the senator should know, as a courtesy," Scott said. "And you, of course."

A chill shot down Landon's spine like a jolt of electricity. For a split second, that same feeling of utter helplessness he'd felt as a nine-year-old threatened to overtake him. He tamped it down, the same way he'd been burying it for years. He tugged the top off the bottle of water, hoping to wash down the bile surging into the back of his throat.

Cyrus Alexander's wiry body and stringy blond hair flashed through his mind. The slapping sound of the back door of the store. Cyrus running away . . . just moments before Landon had walked in to find his mother's body.

Even after Landon had been ferried off to live with his aunt and uncle in Jacksonville and Cyrus was behind bars, that pockmarked face haunted him.

The senator rubbed his chin. "Hate to bring it all up for you again, but I'd rather you find out from us than anyone else."

"I appreciate that, sir." He could barely concentrate on the conversation. Cyrus Alexander had gotten his trial, had his appeals. And Landon knew what he'd seen. Knew it was Cyrus who'd run out the back door. Had seen photos of the cut on Cyrus's hand at the time they'd arrested him.

Gina must have known last night when they'd spent time together at the bar. When he'd kissed her. Hell, all of Tallahassee knew his story. Even the national sports announcers had talked about it during his playing days.

There was no way Gina couldn't know. She must have known the whole time that her organization was trying to get Mama's killer out of prison.

His breathing was shallow. His hands shook. He wasn't sure if it was from the little-boy memories crashing inside him or his anger at Gina. Either way, he had to get out of there. "Is that all?"

"We may need to get in touch with you." The prosecutor slid a business card toward him. "I'll call your mom's sister to let her know, too."

Landon nodded. He hadn't spoken to his aunt and uncle in months.

Not since he'd learned they'd tried to use his name to influence their city councilman on some stupid zoning law Landon knew nothing about.

"The prosecutor's office will keep us apprised of the situation," Scott said.

Landon stood and turned toward the senator. "I need to take some time off this afternoon."

To find out why the hell Gina would do this to me.

"Of course, son." The senator stood, too. "Whatever you need."

Landon thought about returning to his desk to shut down his computer, but wasn't sure he could bear to talk to any of his coworkers. He didn't want anyone asking questions about where he was going. He felt in his pocket for his keys and cell phone, then went straight out the front door of the senator's suite of offices. The friendly guy from the deli downstairs was in the elevator, retrieving a half-empty tray of bagels from some office event on a floor above them. The guy tried to make conversation, but Landon could only grunt in response.

How was a person supposed to act when he learned the man convicted of killing his mom might be let out of prison? How could that even happen, given what Landon had seen? It seemed like the last fifteen years had never happened. Like he'd just found her this morning, her dead eyes staring. Did Gina really think he was that stupid? Did she really think it didn't matter that she was trying to get Mama's killer out of prison?

He was in his truck, driving, before he knew where he was going. He took a left on Apalachee Parkway, then right into the parking lot of the shabby building next to the florist, a building he'd passed nearly every day he'd lived in Tallahassee.

A placard on the handle rattled as he pushed open the door to Morgan's Ladder. The sign read, "Helping the Wrongly Convicted Climb to Freedom."

Gina swiveled in her desk chair to face the door. She was the only one in the tiny, cluttered room.

"Landon." Her smile faded as he approached her.

"What the hell were you thinking?" He crossed the room toward her. A musty smell grew stronger as he passed a cardboard box of old files.

"What are you talking about?" She shrank back as her face registered a mixture of fear and confusion.

"You knew last night, didn't you? You let me kiss you." He shook with anger. "Jesus, I asked you out on a date. And you knew the whole time."

"Knew what?" She rose, as if her full height might be a better match for his ire.

A middle-aged woman raced into the room. Her gray hair surrounded her face like a lion's mane. "What's going on out here?" she asked.

"Suzanne," Gina spoke slowly and held her hands in front of her as if trying to convey that everyone should calm down. "This is Landon Vista. He's here to see me."

"She's the one driving this, isn't she?" He waved his arm toward the older lady. "She's the one trying to get Cyrus Alexander out of jail."

~

Gina held her hands outstretched and flat, waiting for Landon to give her more information. Her thoughts began to click together, like pieces of a puzzle falling into place.

Cyrus Alexander.

The victim, Barbara Landon.

The little boy in the pictures with the dark, curly hair.

Olive-green eyes.

Oh.

My.

God.

Gina sank into her chair. "You're named after your mom's side of the family," she said. It wasn't a question. Not now that all the facts had fallen into place in her mind.

Her throat closed as her hand mechanically fell to the file on her desk. The one detailing the death of Barbara Landon. Her hand was like a shield, hiding from Landon the bloody crime scene photos she'd viewed just days ago. She glanced from the file to Landon and back again, knowing that the little boy in the pictures now stood in front of her, his big body surging with anger.

"Her last name wasn't the same as yours," she said. Her mind grasped for details as she tried to remember what her thought process had been before this news. "How would I have known?"

He stepped closer, breathing as if he'd just finished a marathon. "I'm supposed to believe you had no idea?"

Those accusing eyes bored into her. Their distinctive olive green haunted her. *How could I not have seen it?* The room started to spin.

He stomped around the desk to stand over her. "Did you think it's a complete accident that I work for the guy who takes the toughest stance on crime?"

Anger bubbled in her chest as she realized what he was accusing her of. "It's the state capitol. Half the people here work for the government."

"They're in Tallahassee." His voice quavered. "To make the laws. To decide what happens to criminals when they kill somebody."

Gina's mouth opened, then shut. She'd thought about Landon all night last night. Dreamed of his hands gliding over her skin. Wondered why he made her feel like she hadn't felt in a long time . . . maybe ever.

But as powerful as those dreams were, they were colliding with the mission she'd had for so long. Her reason for being here. To make amends for what she'd done following her brother's death. To find justice for people who'd never found it.

Suzanne seemed to understand that Gina was having trouble continuing the conversation. "We have DNA tests now that didn't exist then."

"He had a big gash on his arm." He motioned to his wrist. "He'd already served time for robbery."

Suzanne thumped the file folder in her hand onto a desk. "That doesn't make him a killer."

Landon squared toward Suzanne. "I saw him running out the back of the store. How much more evidence do you need?"

Suzanne hesitated at the sight of the large man now focused on her. "And if he's the killer, then the DNA test will prove it, once and for all."

"All my life"—the vein in Landon's neck corded beneath his skin—"the one little bit of peace I've had is knowing her killer was in prison."

Gina finally felt like the room had stopped spinning. "Don't you want to make sure the right man was convicted?"

He turned to her, his eyes red-rimmed and hollow. "He had a trial. He's lost all his appeals." His jaw tightened. "I know what I saw that day."

"I'm sorry." Suzanne's voice was calm, but stern. "I know this process will be difficult for you, but it's got to be done. Witness misidentification is the primary reason people are wrongly convicted. People often don't do a good job of describing what they've seen."

His eyes never left Gina's as her boss spoke. In them, Gina saw confusion and pain. She saw the little boy whose mother had been murdered.

She hoped he could read her gaze, too. The confusion. The pain from her past that gave them a common bond. Her desire to reach out and touch him. To make everything better.

But instead, he turned and left, slamming the door behind him.

CHAPTER TWO

Gina dropped to her chair inside Morgan's Ladder and stared at the door Landon had just slammed behind him when he'd exited the building.

"I had no idea." She was mentally processing their argument, so her words were meant for herself as much as for Suzanne. "I should have seen it." Those eyes. How could she have missed those eyes?

"I take it you two have met." Suzanne still stood across the room from her.

Gina nodded, still staring at the front door. "Our volleyball league. Our teams played each other last night."

"You must have made quite an impression." Suzanne crossed the room and pulled out the chair from the empty desk next to Gina's.

Gina turned, her eyes searching her boss's face for what that last comment might mean. No way could Suzanne know Gina had kissed him last night.

Could she?

A wave of heat crept up Gina's neck and she knew she was blushing. She swiveled to rest her elbows on her desk, her head in her hands. How could she have screwed this up so quickly?

Suzanne reached out and touched Gina's shoulder. "There are a lot of emotions surrounding these cases. You, of all people, should know that."

Gina swallowed and nodded, her head still cradled in her hands. It was the reason she'd come here. The reason she'd turned down more prestigious internships to spend her summer at Morgan's Ladder.

She took several deep breaths, gathering herself, then raised her head to look at her boss. "I guess I was just surprised by how quickly he rushed in here. I'll be better prepared next time." She didn't want her boss to think she wasn't up for the job.

"We've cracked open a part of his life he thought was settled years ago. It's a natural reaction," Suzanne said.

Gina nodded. Of course she knew that anger was to be expected, but it was hard to look at things intellectually when a six-foot-four-inch, two-hundred-pound man confronted you with the kind of ire Landon had shown.

Suzanne continued. "I'm sure your family went through much of the same."

"Yes." Her gaze fell to the floor as she steeled herself against the memories. The months following her brother Tommy's death had been like someone rubbing sandpaper on an open wound. It had nearly torn her family apart. "Do you think I should go talk to him?" She motioned toward the door.

The hint of a smile crossed her boss's face. She shook her head. "He doesn't need someone from Morgan's Ladder to console him. I'm sure he's got friends he can talk to. Family, maybe. They'll be able to help him more than a stranger."

And, yes, that's all Gina was. A stranger who'd had her tongue in his mouth last night. A stranger whose life now intersected with his in ways they hadn't known about on the patio of the Twilight Pub.

"This is going to be horrible for him." She knew, because she, too, had lived through the emotions of a trial. A conviction. The determination that the wrong person had been sent to jail. Nick Varnadore had spent eighteen months in a juvenile lockup because of her testimony. He'd gone in a scared, naive teenager and come out an angry, hardened adult, despite the fact that less than two years had passed. He'd grown up while he was in there, and it had changed him forever.

The details of the case on her desk flooded her mind. Like her, Landon had helped send a person to prison. Had his testimony also been wrong? Had he ruined Cyrus Alexander's life the same way she'd ruined Nick Varnadore's?

Even if the right man was in prison, their reopening the Cyrus Alexander case was going to make Landon relive his mother's murder.

As if reading her thoughts, Suzanne spoke up. "Are you rethinking your decision to come here this summer?"

Gina shook her head. "No." There was no way she was going to back out now, despite the run-in with Landon. She'd watched from afar as Nick Varnadore struggled. Gotten snippets of information from others who knew him better than her family had—he'd gotten his GED. Attended one semester at the community college, then dropped out. Had trouble finding a job. Gotten kicked out of welding school.

She'd completely changed the trajectory of his life, and she owed it to him to be here. She'd decided months ago that this was how she would make amends. How she'd pay the world back for her mistake.

Landon Vista could yell at her all her wanted. She had a plan and she was going to stick to it.

∾

Bang. Bang. Bang.

Landon tossed the *Sports Illustrated* onto the coffee table and went to answer the door of his condo. Boomer and Ricardo usually walked right in, but he hadn't unlocked the door yet this morning. Maybe they'd picked up breakfast before the three of them helped Imelda move.

Landon looked through the peephole. The man outside wasn't one of his friends. *Damn.* A fist-size lump of anger and resentment hardened in his chest. Even just the distorted fisheye view told him everything. His dad was coming off a major drunk.

Landon pulled his cell phone from his pocket and glanced at the time. Thirty more minutes before Boomer and Ricardo were due to arrive. He opened the door and blocked the entry with his body as he leaned against the doorjamb. Not very welcoming, he knew, but then, he felt less hospitable the more he saw. Graying whiskers, the sweat-rimmed neckline of his dad's faded T-shirt, jeans that looked almost khaki from the dirt covering them. A smell from Landon's childhood that he tried to forget—the mixture of cigarette smoke and stale whiskey breath.

His dad tipped forward, but caught himself before he leaned too far. "I was beginning to think you weren't home."

"What can I do for you?"

"I'm walking to a friend of mine's who lives down the road." He angled his chin in the direction of the interstate. "Thought I'd stop in to say hello." The older man's grayish skin glistened from the humidity.

As much as Landon hated talking to his dad when he was drunk—which was just about every time he saw him—he wanted to get him out of here before his friends showed up. Embarrassment rose inside him, even though there was no one around to see them. It was the same embarrassment he'd felt about his father most of his life.

Landon opened the door wider and walked into the living room, leaving his dad to stumble in on his own.

"I haven't seen you in a while," his dad slurred. "Been wondering what you've been up to." He sank into the leather recliner. *My recliner.* The one stationed for prime sports viewing at just the right angle in front of the TV. He fought down the rush of irritation that flashed through him.

"I stopped by spring practice the other day," Landon said as he walked around the breakfast bar for a bottle of water. Football was typically a safe subject between them.

His dad raked his hand over the stubble on his face. "They should be pretty good this year."

"Coach needs to make Tompkins the starting quarterback." He handed the bottle to his father. "Grable can't throw anything but a big can of corn."

"Coach doesn't want to admit Grable ain't the wonder boy he thought he was." His dad snorted. "Shoulda let the Gators sign him instead."

"How's your job going?" Landon knew he shouldn't aggravate him, but the stubble on his dad's face told him he hadn't been to work in a few days.

"Damn Dwayne." His dad wiped his hand across his eyes, then took a big swig of water.

The embarrassment of his childhood tightened in Landon's chest. "You got yourself fired, didn't you?"

"What a shithead." The old man wiped his mouth with the back of his hand. "But I got a better deal going, anyway."

A better deal. Landon had heard promises of better deals ever since his father had started hanging around Tallahassee. "Dwayne did me a favor by giving you a chance, Dad. And you blew it? You couldn't just go to work and do what he asked you to do?"

"Me and this buddy of mine—we're gonna lease this old building and open a bait shop. It's right on the road to Cedar Key. Lots of traffic going by . . ."

"Where are you going to get the money to lease a building?" As far as he knew, his dad didn't even have a permanent address.

"My buddy's about to get this big settlement from a car wreck and—"

Landon sighed. "You're here to ask me for money."

The old man's rubbery face slid into a grin. "You want to get in on this? Become an investor?"

"I don't have that kind of money." Landon didn't know how much his dad was looking for, but he wasn't going to give it to him, even if he had it.

"Outdoorsy stuff is big business. Got their own cable channel and everything."

Damn it. Would the man ever stop chasing after these crazy ideas? "I don't want to be an investor."

"I'm not here for money, anyway."

Good. Their last big fight had been because his dad needed to be bailed out of debt. Again.

"I need you to come to the bank with us," his father continued. "Part of our marketing plan. Tell the ol' boys down there you're doing our TV commercials. For free. Can't help but get a bunch of customers come football season." His dad's eyes showed more enthusiasm than he'd seen in them in . . . maybe ever.

"TV commercials for a bait shop?"

The old man's legs stilled. The rocking of the recliner stopped. "So you'll do it?"

Landon grunted. "No way."

"You can't help your old man out? Like I'm not the one who gave you that pretty face to begin with? Or that arm? You wouldn't even be the big stud quarterback if it wasn't for me."

His jaw tightened. "I am not going to risk my reputation . . ."
For a couple of drunks running a bait shop.

"You think you're too good to do this, don't you?"

"You couldn't afford the airtime, even if I agreed to do them."

"You let me figure out the finances."

Landon stood, hoping his dad would understand it was time to go. "And you let me know once you've got the building under contract.

Then we'll talk." He knew it was a safe bet. His dad's schemes never worked out.

His father stood, wobbly at first, then closed the space between them, his breath warm and rancid across Landon's face. "I'd like it if once—just once—you had a little faith in me."

"And I'd like for you to give me a call sometime. Maybe we could have dinner. When you don't need something from me."

He'd gotten used to people using him a long time ago. Latching on to him because he could think in the pocket or throw an accurate pass, but never really looking at him as a person. People who wanted to say they knew him, to say they'd had a beer with Landon Vista, to talk about this game or that, like they'd been as much a part of it as he'd been on the field. He guessed all National Championship towns were like this one—not wanting to let their football heroes go. It was like they thought he belonged to them. To use however they wanted.

He just wasn't sure he'd ever get used to the fact that his dad was the one who tried to use him most of all.

The old man's eyes narrowed. "It's not my fault Dwayne fired me."

Yeah, right.

Landon had never known his dad to have a steady job. He'd even come around the old country store, asking Mama for money. *Even when Mama was alive . . .* Landon's breath caught in his throat. His gaze darted to his father. Maybe the old guy's drunkenness would finally pay off for him. Make him off guard. Maybe a little loose with his information. "What do you know about Cyrus Alexander?"

His father's back stiffened. "Why are you asking me that? Why are you asking *now*?"

"There's a group trying to get him out of prison. They say he might be innocent."

His dad grunted. "Ain't no way he's innocent."

"How much did you know about the case? Did you go to the trial?" Landon's aunt had protected him from the newspapers at the time, but he'd looked it up online as soon as he was old enough to Google without anyone watching him.

"Your aunt and uncle did right by you." His dad looked out the window of the condo at nothing in particular, his gaze distant. "You got no reason to bring all this up."

"You're not going to answer my questions about Mama's death?" The muscles in Landon's throat squeezed tight, then he gasped for air. He rarely talked about her death. Not to Boomer. Not to Ricardo. Not to anyone.

"You should put it all behind you. Not drag it all out again."

Landon paced the room. Desperation coursed through his body like an unwelcome, frigid liquid. "But you knew Cyrus Alexander. You used to go fishing with him."

The older man stepped toward the front door and scrubbed a hand down his face. "I haven't seen the guy in fifteen years."

"Because he's been in prison." He wanted answers to all the questions that had rumbled inside him for years.

His father placed his hand on the doorknob. "And I'd been out of town for two days when she was killed." He slashed his other hand through the air. "I hadn't seen him in a long time before that. Just because I knew the guy doesn't mean I know anything about her murder." He ripped the door open and stomped out, slamming it closed behind him.

Landon rested his forehead on the door as his father's footfalls echoed on the sidewalk outside his condo.

He'd waited years to ask these questions. Stuffed them down inside himself so deeply even he was convinced they shouldn't be dredged up.

His mother would always be dead. Cyrus Alexander would always be in prison. Nothing about those facts would ever change. He'd thought that chapter of his life was over. At least until one night when a redheaded volleyball player had blocked all his shots and seduced him with the softness of her skin and the sweet taste of her lips.

He hated that he couldn't get her out of his mind. That he thought—even on their night at the bar—he could spend a long time with her.

But that was before he'd found out about her involvement in his mom's case. His chest burned as his thoughts jumped to the file folder she'd rested her hand on that day in her office. He'd do anything to get the answers he wanted about his mother's death.

But no way was Gina going to entice him again. No way could he ever be attracted to a woman whose organization would let Cyrus Alexander out of prison. Landon knew what he'd seen that day— the stringy-haired man running out the back of the country store.

Cyrus Alexander had killed his mother. He knew that as well as he knew how to read a defense or lead a passer into the end zone.

He reached in his pocket and pulled out his phone. His thumb scrolled to the number he'd been so excited to get that night in the bar. His motives were different now. He inhaled a deep breath. His shaking finger punched the keypad and he waited for her phone to ring.

If Gina had information about his mother's death, he was going to get it.

~

Gina licked the last bit of apple butter off her finger so she could pick up her cell phone from her kitchen counter. She hesitated when she saw the name on the caller ID.

Landon.

"This is Gina," she said in her best lawyerly tone, immediately wishing she'd done better at hiding the shakiness in her voice.

"We never decided what time I'd pick you up tonight." There was no mistaking the deep voice on the other end of the phone.

"Landon, I . . ."

"How about seven?"

"I assumed after my office the other day . . ." *That you despised me.* ". . . that our date was canceled."

"I'm helping someone move today. Maybe we should make it seven thirty, just to be safe."

She hesitated. Sure, there'd been instant attraction between them at the bar. An immediate bond, sparked by their fun banter, then set ablaze by the kiss she couldn't wipe from her consciousness. The teasing and joking via text later that night had made her even more interested. Made her think even more about the kiss. She still felt his big hands on her hips, pulling her closer. Promising more.

"Look, Landon." She bit her lip. "I'm not comfortable going out with a guy who's a witness in one of our cases." Her curiosity was piqued. Why did he still want to see her?

"It doesn't have to be a date. No drinking. No dancing."

"No kissing." She closed her eyes and remembered the hard planes of his body as it pressed against hers. The first brush of his lips on hers. The soft warmth of his mouth. She shuddered. Even knowing what she'd discovered since then, she longed to feel his touch again.

He scoffed. "Definitely no kissing."

Her sternum contracted as if she'd been hit. Yes, he was a key witness in one of her cases, but she still wanted to see that same hungry look in his eyes that she'd seen on the patio of the bar. She wanted him to want her, even if nothing could happen between them. "So we can call it a business dinner?"

"Sure, if that makes you feel better," he said. "What's your address?"

"I could just meet you there."

"Or I could pick you up."

He was challenging her. Trying to establish his dominance. She hesitated. "8201 Bronough. I live in the apartment over the detached garage."

A loud noise—like a door banging open—sounded on Landon's end of the conversation. "Sorry, man," a male voice said in the background. "Ricardo here yet?"

Landon seemed to ignore him. "I'll pick you up at seven thirty. We have dinner reservations at eight," he said into the phone.

"I'll understand if you change your mind." She still wondered why he'd want to have dinner with her.

"I won't. See you then." He ended the call before she could find out anything more about his intentions.

She punched the button to return to her phone's home screen, then closed her eyes. The churning in her stomach reminded her to take slow, even breaths, to try to center herself like she'd learned in yoga class. It didn't work. She grasped for one of the thoughts that fluttered through her mind like a flock of startled birds.

Would Suzanne approve of her seeing Landon outside the office? Sure, Gina had known she and Landon would eventually talk about the details of the case, but she'd assumed Suzanne would be there, too. She'd envisioned they'd interview him in the rundown conference room at Morgan's Ladder. The one with a corner piled high with boxes of files because they'd long ago run out of filing space.

But she'd assumed her focus would be on getting an innocent man out of prison. She'd known this is what she wanted to do since she'd first learned of organizations like Morgan's Ladder. Like the one that had helped determine that Nick Varnadore had been wrongly convicted. She'd known since then that this would be her way to pay the world back for her mistake.

Maybe meeting with Landon was all part of the same big plan. Cyrus Alexander sat in prison tonight, the possible victim of witness misidentification. It was her duty to help determine the truth. To figure out his guilt or innocence.

The truth was all she wanted and she planned to get it.

Even if there was a two-hundred-pound football player standing in the way.

~

One corner of Boomer's lips rose in a mischievous grin as Landon stuffed his cell phone into his pocket.

"The redhead from the other night?" Boomer said.

"Her name's Gina."

His friend grinned. "You're thinking you're going to get laid tonight."

Landon bent to pick up the tennis shoes he planned to wear to help Imelda and her husband move. Boomer's comment didn't fit Gina. She may be on the wrong side of the Cyrus Alexander case, but she had more class than the girls who normally hung around the bar after volleyball games. Besides, it wasn't really a date.

The front door burst open and Ricardo sauntered in.

A rush of irritation flashed through Landon's body. "Don't you assholes ever knock?"

The pair exchanged a puzzled look. "No," they said in unison.

The truth was, Landon wasn't sure either of them *had* ever knocked. Not in the two years since he'd moved here.

Ricardo raised his hands as if to surrender. "What are you so worked up about?"

Landon tamped down his annoyance. His friends weren't the source of his frustration. Hell, it had never bothered him before that both of them walked right in without knocking. He went back to tying his shoes, hoping the aggravation would pass.

"Predate jitters." Boomer opened the refrigerator and stuck his head in. "He's taking the redhead out tonight. I think he's worried about losing his virginity."

Ricardo laughed. "I thought you were afraid of her." He mimicked a slow motion volleyball spike, his hand landing on top of Landon's head as he was bent over his shoe.

Boomer straightened and tossed Ricardo a bottle of water. "Are you kidding? He was all over her at the bar the other night."

Landon stood and grabbed his car keys, indicating it was time for them to go.

Of course he wasn't afraid of her . . . or was he? Could she really get Cyrus Alexander out of prison? No. No way that would ever happen. But having her work on the case was digging into a wound in his psyche that was better left alone.

"You haven't seen her since the other night?" Ricardo asked.

Landon shook his head as a rush of guilt slashed through his chest. They'd been his best friends for years. He'd never lied to them, but he'd also never talked to them about his mother's murder or his dad's drunkenness or any of the other crap he kept hidden away from them and everyone else. They didn't need to know what he'd discovered about Gina's internship or the fact that he'd confronted her the other day at Morgan's Ladder.

It was none of their business that he was seeing Gina tonight to try to learn what he could about his mother's death. That for the first time in years, he wasn't trying to sleep with the hottest girl he knew.

No, those subjects were off-limits, even for his two best friends.

"Now let's get this move over with." He slapped Boomer on the back. "Unlike you two losers, I have a date tonight."

CHAPTER THREE

Gina fidgeted as she sat in the passenger seat of Landon's truck. Her right side was pressed against the door, creating as much distance between them as possible. This scene seemed too date-like. Too romantic. And her number one goal tonight was to keep it professional. To not do anything to jeopardize her job or her objectivity in the Cyrus Alexander case. Sure, she was only an intern, but she couldn't let her feelings about a case influence the work she did. She'd come here to help Morgan's Ladder, not complicate the issues with some schoolgirl crush on the local football hero.

Besides, the grimness of Landon's jawline reminded her of their reason for seeing each other tonight. He now saw her as the opposition, not the woman he'd kissed on the patio of the pub just a few nights ago.

So why was she so nervous? She'd been on business dinners before. And that was all this was.

She and Landon Vista going out on a business dinner.

Making peace with each other.

And, except for official dealings with the Cyrus Alexander case, saying good-bye.

He'd arrived at her apartment right on time, in creased gray dress pants and a dark green button-down that turned the color of his eyes a couple of shades darker than they'd been when she'd seen him before. She hadn't thought he could look any sexier than the night they'd first met, but she'd been wrong.

"You got your friend moved okay?" she asked, trying to think of anything other than what he'd looked like standing in her doorway.

He shrugged. "She's still got a lot of unpacking to do, but we got all the big stuff in place where she wanted it."

Gina stilled. *She?*

She scolded herself for the tinge of jealousy she felt. Of course he had female friends. A guy who looked like that probably had a different woman clamoring to sleep with him every night. If his lovemaking was anything like the kiss they'd shared . . . Oh, God. What was she thinking? "Maybe you should have stayed to help her unpack."

His gaze slid to hers. He was quiet for a few seconds too long. Gina could tell he was hiding something.

"She'll be okay." His cool gaze returned to the road.

His mentioning that he'd helped a woman move flooded her with memories of Christopher. The way Christopher had vaguely answered her questions when they'd been dating. The way he'd sworn there was nobody else, even after one of her girlfriends had told her he'd been cheating on her. The way he'd looked when she'd flung open the bedroom door at his apartment to find him naked with that goth girl—her watermelon-size boob in his mouth and his—

She squeezed her eyes shut. She wasn't going there. What had happened a few months ago—and hundreds of miles away—had nothing to do with tonight. What mattered now was that she get through this dinner with professionalism and grace, two traits she prided herself on. That alone was going to be tough enough. She opened her eyes and tried to ignore Landon as he drove the truck—the way the skin of his forearm looked even more tan against the dark green of his shirt. The freshly-pressed crease in his pants, so different from the way he'd looked when they first met after the volleyball game. She liked the more casual Landon—the one whose sculpted arms and shoulders were visible on the volleyball court—but this one was nice, too.

He slowed and pulled his truck into the circular drive of a two-story building with the clean, crisp lines of contemporary Asian architecture. A teenage valet moved from behind a podium to greet them as Landon opened the driver-side door. "Welcome to Indochine." The boy's eyes widened as he seemed to recognize Landon. The teen would have been in middle school—maybe high school—during Landon's playing days.

"How's it going?" Landon nodded and smiled, as if trying to put the boy at ease. He handed the teen his keys.

Gina slid from the passenger side and met Landon at the front of the truck.

"This is Thai food," she said with surprise as they headed toward the garden of small trees that led to the front door of the restaurant.

"I keep my promises."

So he did. She liked that in a man.

An unexpected touch startled her. She jerked, then realized it was Landon's fingertips settling on the small of her back as they walked through the garden. She could feel their warmth through the thin fabric of her blouse. She didn't want this to end.

He chuckled behind her. "I'm not going to hurt you," he whispered as they reached the front door. He held it open for her.

She stopped, so close to him she could smell his freshly showered, masculine scent. The curls at the nape of his neck were still wet. "I thought this wasn't a date."

"Southern boys always open doors for a lady." His voice was low. Intimate. Like they were the only two who were supposed to hear it.

She swallowed, suddenly wishing they could be alone together. So what if they shared a little quiet conversation. Maybe a little playful banter. As long as she kept their relationship professional, she wouldn't violate her commitment to her job.

Landon checked in with the hostess, who led them to the opposite side of the restaurant and up an open staircase.

The second-story loft held several tables, a few of them occupied by couples and foursomes. A candle in an amber-colored glass sat in the center of each, creating little islands of light in an otherwise dimly lit area. The hostess led them to a teak two-top by the silver railing, overlooking the diners below. Landon pulled out Gina's chair for her. She smiled at his gesture and sat down.

One corner of his mouth quirked upward as soon as the hostess handed them each a menu and returned down the staircase. "I don't suppose they have a rib eye and some fries?"

"You're a good sport to bring me here." Her gaze slid to a table on the other side of the loft. Some of the couples around them were openly watching, but likely couldn't overhear their conversation. "Though I do think this is good payback for yelling at me in my office the other day."

Landon smirked and returned his gaze to his menu. Gina glanced at the patrons on the level below, some of whom had their heads turned upward, watching Landon.

The server arrived and took their drink orders—a glass of cabernet for Gina and a sweet tea for Landon.

"So my boss asked me to be on a task force," Gina said, ignoring the other diners.

He fiddled with his silverware. "Oh, yeah? What kind of a task force?"

"Its purpose is to bring people together to find common ground on the death penalty issues. Someone from your office is supposed to be on it. Somebody named Scott something?"

"Scott Meredith. The chief of staff."

"You work closely with him?"

"He's my boss." Landon glanced to the diners below.

"He's a good guy?"

His gaze returned to her. "He's probably not going to agree with you on death penalty issues, if that's what you mean."

So there it was again—the difference in values that had separated her and Landon from the beginning. But it was too early in the dinner to talk politics. "I thought it was pretty cool that Suzanne's letting me be on the task force. It'll be a great experience for my internship."

The server returned with their drinks and then took each of their dinner orders.

"Maybe we should get those to go." Gina said to him as soon as they'd both ordered pad Thai.

Landon glanced from her to the server and back again. "Why?"

Gina shrugged. "You don't seem comfortable here." She loved the decor and the buzz of this place, but his unease seemed to be getting worse.

"To go, then," he said to the server. She nodded and left.

He leaned toward Gina. "Is it that bad being seen with me?"

"People are staring at you. I figured you might like to go somewhere else."

"How do you know they're not staring at you?"

Sure, people gawked at her height, but this was different. She'd been seated for several minutes and even newly arrived diners turned to ogle Landon. "I'm not nearly as interesting as you are," she said.

"I guess that's a matter of opinion." His green eyes bored into hers, like they'd done the night they'd first met. Like they'd done right before they'd kissed.

She held his gaze for several seconds, then forced herself to look away. Maybe the rest of Tallahassee was enamored with him, but she wasn't. Her job had to come first.

~

Landon took Gina's empty plate from the opposite side of his break-fast bar and rinsed it off in the sink. The Thai food had actually been not that bad. And she'd pretty much nailed how uncomfortable he'd been in that restaurant.

He watched her as she wandered around his living room. Every other woman he'd ever taken out to dinner had been flattered by the attention, soaking it up like they were proud to be seen with him. Like he was some new piece of jewelry they needed to show off in public. Which was why he rarely took women out to dinner.

Only Gina had sensed his unease and suggested they get out of there.

She leaned over to look at the contents of his coffee table, giv-ing him a moment to admire her strong, sexy build. She wasn't one of those women who felt like they needed to eat so little their ribs showed. No, she was athletic and muscular . . . but soft in all the right places. He'd felt some of those places when they'd kissed. And he wished he could feel all the others, too.

He wondered what she'd deduce from the items laying on his coffee table. That he liked to read, based on the Harlan Coben paperback. That he liked sports—big surprise there—based on the *Sports Illustrated*. And that he needed to pay his cable bill. Besides that, his condo was pretty generic. Even the furniture had come with the place.

"So when do you go back to law school?" he asked, trying to make conversation.

"A few weeks." She picked up the novel off the coffee table and turned it over to read the back. "Classes start August seventeenth."

"Wouldn't you make a ton more money going into corporate law?" He couldn't imagine someone like her wanting to deal in the seediness of criminal law. "Or becoming a partner in a big firm or something like that?"

She returned the paperback to the coffee table. "Sometimes it's not about the money."

He scoffed. "It's always about the money."

She straightened and cocked her head to look at him. "That's a pretty jaded view of the world for someone as young as you."

"I work in politics." He set the salt and pepper back to where he kept them next to the oven. "It's always about the money."

She returned to the breakfast bar and studied his face for a few seconds. "You don't strike me as someone who'd want to work in politics."

There she was, weaseling her way into his psyche again, uncovering things about him that no one else had ever noticed. "Yeah? And why's that?"

She shrugged. "I don't know. It just seems like you wouldn't want to make all the compromises you'd have to make to keep everyone happy in a job like that. You seem too . . . principled."

There'd been a time when he'd felt more principled. Before he'd sold himself out by letting the senator capitalize on his history and his notoriety. "I was about to take a job with an accounting firm, then I met Scott Meredith at a cocktail party. He asked me to hold off a week or so before I made a decision. And they ended up offering me a job."

"What's your title?"

"Statistical analyst." He was fairly certain they'd created the job just for him—or rather, his football notoriety—but she didn't need to know that.

She wrinkled her nose. "Sounds like a lot of numbers."

"That's the best part." People used numbers, not the other way around. And he'd found he was pretty damn good at finding trends, predicting outcomes, using data to find correlations between two seemingly unrelated factors. "Besides, how does a twentysomething decide on a career they could have for the rest of their life?" He didn't have the answer. Maybe she did.

"It shouldn't be based on how much money you'll make."

People with money always said that, but he knew different. Mama probably wouldn't have been murdered had she not been working in that run-down country store in the middle of nowhere. And he'd never forget the other kids making fun of him for wearing the same pair of jeans to elementary school every day during the one cold month of winter. People with money always downplayed its importance.

Gina seemed to sense his silence. "I wanted to be a jockey growing up. But I was five foot eight by the time I was twelve, so I had to find a new career."

He liked the way her laughter snuck into her sentences. "You had horses?"

She picked up her glass and walked into the kitchen. "No, but my friend Julie did. We used to ride them all the time." She filled her cup with water from the dispenser on the front of the fridge, then turned to face him. "So tell me what you were like growing up."

He shrugged. "There's not much to tell." That sounded lame, even to him. He was still the only person he'd ever known whose mom had been murdered.

"When did you realize you were good enough to play college ball?"

"The scouts started paying attention my sophomore year. My high school was a football powerhouse, so they were there every year anyway." He leaned against the counter and stuck his hands in his pockets. "It didn't hurt that we won the state championship when I was a senior." That's about the time his dad had started hanging around for the first time in years, but Gina didn't need to know that.

"No, I guess not." She took a sip of her water. "So it's going to be kind of odd, interviewing you for the Cyrus Alexander case," she said, to fill the awkward silence.

Landon's jaw tightened. "It's the Barbara Landon case." His voice was rougher than he'd expected it to be. "*She's* the one who was murdered."

~

Gina's stomach clenched at the pain in Landon's eyes. Of course he would see it as his mother's case. It was. She shouldn't have referred to it the way she did. "I didn't mean to—"

"There are a lot of guys who've killed someone." His voice cracked at the word *killed*. "How do you choose which convictions you're going to fight?"

"It depends on what's presented to us." Good. A general answer didn't sacrifice the details of the case. "Sometimes it's prosecutorial misconduct. Sometimes a witness recants their testimony. Usually it's witness misidentification."

"You think I didn't really see him running away?" He bent toward her, inches from her face.

"We'll want to interview you." She resisted the urge to lean away from him. "Confirm your testimony."

He gave a humorless laugh as he straightened. "It was fifteen years ago."

But a day she was sure he remembered well. A day he'd probably repeated in his mind like a horror movie that wouldn't end. "We'll talk to everybody involved," she said.

"If you can find them."

"One of the policemen was killed in the line of duty a couple of years ago."

He stood motionless, his hands clutching the counter behind him on either side of his body. "And the old guy who owned the sawmill next door was already about sixty years old when it happened."

"We're studying their original testimony."

"And eventually you test the DNA."

"Yes." She held her breath, wondering where he'd take the conversation next. Silence filled the room.

"So there's"—he looked away for a few seconds—"there's a box with her clothes in it? What she was wearing that day?"

Gina nodded, thinking about how she'd gone into her brother Tommy's room after everyone had left on the day of his funeral. Sat on his bed until late in the evening. Smelled the pillow where he'd rested his head the night before he died.

But Barbara Landon's clothes were packed in evidence bags. Tagged and labeled like lab specimens—brittle with dried blood instead of infused with a mother's special scent and softness.

She wondered if Landon had ever had an opportunity to go through his mother's other belongings. To select items that might have had special meaning to him.

His voice cut into her thoughts. "And her clothes have someone else's DNA on them?"

"Some blood." She wondered if this was new information to him. "Not her type."

He scrubbed a hand over his face. Inhaled, then exhaled a huge breath.

"I didn't see any pictures of her." Gina motioned to where she'd been standing earlier. "In the living room."

He stilled and nailed her with a glare, his demeanor turning her as chilly as if she'd stepped into a walk-in freezer. "That doesn't have anything to do with the case," he said.

She shrugged. "I would have liked to have seen what she looked like." Something other than crime scene photos.

"There aren't many pictures. I have copies of them on my phone." He shoved his hands in his pockets, making it clear he didn't plan to show them to her. "I keep the originals in a safe-deposit box."

She decided to take another approach. "You were adopted by relatives, right?" She'd read it in the file. "In Jacksonville?" She wondered what it must have been like for a nine-year-old to move from rural Pascaloosa County to a large city on the other side of the state.

"They raised me." His gaze settled on hers, steady and unyielding. "They didn't adopt me."

His voice conveyed distance. A lack of belonging. Despite his gruffness, she could sense his pain.

"What do you remember most about your mom?" Her voice was hushed. Reverent. She reached out instinctively, grazing his hand with her fingertips.

He swallowed and pulled away, opening the fridge. His shoulders trembled as he took out a bottle and turned back to face her. At first, she thought it was beer, but then realized it was an old-fashioned grape Nehi. It reminded her that the little boy who'd found his mother's body still stood in front of her.

He twisted off the cap and shot it across the room with a flip of his thumb and forefinger. It pinged off the backsplash and onto the counter, a jarring noise in the silence between them. "This isn't really something I want to talk about," he said.

She waited, hoping he'd change his mind, but instead, he raised the bottle to his lips and took a long drink.

His false bravado didn't fool her. She could see by the way his body quivered that his grief was overwhelming.

"I lost someone close to me, too," she said.

He lowered the bottle and scowled at her. "Then you understand why it's private."

"The more you talk about the person who's died, the more you keep them alive."

He scoffed. "I've got a little more practical view of the world."

"Oh, yeah? Like what?"

"Like once they're dead and their killer's been put in prison, there's nothing you can do about it. It's closed. Done."

She felt like the hot anvil of a blacksmith had been thrust through her midsection. How dare he take such a callous view? These were their loved ones, not some disposable relationship that was gone at the moment of death. "You can at least remember them. Talk about them." It's what her family had decided to do.

"I like to do my remembering in private."

"Then why did you invite me to dinner tonight?"

"You know what?" He grabbed his keys off the counter and walked toward the entryway. "My mistake. I guess it wasn't such a good idea."

She glanced toward the front door, knowing he was signaling an end to their evening together. But Tommy's death had taught her that nothing was more important than reaching out to someone in pain. Her brother's passing had peeled away everything else in life, leaving only the most basic human emotional needs, all of which trumped her professional obligations at Morgan's Ladder.

She headed toward the entryway, but stopped in front of him. "My brother, Tommy." Surely she could tell part of her story without spilling the entire ugliness of it out into Landon's foyer like a bucketful of dirty mop water. "He was murdered when I was a sophomore in high school."

Landon's gaze flickered toward her. She thought maybe she'd gained his trust. That he understood their kinship.

"So you know what it's like," he said.

"I've been right there with you. And I know sometimes you just need someone to give you a hug."

He scoffed at that. "I don't need a hug."

"It could at least make you feel better." Her voice was slow and even. She stepped forward, challenging him. She saw the grief in his eyes and wanted to do something, anything, to make him feel better.

She took another step toward him.

He didn't move.

~

Landon closed his eyes, letting the sensations of Gina's hug settle into his body.

This was not at all what he'd planned when he'd invited her to his condo.

But this wasn't a sexual hug. It had been years since someone—anyone—had held him like this. Since anyone had tried to absorb his pain with their own body.

He wrapped his arms around Gina's back, pulling her tighter against his body. Feeling her kindness and gentleness seep through his skin and into his soul. For the first time in years, tears stung his eyes. Damn it. He squeezed his lids tight, willing the emotion away.

He was supposed to be the tough guy. The one who didn't need anyone else. But Gina had seen through all that. For the first time since his mom died, it felt like someone saw past the facade. Past the guy he pretended to be. Past the persona the outside world expected.

Gina actually saw *him*.

He'd forgotten how good that felt.

Finally, she pulled away and looked up into his eyes. "I hope it's okay that I did that."

He was afraid to speak. Afraid his voice would quiver if he tried to talk. He nodded, but even that simple motion felt choppy and disjointed.

Did she know how deeply she'd shaken him?

She took a step back. His body immediately ached for the closeness again.

"I . . . I'm sorry we have to dig all this up for you," she said.

His chest heaved involuntarily. She was talking about the case, but she didn't realize the impact she'd had on him. "I think you should go," he said.

She stepped toward the front door. "I know it won't be easy for you when we take your testimony."

"You could let it all drop. Take on another case." Good. His voice was steady. He wasn't giving himself away.

"I'm really not such a bad person."

"I didn't say you were." After how she'd made him feel, he wasn't sure what he thought about her. All he knew was that he wanted her out of his house and away from him until he got himself together. He stepped to the door and opened it.

Her gaze held his for several seconds, as if she couldn't decide whether or not she was ready for their evening to end.

Finally, she walked through the open doorway and down the sidewalk, toward his truck. "It really was sweet of you to take me to a Thai restaurant."

"I'm not in this to be sweet." He beeped his truck to unlock the doors as he followed her. "I'm in this to get you to drop the case." He knew his words sounded callous, but for some reason, he felt like she might be the toughest opponent he'd ever faced. And that included the three-hundred-pound linemen who'd wanted to bash in his skull. "I'm in this to win."

"I'm sorry, Landon." She turned on the sidewalk to face him. "But so am I. I'm in it to find the truth."

CHAPTER FOUR

Gina and Suzanne stood silently in the tiny room at the state prison as the guard opened the door. He stepped aside to let the tall, thin prisoner enter first. The interview room, already stuffy, now filled with the smell of a man who was allowed to shower only on certain days of the week.

"Mr. Alexander," Suzanne said as he studied them.

"My buddies call me Cyrus." He winked at Gina. "And if you two are going to get me out of this hellhole, then I reckon you'll be my best friends in the world."

"Why don't we sit down," Suzanne said after the guard had unlocked and removed Cyrus's handcuffs. "I'm Suzanne Holmes, director of Morgan's Ladder. And this is Gina Blanchard."

"You a lawyer, too, pretty lady?" Cyrus rubbed one wrist, then the other. The stringy blond hair she'd seen in his booking photo from years ago was now cropped short. Light from the fixture overhead bounced off his balding forehead.

Gina reminded herself he'd been away from normal society for quite some time. "I'm here to assist."

Suzanne cleared her throat. "We've been reviewing your file, as you requested." Gina had read the letters he'd written to Morgan's Ladder prior to her arrival. She understood why the inconsistencies surrounding his prosecution had piqued Suzanne's interest.

He sat forward, suddenly focused on the reason for their visit. "I know how DNA is clearing all kinds of people. Guys who been in jail for a long time, but didn't do their crimes."

"DNA testing is certainly a possibility," Suzanne said. "But we'd like to ask a few questions today."

"I didn't kill nobody. You understand that, right?" His gaze conveyed an unmistakable certainty as it moved from one woman to the next.

Suzanne opened the tattered leather portfolio in front of her. "Did your defense attorney interview the friends who said they were with you on the boat dock that day?"

He snorted. "My defense attorney was only good at one thing—collectin' a paycheck from the taxpayers. He never did a day of work that I could tell. My buddy, R.J.—who I was fishin' with that day—says the lawyer never even called him. R.J. lived in the same damn house his whole life and the guy couldn't track him down?"

Suzanne flipped through the file. "That would be Randall James Madsen?"

Cyrus nodded. "And Jimbo Cline—the other guy I was fishin' with that day—said that lawyer smelled like a fifth of whiskey when he interviewed him."

Gina watched her boss's reaction. Part of their work had been to research the history of the defense attorney assigned to Cyrus's case. At the time of the trial, he'd already been suspended once for showing up in court drunk. Three months after Cyrus's conviction, he'd been killed in an alcohol-related single-car accident.

"Let's start from the beginning." Suzanne opened her file. "Had you been to the country store before?"

Cyrus snorted. "Everybody'd been to that store. It was the only one around, unless you went into Blackburn, and that was fifteen miles away."

Gina's mind jumped to the crime scene photos she'd seen many times. The bloodied body. The old-fashioned fixtures. Nine-year-old Landon on the front porch with a police officer. The shock in those distinctive green eyes still haunted her.

Suzanne sat forward. "So you knew Barbara Landon?"

He shrugged. "Knew her to say hi, but that was about it. Tried askin' her out once, but just as I got started, her kid—she had this curly-haired little boy—pulled a shelf of green beans down on top of him."

Gina fidgeted in her chair, suddenly uncomfortable as Cyrus talked about Landon. She still lay awake nights trying to think of what he must have been like as a boy, both before and after the incident that had molded him into who he was today.

Suzanne glanced at her before returning her attention back to Cyrus. "Go on."

Cyrus's eyes narrowed. "That little boy's the one who says he saw me runnin' from the store that day."

"Why would he have said that if it isn't true?"

"Hell if I know. I didn't even go there much at the end. I got me a girlfriend right after I was gonna ask his mom out. Somebody else. We moved in together right away."

"So you didn't ask Barbara Landon out? You two had no social connections? No relationship?"

Cyrus held out his hands with a questioning look. "She sold me Skoal. That was all the relationship we ever had."

"This girlfriend you mentioned. She's now your wife?" Suzanne asked.

He stared at his interlaced fingers for several long seconds, then raised his head slowly. He nodded. "We got married. Our son was born twelve days before my sentencing." His eyes glistened with moisture. "I got to hold him. Once."

Gina's throat tightened at the obvious pain on his face. "Where are they now?"

"Back in Pascaloosa County." His voice cracked. "Waiting for me to come home."

~

Landon's gaze shot to the Twilight Pub's front door. Once again, he hated himself for being disappointed when the person who walked in wasn't six feet tall with strawberry-blonde hair.

Boomer looked at the neon Budweiser clock on the wall. "Her game's probably only just now over."

"Whose game?"

"Yeah, right." Boomer raised his beer bottle to his mouth.

Landon ignored him and motioned for the waitress to bring him another. He'd been watching the door like a sentry for the past hour, and his friend knew exactly why. Gina's team had the game after theirs, and she could arrive any minute.

Boomer's eyes raised to someone whose presence Landon felt behind his own chair. Long, manicured fingers smoothed across his collarbone and slid down his chest.

"I haven't seen you in a while," a female voice said through a haze of hair-product smell.

He turned to see Ashley—or was it Amber?—beaming down at him behind pale, shiny lips unnaturally outlined in dark plum. "I . . . been around."

Boomer craned his neck to look around the tavern, as if trying to distance himself from their conversation.

"You going to be around all night?" Her forefinger flitted up to trace his jaw. "Maybe later?"

"I . . . um . . ." The door swung open again, but Ashley's ample bosom blocked his view of who came in. He fumbled for words. "I'm waiting for someone."

Ashley's ultrashiny lips tensed, then spread into a forced half smile.

"Shame," she said as she hoisted her breasts out of his face and stood upright. "Would have been nice to spend some more time together."

Boomer leaned forward as she slinked away. He watched her shimmy to her next conversation. "Who the hell was that?"

Landon shrugged. Some girl he'd slept with six months, maybe a year, ago. She'd provided an opportunity for sexual release, followed by that same feeling of hollowness. The one that always settled into his chest when he knew the hookup was little more than him using her. And vice versa.

His friend shook his head and laughed. "You must really like this Gina girl. She's got you messed up bad if you're going to turn away someone like that." He nodded in the direction Ashley had gone.

Boomer didn't have any idea the number of ways Gina was screwing with his mind—and not all of them had to do with Cyrus Alexander. "She works for a nonprofit that tries to get people out of prison."

"I thought she was in law school."

"She's in Tallahassee for the summer. An internship." He took a long swig of his beer as he decided how much information to share with his friend. "They're looking into Cyrus Alexander's case."

"The guy who . . . ?" Boomer's eyes widened.

"Yeah." Landon was glad Boomer knew who Cyrus Alexander was. They'd never talked about it, though the media often talked about Landon's past. "That one."

Boomer shook his head. "No wonder you've been so hard to get along with. You don't know whether to hate her or sleep with her."

Landon glared at his friend, not wanting to admit—even to himself—how close Boomer was to being right. "I need to keep an eye on her. See what they're doing with the case."

Boomer chuckled. "And if she doesn't get here soon, you're going to track her down like a bloodhound." He tipped up his beer and took a swig. "Desperation isn't a good look on you, my friend."

"Up yours." Landon pushed his chair back and walked away, hoping they'd have a new topic when he got back.

He rounded the corner on his return trip from the bathroom and stopped midstride. Gina stood talking to her teammates near the door. She laughed at something one of them said. God, she was beautiful. Not in the made-up way that girls like Ashley tried so hard to copy, but in a natural, flowing, the-kind-of-girl-you-wanted-to-hold-all-night sort of way.

Gina looked over her friend's head, her eyes locking on his as he moved toward his table. She said something to the group, then walked toward him. Landon took his seat, across from Boomer.

"Hey, guys," she said, standing next to them.

Boomer's gaze moved from her to him. "Aren't you going to ask her to sit down?"

"We have a difference of opinion on something," Landon said.

She sat down anyway. Gutsy woman.

"Doesn't mean you can't have a beer together." Boomer held his beer bottle up to a passing waitress, signaling her to bring another one.

Landon glared at his friend. Since when did he need Boomer's help in talking to girls?

Gina turned to Boomer. "The organization I work for is trying to get—"

"I already told him." Damn it if she was going to drag Boomer into this. Landon kept his life private for a reason.

"Maybe you two should just . . . agree to disagree," Boomer said.

"It's not like I'm a Red Sox fan and she's a Yankee fan," Landon said. "Something minor like that."

"You spent the whole night watching the door for her and now that she's here, you pick a fight?" Boomer asked. Landon made a mental note to kick his friend's ass next time they were somewhere with a little more room.

A half smile crept across Gina's face. "You watched the door for me?"

Landon glared at Boomer as he spoke. "Keep your friends close and your enemies closer."

Gina leaned in and ground out her words. "I am not the enemy."

"You're in trouble now," Boomer said under his breath, his beer bottle poised at his lips.

"You're not really helping here," Landon said to him.

Gina ignored them. "How can I be the enemy if all I want is the truth? How can someone think the truth is wrong?"

The breath in his chest quickened. "The truth has already been established. The truth"—he leaned in closer—"is what I saw running out of the back of that country store."

Her bottom lip trembled. "Eyewitnesses can be wrong sometimes. Actually, they're wrong a lot of the time."

"Oh, yeah? And how do you know that?" Landon didn't raise his voice, but knew his low, close tone was more menacing than any shout. "Because you've worked at Morgan's Ladder for a whole three weeks now? I don't think that makes you an expert."

The server arrived with a round of beer on her tray. Gina grabbed one, squeezed her eyes closed, and took a long sip. She slowly lowered the bottle. "I have to go."

Landon watched her hurry to the door. The guy at the next table craned his neck to follow the sight of her butt.

"You're a total fuckup," Boomer said to Landon.

Landon raked his hand down his face. His stubble rasped. Why did he feel the need to go after her? "I'll deal with you later," he said as he rose to follow her.

"And you"—he pointed his forefinger in the face of the guy at the next table who'd leered at her ass—"you stay away from her." The guy held both hands up in the air and scooted his chair as far away from Landon as he could.

Landon turned and rushed toward the door as a voice rose from the table full of guys. "Hey, wasn't that Landon Vista?"

He ripped open the door to the bar and glanced around the parking lot. A group of drunken college-age women bumped into him as they passed, arm in arm. A Dodge Charger roared out of the entrance and onto the road.

His chest clutched. Had he missed her? And why did he care so much? He turned to go back inside when Gina came into his view, across the parking lot. He broke into a sprint before he knew what he was doing.

"Wasn't that Landon Vista?" he heard the guy say as a couple walked toward their car. Jeez. These people really needed to get a life.

Gina sniffed as he approached, trying to hide her emotions. She held her chin high.

He reached out to touch her arm. "Kind of tough to be a badass if you can't find your car."

She smiled a bit, though he could tell she didn't want to. "I never said I was a badass." She held up her key fob and watched as the lights of her SUV blinked a couple of rows over.

"So what did I say in there that made you leave?"

"Nothing." She shook her head. Her hair glinted in the light of the streetlamp. Tears glistened in her eyes. She started walking.

He followed alongside her. "Seriously. You always want me to talk about my private stuff. Now it's your turn."

She took a deep breath and blew it out. He got the impression she was thinking about telling him.

"Something about eyewitnesses . . ." he said, coaxing her.

They arrived at her SUV and she leaned against it. "You said I didn't know anything about it. That I'd only worked for Morgan's Ladder for three weeks."

Yeah? And?

He would never understand women. "How long have you worked

there?" Maybe he had the time frame mixed up. He thought she'd only gotten here this summer, but maybe he was wrong.

"Four weeks," she said.

Crazy. All of them.

He couldn't think of anything to say. And he sure as hell didn't want to make her start crying. He'd never known how to deal with women's tears.

"But that doesn't mean"—she took a ragged breath—"that doesn't mean I didn't know about eyewitnesses before then."

His head shot up. What was she talking about? Had she been the victim of some violent crime? A protectiveness he'd never felt before washed over him.

She closed her eyes and looked like the most vulnerable, innocent person he'd ever met. The made-up woman who'd tried to hook up with him inside was nothing compared to Gina's wholesomeness. How could wholesomeness be so damn sexy?

He reached out and took her hand. "What are you talking about?"

"I thought I knew who killed my brother." Her voice quavered. "But I was wrong."

"*You* were the eyewitness?" A sense of relief washed over him. No one had harmed her. At least, not that he knew of.

Her nod was barely visible. "A kid went to prison for eighteen months." A single tear streaked down each of her cheeks. "Because of me."

He rubbed the back of her hand with his thumb. "People make mistakes. They don't always see what they think they see." *He* hadn't made a mistake in tagging Cyrus Alexander, but perhaps other people misidentified suspects.

"He was sixteen when he went in." Her voice pleaded with him to understand. "Can you imagine what happened to him in there? How his life was ruined?"

"So this is why you work for Morgan's Ladder?" He stepped closer to her, the intimacy of the moment drawing him near.

She sniffed and nodded.

No wonder she brought so much passion to her work.

"So where do we go from here?" he asked.

"I continue to do my job."

He'd never seen her look so tired. So defeated. He tipped her face up with his finger. Just touching her made the connection between them more real. More alive. "And I continue to be the asshole on the other side of the case, making your life miserable?"

"Something like that." Her eyes studied his. Questioning him. As if trying to share things that were far different—far deeper—than her superficial words conveyed.

"That doesn't seem like a very good arrangement," he said.

"It's why I came to Tallahassee. What I was meant to do."

He bent his head next to hers, reveling in their closeness. He wished it could be different between them. "But what if you're wrong?" His mouth lingered near her ear. The scent of her beckoned him closer. "What if it's not why you're here?"

"We're not talking about the case anymore, are we?" she whispered.

"I don't know what I'm supposed to do." His nose skimmed the soft skin in front of her ear. "Or what I'm not supposed to do."

She pulled away from him far enough to look into his eyes. "We probably . . ." She brushed her lips on his. "Shouldn't . . ." She grazed her lips on his again. "Do this." She grasped the front of his shirt with her fingers and pulled him toward her. His hands immediately went to the top of her SUV, bracing him as he leaned into her kiss. She clutched the fabric of his shirt tighter. A release of tension trembled through his body as he realized that she wanted him as badly as he wanted her.

A shiver raced down his spine as his lips settled onto hers. He'd wanted to do this ever since that first kiss they'd shared on the night they met. He moved his hand to her jaw and felt the dampness of her tears. The softness of her skin. The magnetic pull he couldn't seem to escape.

He brushed his tongue against her lips and she parted them as a soft moan escaped from her chest. He took a step forward, pinning her against the SUV with his body. Her hands skimmed his rib cage. His shoulders. Came to rest on his backside and pressed him forward, molding their bodies together as their tongues explored each other.

A bright light flashed over them as tires crunched on gravel a few feet from them. Her hands rushed to his chest and pushed him away as the headlights to a car pulled into the space facing her SUV, illuminating them like a spotlight.

She pushed against his chest even harder and he stepped back. He wanted to punch the asshole who'd ruined their kiss. Gina squinted and held up her hand to block the headlights. He stepped into the path of the beam, blocking it for her with his body as he sidled up beside her.

"I've got to go," she said.

"You're not going back inside?" He'd waited all night for her to get here and he sure as hell didn't want her to go. Not until he'd spent more time with her. Not until he understood what made him so drawn to her.

She motioned to her tear-streaked face, then removed the set of keys she'd tucked in the waistband of her volleyball shorts. The lights on her SUV flashed behind her again as she beeped the locks open. "Can you tell someone on my team I've gone home?"

"I don't feel much like partying anymore, either." He toed a rock beneath his feet. He wanted to spend more time with her, though he wasn't sure which of his motives drove his desire. Was it Gina, the woman, or Gina, the employee of Morgan's Ladder, who made him feel like he had to keep an eye on her? "Give me a ride to my condo? I rode here with Boomer."

"We shouldn't have done that."

"This?" He motioned from her to him, then back again in the space between them.

"Yes. This. It can't happen again."

Her resolute demeanor felt like cold steel slicing into him. "I'm just asking for a ride home."

"I'm not coming inside." She held a hand up, as if to accentuate her point. "Just dropping you off."

He wished like hell it was different between them, but wasn't about to push himself on her, regardless of how much he wanted to kiss her again. "That's all I'm asking for."

She jerked her head toward the SUV, motioning for him to join her, and they both climbed in. Her car smelled like lavender. A clear droplet of crystal hung from the rearview mirror, sending sparkles of light throughout the interior. He looked around the SUV while she texted her friend inside to let her know she was leaving. A gym bag and a briefcase sat on the backseat. A pair of Nikes were tossed on the back floorboard.

By the time he'd texted Boomer to let him know he wasn't coming back inside, they were cruising through the streets of Tallahassee.

He settled back in his seat and tried to sort through what had just happened. She'd kissed him—and it was clearly her doing—but now acted like they'd committed some horrible sin. She didn't want to get involved with him because of the case, but she'd been the one to clutch his shirt and pull him toward her.

It wasn't like there could ever be anything between him and Gina, even without the case. But he wanted to pretend that things were different.

She'd eventually realize he wasn't good enough for her. Sure, he got to play football for a few years, but he would always be the one with the sordid past.

He knew he made a good first impression. *Sports Illustrated* had called him "ruggedly handsome." The wives of booster club members fawned over him. He'd never had trouble going home with a woman when he had a need for sex.

But Gina would learn soon enough that outward appearances didn't solve everything. Sometimes they just hid the reality inside. A reality that would never live up to the promise. That would never make him good enough for a girl like Gina.

"So I talked to my boss about the death penalty task force," he said, trying to get his mind off of their kiss.

"And?"

"He's asked me to be the representative for his office." Okay, that wasn't the complete truth. Landon had first *asked* Scott Meredith to recommend him to the senator for the assignment, but she didn't need to know that.

She jerked her head to face him. "On the task force?"

He nodded. "I'm scheduled to go on an interview with you the day after tomorrow."

"The one in Tampa?"

"Yep." They'd be interviewing a college professor who specialized in eyewitness misidentification.

"You're sure you're up for this? Discussing crime scenes and murders and stuff?"

No, he wasn't sure. But he'd volunteered for the task force before he'd known what all was involved. He'd thought it would be committee meetings. Debates. Statistics for and against the death penalty. He'd had no idea he'd have to interview people about the accuracy of eyewitness testimony. "I can handle it."

She nodded and seemed to think about his response for a minute. Then, as if the thought had just leapt into her mind, she turned toward him. "No one can know what we just did."

"I understand."

"No one." She emphasized her words with a slice of her hand through the air.

"I got it." God, did she have to act like it was the most embarrassing thing that could ever happen to her? It was a goddamn kiss. And a nice one at that.

They fell into silence. His eyes darted to the curve of her breast as the faint glow from the dashboard shadowed her body. Headlights from each passing car shot a swath of light through the interior, illuminating her face for a brief moment. He shifted his body to look out his window, away from her. Surely he could keep his libido in check long enough to talk to her about all the reasons Cyrus Alexander should stay in prison. They'd had no business kissing. It conflicted with her professional obligations and sure as hell wasn't a good idea for him, either.

But he'd known from her reaction—the way she'd pressed her body to his, the way she'd opened her mouth and let his tongue explore hers—that she'd enjoyed it as much as he had.

~

Gina felt Landon's gaze on her from the other side of the car. She'd seen his eyes flash both passion and annoyance—and she wondered what was in them now.

But she was driving him home. Period. And doing her best to forget the fantastic kiss they'd just shared. She tried to force herself to think of him as the forlorn child in the crime scene photos and not the sexy-as-hell man whose hands had molded to her hips, urging them closer as his mouth devoured hers.

That first kiss, more than a week ago, had been innocent. She hadn't known who he was then. But this one—this one she'd asked for, knowing exactly who he was and how he was connected to one of the cases at Morgan's Ladder.

Just her luck, the car that pulled up when they were in each other's arms would probably end up belonging to a Florida State Supreme

Court justice. Yeah, right. Like they hung out at the Twilight on Thursday nights. The end of her legal career before it ever got started.

She couldn't believe she hadn't been more careful, especially on the heels of the fiasco with Christopher. She'd dated the guy a year and a half, then caught him in bed with a girl he'd met at the pizza place that same day. She'd been humiliated. Heartbroken. And worse—she'd been made to feel like she was disposable. Their relationship had meant so little to him that he'd slept with a girl he'd met two fricking hours earlier.

She'd promised herself that she'd be much smarter with guys after that. So why was she kissing Landon Vista again? And she'd been the one to initiate it.

He grunted brief directions to guide her way. She turned into the driveway of the condo complex where he lived and pulled her car along the edge of the asphalt. A streetlight shone from above, creating a bright pool of light in an otherwise inky-black night.

A tall, thin man stepped into the beam of the streetlight, one of his hands raised in greeting.

Landon groaned. "You should just floor it now."

"And run over him?" Sure, he looked kind of scary in his faded T-shirt and wrinkled pants, but she had Landon Vista with her. Tallahassee's answer to Superman.

Landon got out of the car, slammed the door shut a little harder than necessary, and stalked toward the man. The guy was almost as tall as Landon, but much skinnier, in a sickly sort of way. The two exchanged words, then both sets of eyes turned to look at her.

Why was she a part of their conversation? And who was this guy?

She shifted into park and slipped out of her side of the car, eager to find out.

CHAPTER FIVE

Landon stood in front of Gina's SUV, frozen in place, dreading the introduction he would have to make as soon as she crossed in front of the car toward them.

As usual, his dad ruined everything.

Her questioning look moved from one man to the other, then back again. His dad ogled her like some drunk at a strip club, stopping far too long on those shapely breasts. Landon's possessiveness kicked in again. Even more than usual, he was disgusted with his old man.

"You're not going to introduce us?" His dad's voice sounded wolfish. Sinister.

"This is Gina," he said. "She gave me a ride home."

She shot Landon a questioning look, then stuck out her hand. "Nice to meet you." Landon liked the way she didn't shy away from someone who was obviously dirty and disheveled. He'd always believed people needed to help others. But this was his goddamn father. A man who didn't even try to help himself.

His dad's lips parted into a Wile E. Coyote grin, his tobacco-stained teeth yellow, even in the dim light. "Martin Vista." His hand nervously smoothed his hair as soon as he'd released her grip.

Her searching eyes met Landon's. "Your father?"

Years of memories cascaded through his mind. The time his kindergarten teacher wouldn't release him to a drunken dad. The pitying whispers at his mother's funeral, wondering why his dad wasn't there for him, even though his parents had never married. The headline in the newspaper the time Martin had gotten banned from Landon's high school football games for yelling obscenities at the opposing team.

"You didn't tell me you had a girlfriend." His dad chuckled and slapped him on the back.

"We met through our volleyball league." She seemed to understand the strained relationship between the two of them. "I'm not his—"

"What can I help you with, Dad?" It was a standard conversation opener for the two of them, but Gina frowned at him.

"I stopped by to see if you'd thought about my . . . investment opportunity."

Investment opportunity? He hated his dad for trying to sound so important. It was a fucking bait shop. "I haven't changed my mind."

"We're meeting with the bank tomorrow."

He wondered how long it would take Gina to figure out his dad was drunk. Sure, her past wasn't as pristine as he'd once thought it might be, but she still seemed rich and classy. Drunks in those families were called alcoholics. And they were still rich and classy. His dad would never be either. "I'm not doing the commercials."

"One afternoon of taping? You can't spare that for your old man?"

"I'll let you two talk." She tipped her head in Martin's direction. "Pleasure meeting you."

The older man waggled his eyebrows at Landon once she'd gotten in her SUV and was backing up. "Ni-i-ce."

"Stop it."

"You don't want to talk about her"—he motioned toward her SUV as she pulled away—"then let's talk about my new business venture."

"Don't mention my name when you're out there talking to people about it." He didn't want to be associated with this.

Martin's eyes narrowed. "I wish I could remember the exact time you became too goddamn high and mighty for your own father."

"Good-bye." Landon took a step up the sidewalk toward his front door, mad that his dad hadn't asked about the Cyrus Alexander case. He didn't want to talk to Martin about it, but it would have been nice for him to care enough to ask.

"Don't have time for me now that you got a sweet little squeeze like that around?"

Landon returned to face his dad. Gina wasn't his "squeeze," but that wasn't any of his dad's business. "The invitation's still open. Dinner and a ball game. Anytime you want to come over without some agenda."

Martin's jaw twitched in the moonlight. He stared at his son for several seconds, then stuck his hands in the pockets of his jeans and walked toward the street.

Landon exhaled, trying to rid himself of the toxic tension that thrummed through his veins when his dad was around. This wasn't at all how he'd wanted the night to go. Granted, the kiss with Gina had been fantastic. Better than fantastic.

But what had he been thinking, kissing her back? And why had he felt so offended when she'd pulled away? To make things worse, he hadn't been able to form a rational thought in her SUV—hadn't tried to talk with her about Cyrus Alexander. Hadn't emphasized the fact that the guy had lost all his appeals. He'd just sat there like some horny teenager, unable to talk when the head cheerleader was nearby.

His cell phone rang in his pocket as he trudged to the fridge for a bottle of water.

"You okay?" Gina asked without a greeting as soon as he answered. "I wasn't sure if I should stay . . . or go . . . or what."

"Visits from my dad are always such a pleasure. You did the right thing—got out while you could."

"You want to talk about it?"

"No." He pulled the last grape Nehi out of the fridge. He really wanted a beer, but with his father's history of drinking, he stuck to the nonalcoholic stuff when he wasn't out with his friends.

"You sure?"

"Not now." He cradled the phone against his shoulder as he tugged the cap off the bottle. "Not ever."

"You two don't get along very well."

No shit.

He took a big gulp, knowing he needed to say something nicer to her than what he was thinking.

"Not a great history there?" she said before he could come up with a response.

"I don't want to be rude or anything, but this isn't something I like to talk about." He'd realized since he was a kid that other people had different experiences. Other people had families. He'd always be the kid whose mom had to work in a run-down country store and whose dad hadn't wanted him. Even with his football success, he'd always be the kid who didn't belong.

"You should treat him with a little more respect."

He scoffed. "Did your dad live with you growing up?"

"Yes."

He could almost imagine her nose rising into the air as if to say "Of course my father lived with us." He'd learned a long time ago that people like her took family for granted. That they assumed everyone had one.

"And what does your father do for a living?" he asked her.

"He's a hospital administrator."

"So he goes to work, brings home a paycheck, stays sober long enough that they want to keep him working there?"

"Yeah . . ." Her voice had a questioning tone.

"Then don't tell me how to treat my dad," he said. "You don't know anything about it."

~

Gina and Landon stood as the professor from the university in Tampa entered her office.

"Dr. Stanton." Gina extended her hand and the older woman shook it. "I'm Gina Blanchard. The administrative assistant asked us to wait in here."

"That's fine," the woman said as she turned toward Landon.

"Landon Vista," he said as he shook her hand.

"I didn't expect people who were so"—Dr. Stanton motioned for them to sit as she circled behind her desk—"young."

"Landon—I mean, Mr. Vista—works for Senator Byers," Gina said. "And I work for an organization that gets wrongly convicted people out of prison."

"Which must make my work particularly interesting to you," Dr. Stanton said. Gina watched her movements, trying to figure out if she knew Landon's history as an eyewitness to a crime, but Dr. Stanton appeared to be unaware.

"Yes," Gina said. "I read up on your work once I found out we'd be interviewing you." The professor's research on false memories made her one of the leaders in the field.

Dr. Stanton turned to Landon. "And you?"

"I . . . ummm . . ." Landon fidgeted. Gina had e-mailed him links to all the articles she'd read online, but she wasn't sure he'd read any of them. "I'm familiar with your research."

"Good," the professor said. "Then we don't have to start with the basics." She rested her elbows on her desk. "So what do you want to know from me?"

Gina opened her notebook and dug a pen out of her purse as she spoke. "In my line of work, we know that eyewitnesses are often wrong." She avoided looking at Landon.

The professor nodded.

"But *why* are they wrong?" Gina continued. "How do they think they saw something they really didn't see?" God, if she'd only known the answer to that after Tommy's murder. Before she'd sent Nick Varnadore to prison.

The professor sat back in her chair. "The mind has a tricky retrieval system. People under stress—like those witnessing a robbery or a homicide—sometimes don't capture the right details. And if they do, the mind may not retrieve them correctly. That's why the witnesses often don't get even the most basic details correct, like whether the perpetrator was bald or had a complete head of hair. Sometimes they don't know whether the guy's white or black or Latino."

Landon sat forward in his chair. "But what if they saw something before they knew the crime had taken place? Doesn't that increase their level of accuracy?"

Gina shot him a warning glance. He was asking about his own testimony, though the professor didn't know it.

"Being under stress is only one of the ways our memories are bastardized," Dr. Stanton said to Landon. Gina wanted to look at Landon's reaction, but she didn't.

The professor continued. "The biggest finding in recent years is that other people can plant false memories into our brains. Sometimes it's on purpose and sometimes it's by suggestion. An accident."

"Can you give us some examples?" Gina had read about this in the articles online. She'd spent time rehashing the days after Tommy's death, as if hoping to find someone else who'd first planted the thought that Nick Varnadore was the one who'd pushed Tommy off the train trestle. But no. It had been all her doing.

"I studied a woman last year who claimed to have been on the Jersey Shore during Hurricane Sandy. She was seeking medical help for what she claimed to be PTSD from the storm." Dr. Stanton opened her desk drawer and pulled out a file folder. "Except the insurance company didn't buy it. She was having a hysterectomy in Omaha during Hurricane Sandy. They knew it because they'd paid the hospital bill."

"So why would she claim to have been in New Jersey?" Gina asked.

"She'd spent days during her recovery with nothing to do but watch TV. She'd seen the videos so much she actually believed she was there." Dr. Stanton opened the file she'd retrieved from the drawer. "And this man." She spun the file so that a man's mug shot was facing Gina and Landon.

Gina thought she'd seen the picture before, but couldn't remember the story behind it.

"William Thomas. His neighbor suspected him of having an affair with his wife, so the neighbor kept asking his own daughter about the times that Mr. Thomas had touched her inappropriately. After a while the little girl had false memories of being molested by Mr. Thomas."

Landon frowned. "He did that to his own daughter?"

Dr. Stanton nodded. "Sad, isn't it?"

More like sickening. Or evil. "How'd they figure out it didn't happen?"

"The neighbor eventually turned himself in. The wife threatened to leave if he didn't tell the truth." The professor shrugged. "He ended up admitting he'd talked the little girl into it."

"I hope the wife left him anyway," Gina said. "And kept the daughter away from him."

"I think she did." Dr. Stanton stood. "Come on. I'll show you our research lab."

They spent the next two hours touring the school's facilities for the study of how the brain recalls facts, experiences, smells, and other stimuli. They listened to the professor's stories about how false memories had been planted in people's minds by therapists, well-meaning friends or family members, and even television shows.

"So," Gina said later as she and Landon walked through the parking lot toward his truck. "What do you think?" He'd been quiet all afternoon, asking questions of Dr. Stanton only a couple of times.

"It's . . . a lot to absorb."

She glanced sideways at him. He looked a bit shaken. So he *did* realize how Dr. Stanton's work could apply to his own testimony. Gina decided not to push it with him. Not until he'd had a chance to process everything they'd learned today. At least she'd had a few days to think about what she'd learned in the articles. And a much longer time to think about how her testimony had locked up the wrong guy.

They walked in silence, both engrossed in their own thoughts.

It had been dark the night of Tommy's death. She'd just pulled up to their regular gathering spot—the old train trestle out off Highway 63. She'd turned her headlights off as she approached—everyone did when they came here so that Rachel Crawford's grandma wouldn't see them from across the river and call the sheriff on them again. Like it mattered when her house was so far away.

But that's what teenagers in her hometown had been doing for years. And that's what she'd done that night. It was why it had been so dark. Why it had taken her a minute or two to realize that someone had plunged off the trestle and into the river. Even longer—oh, God, much longer—to realize it had been Tommy. She'd been certain it was Nick Varnadore who'd pushed him. The crowd of teenage boys had been laughing and joking as they drank beer on the trestle. The sheriff found out later they'd also been passing around a bottle of tequila someone's big brother had bought them.

She'd seen the guy in the dark green hoodie—Nick's hoodie—step toward Tommy in the dark. He shoved Tommy with both hands, knocking him onto the boulders on the riverbank below. Traumatic head injury had been the cause of her brother's death, and she'd been there to witness his last few seconds of life.

She got the sense that Landon was watching her and glanced sideways at him.

"Sucks, doesn't it?" he asked.

"What's that?" They kept walking.

"How you can never forget what happened." His face was solemn. "How it's always there. With you."

"Yeah." She took a deep breath. "It really does suck." She wanted to share her story with him, though she wasn't sure why. "Every now and then I have a few minutes when I forget about it." She took a few more steps. "But it's always there."

"They use DNA to figure out who really killed your brother?"

She shook her head. "The other guy finally came forward. Couldn't live with himself knowing the wrong guy had been convicted." She swallowed. "It was dark. I didn't know."

He reached over and gave her hand a quick squeeze—a sign of solidarity—as they continued through the parking lot. She liked that he was there for her. That he knew that she, too, had demons that she wrestled with.

"I'm glad you're here with me," she whispered when they'd finally reached his truck. Though no one else was around to hear her, just saying it out loud felt a little rebellious.

He brushed against her as he reached to open the passenger door for her. "The next time we come to Tampa, we need a better plan."

"Yeah? How so?"

They were so close she could see a bead of sweat trickle down his temple. She lifted her hair off the back of her neck. The damn Florida heat made even a walk across a parking lot unbearable.

"There are world-class resorts here, but we're making a five-hour drive back tonight," he said.

She chuckled. "The state isn't going to pay for us to stay at a resort in Tampa." But maybe Landon would. She glanced sideways at him. Was that what he was implying? That they spend the night here? Together?

She rushed into her seat, eager to get some distance between them. She needed time to contemplate that thought.

What would she say if he asked her to spend the night here? It was a conflict of interest with her job—that was for certain. But they were hours away from Tallahassee. No one would ever know. And this was a vacation destination, where people came to relax. To unwind. To go a little bit crazy.

She certainly wouldn't suggest it herself.

But if he offered, would she accept?

Landon glanced over at Gina where she slept in the passenger seat of his truck as he drove. The rays of the setting sun glinted off her hair. Her eyelids fluttered a bit, then settled. She'd taken off her jacket, and her rose-colored blouse fell open just enough for him to see the sprinkling of freckles across her sternum.

Would she have spent the night in Tampa with him if he'd asked?

Any other time, he would have jumped at the chance for a spontaneous rendezvous with a beautiful woman. But this was Gina, the woman who felt guilty just for kissing him. His self-esteem didn't need the kick to the groin he would have gotten if she'd turned him down. He'd already decided he wasn't good enough for her, but no woman had ever complained about his performance in the sack. A night in Tampa might have been good for both of them.

But today's visit to Dr. Stanton had shaken him up. Hell, he was a math-and-science guy himself. Those were the two subjects that had right and wrong answers. Period. Not that mumbo jumbo about identifying themes in literature or trying to figure out which ad campaign would make the fickle public buy more of a certain brand of ketchup. He liked when there were solid answers. And scientific research proved things that couldn't be disputed.

Dr. Stanton's research on false memories had proven, time after time, that the human brain was fallible. That someone could believe they'd experienced things they'd never experienced.

Had someone involved in Mama's murder case convinced him he'd seen Cyrus Alexander running from the country store? He tried to remember the officers and social workers he'd talked to that day, but their faces all ran together in his mind, like a kaleidoscope of eyes and noses and lips all tumbling together into a memory that couldn't be trusted. He'd been scared, not knowing if his mom would go to heaven or not. Not knowing what they'd do with her body. Not knowing where he'd live or if his dad would come after him.

He gripped the steering wheel harder, thankful that Gina was asleep so he could be alone while he thought all this through.

If other people remembered things they hadn't seen, was it possible that he hadn't seen Cyrus Alexander running from the country store?

What if his testimony had helped put an innocent man in prison all those years ago?

What if Mama's killer was still out there?

CHAPTER SIX

Landon rolled over in his bed, trying to get back to sleep for the third time since he'd finally dozed off at about 4 a.m. They'd gotten home from Tampa close to midnight. He'd gone straight to bed after dropping Gina off at her apartment, but the visit with Dr. Stanton—and the time he'd spent with Gina—had kept his mind churning like a blender.

When he'd finally dozed off, she haunted his sleep, luring him like one of the sirens they'd learned about in that mythology class he had to take sophomore year. Twice, he'd startled awake, sure he could smell her perfume and hear her rustling the sheets beside him. Positive it had been her hair tickling his face as she straddled him. Absolutely certain he'd felt himself inside her. But it had been only dreams.

God, he really needed to get a grip.

She wasn't someone he should be lusting after. She was the woman who was trying to prove that every important fact in his life was wrong.

And worse yet, she and her stupid task force had made him start doubting what he'd seen the day Mama was murdered. For fifteen years he'd been certain the right guy was in prison. Certain that, though he could never get his mother back, at least justice had been served. At least he'd helped nail the guy who'd killed the one person who'd ever loved him.

Yet Dr. Stanton's research had given him doubts. Doubts on the one topic he'd been absolutely certain about since he was nine years old.

Finally, he rolled himself out of bed, showered, and headed for Ace's, the pool hall and bar that had been his dad's hangout when he last went looking for him two years ago.

The inside of Ace's was dark and dingy, even though the Florida sun pounded every other corner of the state with its unrelenting glare. A wall of stale odor made him pause at the door, evidence that Ace had gotten around the state's "no smoking" ban that covered most food-and-beverage establishments.

"Hey, hey. Landon Vista." The bartender, a dark-haired man with his hair pulled back in a slick braid, smiled with recognition. "I've seen that face on TV a thousand times."

He nodded an acknowledgment as he approached the scarred wooden bar. "How's it going?"

The bartender tossed a cardboard coaster in front of him. "You looking for your dad?"

"He around?"

"Went down the street for some breakfast. He's looking pretty rough this morning."

My dad? Hung over? Say it ain't so. But he kept his sarcasm to himself.

"Been gone awhile, so he should get back any minute," the other man continued.

Landon pulled out a bar stool. Yellowish stuffing peeked out of slices in the faux leather cushion. "Maybe I'll hang here and wait for him."

"Get you a brew?"

Landon shook his head. Did the guy really think he'd drink a beer at nine o'clock in the morning? "Sweet tea, if you've got it."

The bartender turned to the counter behind him as the front door scraped open. A tall, thin silhouette stepped inside, the only shield from the ray of sunlight that tried to barge its way into the dank room.

"You got a visitor, Martin." The bartender's gaze went from his dad to Landon.

His dad squinted, as if trying to let his eyes adjust to the dark interior. A look of realization spread across his face. He hesitated a couple more seconds, then shuffled to the bar and plopped down two stools away from Landon. "What brings you to the dark side?" he said, not making eye contact with his son.

The bartender set a glass of sweet tea in front of Landon and a pint of beer in front of Martin. Landon snatched the beer, suddenly needing to calm his frayed nerves, and downed most of it. Not a great example, considering that one thing he'd always wanted was for his dad to stop drinking. But after the last few days, he felt like getting drunker than he'd ever been. To forget. To dull the pain. To try to believe his mom could remain at peace, her memory not mired in a total screwup with the wrong man in prison.

His dad motioned for the bartender to get him another beer. The guy set another draft in front of Martin and then ambled off to a back room.

Landon wiped his mouth on the sleeve of his T-shirt. "I'm here to ask you some more questions about Mama's murder."

The corner of his dad's mouth tensed. Martin still didn't face him. "Son, it ain't my fault if the Florida court system screwed it all up."

The back of Landon's neck tightened with anger. "That's all you have to say?" A faint crinkling sound filled the silence between them as he peeled his forearms off the sticky bar. "All you can do is criticize the court system?"

"What do you want me to say?" Martin asked.

"I don't know. Have a reaction. Act like you care. Act like it affects you in some minor way."

"That was almost twenty years ago. We weren't married. Once they realized I didn't do it, they didn't want me to have anything to do with it."

"She was the mother of your child." Landon hated the pleading tone in his voice, as if all the years he'd wished his dad would care were focused into this one moment.

His dad finally turned to face him, surveying him from his shoes to his head. "You seem to do pretty good for yourself."

And this was what bothered Landon most about his dad. Not that Martin hated his son. Not that he was mean to him. Hell, a couple of beatings would have meant he'd been around a few times. No, what hurt most of all was the indifference, to both him and his mother.

"It doesn't bother you that it's all coming back? That Cyrus Alexander may have spent fifteen years in prison for something he didn't do?" *That your son might be pretty messed up in the head if he helped convict the wrong man?*

His dad raised his mug to his mouth and drained the beer. "Good thing he didn't get the death penalty, huh?"

"He's been taken away from his family"—Landon's gaze locked on his father's—"just like I was."

His dad broke the eye contact by taking a pack of cigarettes from his shirt pocket. He tapped it on the back of his other hand, then slid one out and inserted it between his dry, cracked lips.

"If Cyrus is innocent," Landon said, "the guy who did it is still out there."

Martin lit his cigarette and took a long drag. "But the courts have ruled him guilty."

"I may have helped put an innocent man in prison." Landon rested his elbows on the bar and cradled his forehead in his outstretched fingertips. "And if he didn't do it, then there will be another investigation. Another period of not knowing."

"Ain't gonna make her any less dead."

Landon's head shot up as his jaw locked and his body stiffened. "Don't talk about her like she's a"—his mind spun—"a side of beef or some possum that somebody ran over in the middle of the road."

"Why don't you tell me how you want me to act?" His dad's eyes narrowed. "Then it'll be easier on both of us."

"Act like you have some inkling that this is important. You sit over there"—he swept his arm toward Martin—"like we're talking about the weather or the stock market or something."

His father leaned toward him. "How come what I do is never good enough for you?"

"I just want you to care." Landon ran his fingers through his hair. "Care about whether or not the right guy's in prison. Care about how this affects other people."

"Why do you need me involved in this? Why do I all of a sudden have to change because of all this?"

Landon felt his eyes mist up. Damn if he was going to let his dad see how much this meant to him. "Because I'm tired of being the son of a drunk." *The kid whose mom got murdered and whose dad wouldn't even take him in.*

Martin shook his head and chuckled. "Those football fans fed you a bunch of hooey. Sure they loved you while you was playing ball, but where are they now?" He looked around the empty bar. "Don't you go thinking you're so much better than me."

Landon's bar stool toppled backward as he stood. He couldn't say another word. Couldn't face his father anymore.

He'd known for a long time that while he was some guy with quick feet and a good arm, he would always be the son of a murdered woman, the son shipped off to live with an aunt and uncle, raised in a place where he never felt like he actually belonged.

He knew he was an imposter. Someone who'd been touted as important, but who—in the end—didn't really matter.

He hated that his dad was right.

~

Gina had known something was wrong by the tone of Landon's voice on the phone. She'd agreed he could come over, but she wasn't prepared for the disheveled way he looked. The dark circles under his eyes told her he hadn't slept much since they'd returned from Tampa last night.

"I want to ask you some questions," he said as soon as she opened the door.

His normal, casual posture had been replaced by a combative stance—shoulders squared, arms bowed wide beside his body.

"About your mom's case?"

His jaw twitched. "About my dad."

Gina swallowed. "You want to come in?"

He stood there silently for too long. She watched the rise and fall of his chest under his faded T-shirt. "Yeah," he finally said, his voice a whisper. "I do."

This was the first time he'd been inside her apartment and he looked around. He picked up a framed picture of her family from the table next to the couch—the one with her, Mom, Dad, and Tommy snow-skiing, right before they all went down their first black-diamond slope.

"That was the year before he died." If he was here to talk about his mom's murder, then maybe it would be good for her to open up, too.

"The Rockies?"

She nodded. "Breckenridge." Then she remembered his upbringing had been far less privileged than her own. "Colorado."

"You must miss him."

"I do." Tommy had been the one she built forts with in the living room. And told ghost stories with at night. The one who'd challenged her at running and jumping and climbing trees, all of which helped her become the athlete she'd been in high school and college. "Every single day."

He set the frame back on the table and turned to her. "I know what you mean."

"You want to sit down?" She motioned to the couch.

He hesitated, but soon made his way to the sofa. He rested his elbows on his knees.

"You want to talk about your dad?" she asked.

"I think he knows something." His words rushed out as if he'd been holding them in too long.

"About the case?"

Landon nodded.

"How long have you thought this?" Or had Landon been a nine-year-old child afraid to tell the truth because of what his father might say or do? Her mind whirled. Martin Vista had been questioned by police and had been cleared as a suspect. Surely Landon knew that.

"He's just too . . . evasive. He won't even talk about the time frame when it happened."

"He had an alibi. He was out of town with the guy who owned the sawmill next door."

"The guy was fifteen or twenty years older than he was. Why'd they even hang out together?"

"The police verified it with the man's daughter. She was home from college. Your dad and Grady Buchanan liked to gamble together. Your dad would go with him whenever a load of wood had to be delivered near a casino—Biloxi, Mississippi. Cherokee, North Carolina. They'd done that a few times before." She wondered if she should be sharing that information.

"He just . . ." His voice cracked. "He won't even enter into a conversation with me about it."

She didn't have an answer, but assumed he didn't expect one from her. She walked over and sat on the chair next to the couch. Her knees touched Landon's. She knew from Tommy's death that sometimes words just got in the way. Sometimes the best comfort was a friend who was just . . . there.

She rested her hand on his knee and caressed his skin with her thumb. Landon let his long torso fall against the back of the couch and covered his eyes with the backs of his hands.

Still, she sat there. Making her presence known. Letting him decide when the time was right for them to talk.

After several minutes, he lowered his arms and let out a big sigh. "I don't understand how he can be so detached from it all. Like he doesn't even care."

She thought of how she might respond, but everything sounded so lame. She slid onto the couch next to Landon. "Maybe that's a defense mechanism. His way of dealing with it."

"I got used to him not being around much. I learned never to expect anything from him." His chest shuddered. "But that was about me. The kid he never wanted and didn't take care of. I'd have thought he'd at least give a damn about who killed my mom." He braced his elbows on his thighs and rested his head in the palms of his hands. "But he doesn't care if Cyrus Alexander's the guy or not."

"So you go on without him," Gina pulled her knees to her chest. "You've made it this far. Why do you need him now?"

Sure, she'd reread the file tomorrow, focusing on Martin Vista's testimony, but Landon didn't need to know that.

"I've just always wanted—" Landon stopped, as if he didn't have the power to go on. "Never mind."

She smoothed one of the dark curls on his head. Sure, he was someone involved in one of her cases, but somehow touching him this way felt . . . natural. "I'm always here if you want to talk."

"Yeah. How sad is that? Being consoled by the opposition because my dad lets me down again."

"But I'm a good listener. About anything." Her gaze rose to his and held there. A growling sound gurgled in his midsection. His palm clapped against his belly.

She laughed. "Was that your stomach?"

"I might have forgotten to eat the last couple of days." They'd stopped for burgers on the drive home from Tampa last night, but he hadn't eaten much of his.

"Yeah?" She popped up off the couch. "Well, it's a good thing you're with one of the best omelet makers in Tallahassee."

He held his hands up and shook his head. "No. I didn't come here to mooch a meal off you."

She grabbed one of his arms and pulled it, encouraging him to get up and come with her. "Come on. I never cook for myself. It doesn't make sense when there's only one person. And I love a big breakfast."

He hesitated.

"Sausage links," she said in a singsong voice. She'd bought a packet of them a few days ago, thinking they'd keep forever in the freezer. "Fried potatoes. Omelets."

He laughed as he stood. "How many people are coming over?"

He now stood inches from her, almost nose to nose. The closeness of him made her feel giddy. "I told you—I like breakfast."

"I just never knew a girl who could eat more than I can," he teased.

She grinned. She'd always been grateful for her physicality and strength. Had never gone through the body hang-ups that some girls had. She tilted her head playfully. "Are you calling me fat?"

His hands traveled to her hips as his eyes met hers. The fun, flirty atmosphere was replaced by a silent connection between them. "I'm definitely not calling you fat."

She took a deep breath. Her gaze fell to his lips as the manly smell of him swirled around her. She immediately jerked her gaze back up to his olive-green eyes. God, would he think she wanted him to kiss her? This was all so . . . inappropriate. She couldn't be making out in her apartment with someone involved in one of her cases. She could almost hear Dr. Howard's class lecture on conflicts of interest. Still, she didn't want the moment to end. "Then what are you saying?"

He took a tiny step forward, drawing their bodies even closer together. "What I'm saying . . ."

∼

Landon's mind whirred as he stood with his hands on Gina's hips. He'd come here to talk about his dad, yet here he was, unable to keep from touching her. "What I'm saying is . . . that you confuse me."

She seemed to know what he was talking about. "Because you don't know whether to run me over in the parking lot . . . ?"

He nodded, waiting for her to finish her sentence. The only sound in the room was the pounding of his heart in his ears.

". . . or kiss me?"

He nodded again.

"I think the kissing would be a bad idea." Her soft whisper filled the few inches between them. Despite her words, she didn't pull away.

"Because of the case?"

"And because I confuse you."

"Maybe the kissing would help." He was for damn sure willing to give it a try.

"But I could lose my job."

The sweet scent of her beckoned him closer. "It's just a summer gig anyway."

Her mouth fell open in mock surprise. "You want me to risk my career to kiss you?"

"It would probably be worth your while." And if it led to other things . . . well, he'd definitely make sure she enjoyed that, too.

She covered his hands with hers and gently pulled them away from her hips. "Maybe we should stick with breakfast."

She turned and walked toward the kitchen, giving him a great view of that sweet ass in tiny yellow shorts. He stood for a minute, wishing that little scene had turned out differently, then followed her into the kitchen.

She handed him a cutting board and two potatoes. "You're in charge of these. Wash them first, then cut them into thin slices. Leave the skin on." She opened the fridge and bent over to rummage through one of the drawers.

Again, the yellow shorts caught his attention, but he needed to stop staring and keep up with his end of the conversation. "You're kind of bossy."

"You want to help or do you want to complain?"

What he wanted to do was stay right here with her, whatever that took. And he hated himself for it. He hated that he'd started out wanting to find out more about his mother's case and ended up enjoying—way more than he wanted to—his time with Gina.

He turned on the water to wash the potatoes as she pulled something from the fridge and closed the door. She walked over beside him and stuck a green pepper under the stream of water. There she was, close again. Leaning against him. Her breast grazed the back of his arm.

"This okay in your omelet?" she asked as she stepped away from him.

"Sure." His throat was thick. He cleared it, feeling like a horny eighth grader who got all flustered at the thought of a boob touching him. "Sure," he said again, with more conviction this time.

"Mozzarella or cheddar?"

"Are you always this prepared to fix a guy breakfast?" He didn't want to think about another man standing in her kitchen. And he *really* didn't want to think about what they might have done the night before.

She paused and grinned at him, as if she was on to his little tinge of jealousy. "I haven't fixed breakfast for any guys since I've been in Tallahassee."

"That wasn't what I was asking."

She pulled two knives from the silverware drawer. "I'm pretty sure it was," she said as she turned toward him.

"Your sex life is none of my business." He grasped the knife she held out for him.

She didn't let go of the utensil. "Then why are you asking about it?"

He held her gaze for several seconds, challenging her. He didn't want her to know how much he thought about having sex with her. "Cheddar."

She released the knife and motioned to the cutting board. "Cut your potatoes. Thin. Like potato chips."

"Yes, ma'am." He'd do just about anything, he realized, to stay here with her.

"And no more looking at my ass."

His eyes widened. She'd caught him.

"I'll just . . . ummmm"—he motioned toward the cutting board behind him—"cut these potatoes now." He turned around, ready to get to work before she nailed him again.

CHAPTER SEVEN

Gina watched as Landon sliced the potatoes. How adept a person was in the kitchen told a lot about how they'd been raised. Though Gina's family was fairly well-off, she'd learned to cook from both her parents, unlike her wealthy roommate, Caitlyn, from sophomore year, who'd grown up with a housekeeper and didn't even know how an electric can opener worked.

"You've done this before," Gina said as she scooped from the margarine tub.

He chuckled. "Only a few thousand times."

"You worked in a restaurant?"

"My aunt used to leave a note for me every day after school, telling me what I needed to do to get supper started."

"I would have thought you had football practice." She plopped the margarine into the skillet.

He reached for the second potato. "And basketball. And baseball."

The rhythmic sound of the knife thwacking on the cutting board was relaxing. Homey. "So when did you have time to start dinner?"

He shrugged. "She was out even later than I was."

"So what's your specialty?" She loved the camaraderie with him. Their closeness. It was comfortable. Almost . . . intimate.

He turned to face her as he chuckled. "My specialty?"

"What do you like to cook?" She slid the mound of margarine around in the skillet, trying to get it to melt faster.

He turned back toward the cutting board and sliced some more. "Chili. Beef roast. Frozen pizzas."

She laughed. "Frozen pizzas aren't really cooking."

"They are when your job keeps you out a lot of evenings."

"What is it you do for the senator exactly?"

He straightened his back. "Senior statistical analyst," he said in an official-sounding voice, but with a touch of sarcasm.

"You don't like it?"

"The statistics part is fine. I was a math major, so it's a pretty good gig."

So, good looks, athleticism, *and* brains. The whole package. But there was something he wasn't telling her. "What's the part you don't like?"

He stood motionless, no longer chopping the potatoes. It was as if he wasn't making eye contact with her on purpose. "Never mind." He started slicing again. "I like it all."

She hesitated for a few seconds, wondering if what she'd sensed for a while now was really true. Finally, she decided to dive in. To test the deep, still waters known as Landon Vista. "You don't like that there's so much focus on your mom's murder. That you're their poster child for tougher sentencing guidelines."

His shoulders rose and fell in an exaggerated shrug.

She turned down the burner and set the spatula on the counter. Dare she comfort him? Dare she try to get beneath his facade?

She walked up behind him and placed her hand on his back. He stiffened, then slowly relaxed.

"You don't have to work there," she said. A shoulder muscle rippled underneath his shirt.

He set the knife the counter, finished with his task. "I don't want to talk about this."

She paused, thinking about that TED Talk she'd watched on her computer—the presentation about how everyone felt vulnerable. But should she share her own fears with him? She swallowed. "I hate going into the prisons."

He turned to look at her. "What?"

"I love knowing that I'm helping innocent people get out, but I hate going in there. It's scary and claustrophobic and . . . without hope."

"Why are you telling me this?"

So maybe you'll open up to me.

She shrugged. "I don't know. I guess everyone hates something about their job." She reached around him and took the cutting board full of potatoes from him and slid them into the skillet. They sizzled in the melted margarine.

"Seems like a tough career for someone whose clients are, by definition, in prison."

She had to agree, but she'd promised herself she'd do it. It was her way to make amends.

But Landon didn't need to know that. She'd never told anybody how strongly she felt about why she had to do it.

"Can you get another skillet from there?" She pointed to a lower cabinet with her toe. "And then get the eggs out of the fridge?"

They worked steadily beside each other until the huge breakfast was ready. "If you need ketchup for your potatoes, it's in the fridge." She set the heaping plates on the table next to the glasses of orange juice she'd asked him to pour.

He retrieved the bottle and rushed over to the little nook to pull a chair out for her.

She smiled. "You really were raised a good Southern boy, weren't you?"

He shrugged. "It's the least I can do since you're feeding me so well." He pushed her chair in and sat in the other one.

She sipped her orange juice, then set her glass on the table. "Taste your omelet," she said, eager for his opinion.

He took a bite and nodded as he chewed. "Good."

Satisfied, she picked up her own fork and started eating. They ate silently for a long while. The hum of a car passing by on Bronough Street was the only sound in the kitchen.

"I hate being the guy everybody thinks they know," Landon said, finally breaking the silence.

She lowered her fork slowly as her gaze met his. She could tell the conversation had taken a turn.

"It's what I hate about my job," he continued. "People fawning over me because I used to play football. They don't even know me."

She nodded. She'd gotten a taste of that from her own playing days. Groupies who wanted a piece of her, even though they knew nothing about her. And that was women's volleyball. It had to have been a hundred times worse for a guy who won Division I football games on TV every Saturday afternoon.

"Some days I wish I could just sneak away. Go become a river guide or work for the fish and wildlife commission"—he waved his fork in the air—"or something else deep in the woods."

"You don't have to stay in such a public job. Or even stay in Tallahassee, for that matter."

"Oh yeah? Where else would I live?" He reached for the ketchup bottle and twisted off the lid.

"I once read that Wyoming has the fewest people per square mile." She wondered where—ten years from now—each of them would be.

"Sounds like the perfect spot." He shook the ketchup bottle over his potatoes, which were the only thing remaining on his plate. Nothing came out. He shook it again. Still nothing.

"Here. Let me. I used to have to do this when I worked summers in a restaurant." She took the bottle from him and beat it against the heel of her hand as she aimed it toward his plate.

Nothing came out.

She stood up for a better angle and leaned over the table. Yes, she'd hated it when the male customers used to leer at her boobs when she did this as a waitress, but her shirt today wasn't as low cut as her uniform had been at the steakhouse back home.

She shook the bottle and then raised her head. Landon looked up from her chest to her face. He held her gaze. Silent heat simmered between them.

She looked down again, fully aware that Landon's attention would drop back to her cleavage. But she liked that he was attracted to her. That she had something he wanted. Something that would at least keep him interested.

She pounded the bottle on the heel of her hand, harder this time. A giant mass of ketchup burst out and onto his lap, spreading across his light khaki shorts. His jaw dropped open as he scooted his chair back.

She clapped a hand over her mouth. "I am so sorry."

"Didn't keep your restaurant job long, did you?"

"That never happened before." She grabbed a wad of paper towels to mop up the puddle on top of his zipper, then realized she couldn't really . . . dab . . . there. She pulled back instinctively.

"I've got it." He took the paper towels from her and scooted the red mass around on his lap. There was so much of it that sopping it up seemed like a futile effort.

She jumped up. "Let me get you some other pants to wear home."

"No. I'm pretty sure I'll be okay."

She motioned to his pants. "I'll wash those for you—make sure the stain comes out."

"You don't have pants big enough—" He stood.

She held in a giggle as the ketchup ran down his shorts and onto his legs. "I do. I have this huge pair of sweatpants." She glanced at his sopping-wet crotch. "Never mind. I'll be back," she said as she dashed into her bedroom.

∽

Landon hoped to God no one in Tallahassee saw him in the sweatpants Gina had insisted he wear home. Could a guy look any more stupid than he did, with huge orange letters emblazoned across his ass? Especially the words *Tennessee Volunteers* when everyone in town was a Seminoles fan?

But he'd told Calvin he'd return his cordless drill this morning, and after all the guy had done for him—as both a coach and a friend—he didn't want to let him down. Calvin had bought his wife a new wine rack for her birthday and he needed to put it together.

Landon knocked on the front door of Calvin's house and turned toward the street behind him, checking again to make sure none of the neighbors were in their yards.

Calvin answered the door in a pair of gym shorts and a T-shirt. He'd gone two-ninety in his playing days, but had slimmed down to two-thirty or so since he'd been coaching at Florida State.

"Hey." His friend opened the door wide for Landon to enter. The ebony-colored skin on his forearms glistened in the morning sun. "Rachel's making pancakes. You want to come in and have some?"

"I already had a big breakfast, but thanks." He handed Calvin the drill. "I've . . . got to be somewhere." Back home. Where he could change out of these ridiculous pants.

"Why you in such a hurry?" Calvin stepped out onto the front porch. "You want to at least come in for a glass of juice or something? Sweet tea?"

Landon backed down the sidewalk, looking over his shoulder to see where he was going, unwilling to turn around. "No. Thanks." He stuck his hand in the air in a sort of half wave. "Got to go."

When he'd gotten around to the corner of the garage, he'd turned and rushed toward his truck, thankful he heard the door close behind Calvin.

"Hey, Vista." The deep voice of his former coach thundered from the front porch.

Landon turned to see that Calvin had closed the door, but remained on the outside.

Calvin chuckled. "Nice pants."

Landon cringed as Calvin's big, booming voice ricocheted off the other houses in the neighborhood.

"I guess we know where you were last night." Calvin called, his voice even louder than before.

"Screw you."

"Screw somebody," Calvin called.

Landon heard Rachel on the front porch chastising Calvin for shouting across the front lawn, but Landon didn't turn around. He liked Calvin's wife, but he sure as hell wanted to get out of there before the entire neighborhood came outside to see what all the yelling was about. Before they saw the big orange letters across his ass.

He turned on his truck and slammed it into reverse. Out of the corner of his eye, he saw that Rachel stood toe-to-toe with Calvin, leaning toward him as she waved a finger in his face and did all the talking. At least Calvin was getting what he deserved. Good.

Landon pressed the gas pedal to get out of there and . . .

Crunch.

Metal crashed against metal.

His body jarred forward.

Shit.

CHAPTER EIGHT

A high-pitched alarm screamed in Landon's ears. His heart raced. He glanced in the rearview mirror and saw nothing but the black metal of the F150 he'd seen parked on the other side of Calvin's street.

He'd backed into a truck that wasn't even moving. He pounded his steering wheel with the heel of his hand. "Shit. Shit. Shit." The hassle of fixing both vehicles was a bother he didn't need right now, not to mention the deductible he'd have to pay. Could this day get any worse?

Calvin ripped open the driver-side door and thrust his face down next to Landon's. "You okay, man?" The smell of maple syrup tinged his breath. Rachel was right behind him, her brows knit with worry.

"Peachy." He was more embarrassed than anything. Like some sixteen-year-old learning how to drive. What kind of an idiot backs into a parked car?

Both men and Rachel walked to the back of the truck to look at the damage, the ugly sweatpants forgotten for now. A dent the size of a bathtub marred the side panel of the pickup truck. Landon's bumper had buckled. The end of it punctured through the metal of the other vehicle.

An old couple in a Camry turned the corner and inched toward them, unable to get by.

Landon returned to the open door of his truck. "I guess I should get it out of the middle of the road." He sat down and shifted into gear. The grating sound of metal filled the air as he inched forward.

"Hey, my truck!" A pajama-clad neighbor ran out of the house behind them.

Calvin held a hand in the air like a superhero ready to stop the man in his tracks. "Give it a rest, Phillip. It's just a truck."

Phillip continued, picking his way through the yard as if he'd never walked outside barefoot before. "He's fleeing the scene of an accident."

Calvin rolled his eyes. "He's getting his truck out of the street." He stood aside and motioned to let the Camry pass.

The neighbor approached the open door of Landon's truck. "What kind of an idiot—" His eyebrows rose. "Landon Vista?"

Calvin's big hands each grasped one of the man's scrawny shoulders from behind and straightened him up. He turned the man toward his own house. "Nothing to see here. Now go inside and call the police so they can file a report."

"But my truck." Phillip squirmed. He tried to turn around, but Calvin's grip was solid. The bigger man marched Phillip to his front door and opened it for him, guiding him until he was inside.

Calvin shut the door and returned to where Landon sat inside his truck. "Remember the guy I told you started a petition to keep the ice cream man off our street?"

Landon jabbed a thumb toward Phillip's house. "That guy?"

Calvin nodded. "What kind of a guy doesn't like ice cream? Now pull it into my driveway and we'll wait inside until the police come." He nodded toward the pants Landon was wearing. "I don't want any of my neighbors seeing you wearing those bad pants."

Thirty minutes later they were back in Calvin's driveway as a middle-aged policeman wrote Landon a ticket. Calvin had loaned Landon a pair of nylon shorts to wear.

Phillip sat on his own front porch in a faded wicker chair. Each time he stood up and started down the stairs, Calvin glared at him and Phillip scurried back to his seat like a scared puppy.

The cop handed Landon the ticket. "Some guys at the station were talkin' the other day. Said they might let Cyrus Alexander out of jail."

Calvin cleared his throat and frowned at the policeman.

"What?" The cop held his hands out in a questioning pose. "The kid should know if they're gonna let his mom's killer out of prison."

Landon crumpled the ticket in his hand and tried to get a grip on his anger.

The policeman squared himself in front of Calvin. "Don't be glaring at me like that. I got nothin' to do with this."

"I know they're trying to get him out of prison." Landon stepped between his coach and the officer. *I live it every goddamn day.*

"So if the DNA shows Cyrus Alexander is innocent"—the policeman turned his attention to Landon—"they open the case back up. Find the real killer."

Landon glared at him. "Yes. I know." This is why he hated living here—so many people in his business. So many people thinking they could talk about his private life as if it were part of the public domain.

The police officer took off his hat and scratched the top of his head. "I hate like hell that there are scumbags out there, holding down a job, having a family . . . and all the time they know they killed someone or raped some little girl or . . ."

"Is that all you need from us, Officer?" Calvin asked.

The cop glanced from Landon to Calvin and back again. Finally, he jabbed a thumb toward Phillip, who still sat on his front porch. "That guy do everything you tell him to?"

Calvin's dark eyes stayed on the policeman. "If he knows what's good for him."

The policeman tipped his hat. "I'm just going to be in my car over there, finishing up my paperwork." He held his hand out to Landon. "Good luck to you, son."

Landon shook his hand. "Thanks."

"Thank you, sir," Calvin said as he, too, shook the officer's hand.

Landon and Calvin waited in silence as the officer walked toward his car.

"You know, I don't need you to protect me anymore," Landon said, though he appreciated his friend looking out for him.

"What are you talking about?"

"I don't need you sticking up for me every time someone brings up my mom's murder."

"I'm just trying to help you out. I know it must suck."

Landon nodded as he fiddled with the tangled bumper, trying to see if it might fall off as he drove down the road. He took a deep breath. Normally he didn't talk about these things, but Calvin was his friend and mentor. "They're taking my testimony tomorrow." He messed with the bumper some more, not wanting to look at Calvin.

"The girl you told me about?"

Landon straightened and took his keys from his pocket. "Her boss." He shrugged. "I don't know if Gina will be there or not."

"Did you talk to the police the day it happened? Or were you too young then?"

Landon nodded. Surely Calvin knew Landon had been the one to find his mother's body, but he wasn't sure. He tried to swallow the lump in his throat. "I testified at the trial."

Calvin stayed silent.

Landon looked at the ground. "What if I helped put an innocent man in prison?"

"You think there's a chance of that?"

After what he'd learned from Gina and Dr. Stanton, he was beginning to wonder. He kicked a piece of gravel on the road. "I never thought it before."

"And now?"

"I just want to be certain." He took a deep breath. "I don't want to be one of those witnesses who put the wrong guy behind bars."

"You want me to be there with you tomorrow? A little moral support?"

"Thanks." Landon had appreciated Calvin's being there for him when he'd gotten into trouble in the past, but he was a college kid then, busted for underage drinking, and once for shoving a reporter who'd gotten too aggressive with his questions about Mama's murder. But Landon was twenty-four years old now. Old enough to handle things on his own. He gave his friend a good-natured look. "But I'm a big boy now."

Calvin nodded. "Let me know if you change your mind."

Landon held out his hand. They shook hands. Did the shoulder bump.

"Good luck tomorrow," Calvin said. "Call me if you want to go out for a steak and a beer afterwards."

"I will." Landon walked toward his truck, then turned to make sure Calvin heard him. "Thanks again for the offer."

Calvin held up a fist of solidarity. "You're the man."

Landon chuckled and opened the truck door.

"Hey, big boy," Calvin called across the yard.

Landon paused to look at his coach before he lowered himself into the driver's seat.

Calvin grabbed something off the chair on his front porch and started to walk toward him. "Don't forget your girly pants."

CHAPTER NINE

Landon sat in the main office area of Morgan's Ladder, scared as hell about revisiting the testimony he'd given fifteen years ago.

Gina's boss opened the door to the office near the back of the room. "Mr. Vista," she said. "We're ready for you now."

Behind Suzanne, Gina stood with her hands clasped in front of her.

How the hell was he supposed to act around her? Yesterday, he'd had his hands on her hips, inches from a bedroom where he'd like to lie with her. To smell that sexy curve at the base of her neck. To hear her soft moans as they pressed their bodies together. To do things that would make them both forget everything else in the world.

And today he'd be reciting the details of his worst nightmare in front of her. He had no idea if he'd even be able to talk about what he'd seen that day. He hadn't spoken to anyone about what he'd witnessed since the trial. Not his aunt and uncle. Not Boomer or Ricardo. Not even Calvin.

But he was also scared as hell that he was wrong. For a decade and a half, he'd been certain about what he'd seen. Absolutely sure the right man was in prison. But then Gina had come along and made him wonder. Made him ask his dad questions that were still unanswered. Made him wonder if he'd ruined an innocent man's life.

He stood mechanically and walked toward them. The older woman offered her hand as he entered the tiny room.

"Call me Landon," he said as he shook her hand.

"And you can call me Suzanne." She motioned for him to sit in a chair around a small round table. "I believe you know Gina?"

His gaze met Gina's for the first time since he'd entered the room. Her eyes narrowed slightly. What did she think he was going to do? Tattle on her for inviting him to breakfast? He was a better man than that, and he hoped Gina understood that. "Yes." He cleared his throat. "We've met."

"Have a seat, then," Suzanne said.

The three of them sat and Suzanne rested a leather portfolio on the edge of the table at an angle so that Landon couldn't see its contents.

"I'm sorry to have to put you through this," Suzanne said.

She paused as if for a response, but he'd be damned if he was going to make this easy on her. He clasped his hands on the top of the table, waiting for her to fill the awkward silence. Gina fidgeted in her chair.

"We know this will be difficult." Suzanne's voice was calm and quiet. Tinged with sympathy.

Landon's gaze shot to Gina before he realized what he was doing. He'd known in advance that she might be a part of this, but somehow her presence unnerved him.

Suzanne laid her pen on the table. "Does Gina's being here make you uncomfortable?"

He held his hands in the air. "No. No. I'm fine." The only thing that mattered here was finding the truth. If there was any chance at all that he'd helped put an innocent man in prison, then he wanted to help get the guy out, too.

"Do you need a bottle of water?" Suzanne asked. "A bit of fresh air before we get started?"

He blew out a long breath and rubbed his hands down his thighs. "I'd rather just get it over with."

Suzanne picked up her pen again. "Okay, then. Tell us what you were doing that morning. Before you found your mother had been murdered."

He closed his eyes briefly and was immediately whisked back to the little grove of trees near the river. "There was this stand of trees. Back behind the store." He opened his eyes. "It got really boring hanging around the store, so I'd fish there a lot."

"You and your mother lived in the back of the store?"

Landon realized how pathetic he must look in front of Gina. She had her family ski trips to Breckenridge and he had—what?— a cot in the back of his mom's place of employment. "Not at first. We'd had a duplex. In town. This old lady owned it and lived in the other side. My mom helped take care of her."

"Did you both live with your father then?" Suzanne asked.

Out of the corner of his eye, he saw Gina's gaze fall to her lap. She'd met the guy. She had an idea of what Landon's childhood had been like. Embarrassment welled inside him, like it had in elementary school when the other kids had asked what he planned to do with the Father's Day card each of them had made during art. "I'm not sure we ever lived with him."

"Why did you move out of the duplex?" Suzanne's tone was patient and kind.

"I remember that the old lady's relatives came and moved her out. I think they put the duplex up for sale or something." Anger roiled inside him. Entire swaths of his childhood were missing from his memory because he hadn't grown up with adults who could reminisce and fill in the missing pieces. "Why does this matter?" He wanted to get this over with as quickly as possible.

"I'm just trying to set the stage." Suzanne's calm voice told him she'd done this many times before. "Trying to find out anything I can about that day."

"We lived in a room in the back of the store. We had two cots, a sink, and a hot plate."

The old man who owned the store had let them eat bananas once they got brown and lettuce once it wilted, but Suzanne and Gina didn't need to know that.

"Is that what you need to know?" he asked.

Suzanne glanced at Gina. "So the day your mother was killed?" the older woman continued. "Let's go back to that day."

Landon closed his eyes. He could almost feel the unbearable heat of the South in the summertime. "I had to get out of the store. It was hot and sticky and . . ." God, he'd hated the hours he'd spent cooped up there that summer. "My mom and I had played about fifty games of Crazy Eights." He could still see the wrinkled playing cards with the Piggly Wiggly logo on the back. "I went to the creek to go fishing."

"By yourself?" Suzanne asked.

He nodded.

"Tell me about your fishing that day."

He gave her an impatient look. "I didn't usually catch anything."

The older woman shook her head. "I'm not talking about what you caught. I'm talking about what you saw. What you heard." She reached out and touched his hand where it rested on the table. "Close your eyes and try to remember that day. The sights. The sounds. The smells."

He did as he was told—half afraid of what he'd remember and half afraid of what he might forget. "Doc Barker's car pulled up. He stopped by every Sunday for a newspaper. He used a walker, so Mama would take his paper out to him. She waved to me as he was pulling away." Landon felt his fingers raise off the table as if he waved back.

"Go on."

"There was that smell you get at low tide. Kind of muddy and"—his nose curled up; anyone who'd been around a marsh at low tide would know the smell—"like dead fish."

"What sounds do you hear?" Suzanne's voice got more distant the more he let himself sink into his memory.

"Quiet, mainly." He sat for several seconds. "Mosquitoes buzzing. A boat going by way off in the distance. And this . . ." He paused. A fact he'd forgotten before leapt to the forefront of his mind. His heart beat faster. "This high-pitched whir."

"Any idea what the whirring was?"

He waited a moment, listening for anything his memory might serve up. "I don't know. A boat motor, maybe. The marsh led out to the intracoastal. A lot of boats went by in the distance." He frowned. "But it was more high-pitched." He opened his eyes.

"So you were fishing. What happened next?"

He sat back in his chair and rolled his head around to loosen up his neck. He needed to at least *tell* his body to relax, even if he knew it wouldn't. "I packed up my stuff to go inside." He'd used an old shoe box for a tackle box, even though he had only three lures that he'd found in the marsh grasses, left by fishermen who didn't have the patience to untangle them. "I hadn't caught anything and had been out there for a while." He sucked in a deep breath and let it out slowly. "I heard the back door slap closed." He banged his hand on the table, replicating the noise. "And saw Cyrus Alexander running out of the back of the store."

"You mean a man you thought looked like Cyrus Alexander?"

Landon turned toward Suzanne. His body quivered. Felt like it might cave in on itself. This was the part that put the right man in prison.

Or not.

"No. He came into the store sometimes." Landon's voice shook. "I knew who he was."

Suzanne shifted in her seat. "When he ran out of the store, where did he go?"

"He ran through this field—there was this dock down there where guys used to fish and drink beer and stuff. He ran in that direction."

"How soon after he ran that you arrived in the store?" Suzanne asked.

Landon looked down at his lap. Beside him, Gina sat forward. Yes, now they were getting to the part they all knew would be most difficult.

"I walked right there." His voice was barely a whisper. "I mean, I didn't think Cyrus had done anything. I didn't know . . . anything was wrong. I'd seen her walk out to Doc Barker's car a little while earlier." He hesitated. Thought he might throw up. It was the last time he'd seen his mother alive. He'd replayed this scene over and over in his mind through the years, but he'd only spoken about it two other times—once for the police on the day she'd died and once in court. "That's why it was such a surprise . . . to . . . find her."

He heard the blood sloshing around in his head. Heard Gina's quick breathing beside him. He continued to look down at his lap. He didn't want to see the look on either of their faces.

"I know this is hard." Suzanne's voice was as soft as his. "But can you tell me what you saw?"

He swallowed. If he hurried through this, it would be over more quickly. God, he hated this. "She was there. Draped over the counter. There was a puddle of blood on the floor."

"Was she alive?"

He closed his eyes and shook his head. Those eyes. *Her* eyes. Staring blankly at him. Lifeless. Like Cyrus Alexander had stolen her breath and taken it with him as he dashed out the back door. "No."

"What did you do next?"

He didn't want to think about Gina sitting over there, staring at him, so he kept his eyes on her boss. "I shook her and cried and shook her some more. Finally, I ran down the street to the neighbors' house and got them to call 9-1-1."

"You didn't have a phone at the store?"

They took sponge baths in the sink and cooked cans of soup on a hot plate, but he didn't want to share those details. "We barely had running water." It hadn't dawned on him back then that it was odd, even for a backwoods business, to not have a phone.

Suzanne gave a single nod. "How far away was the neighbors' house?"

He remembered panting by the time he got there—hotter, sweatier than he'd been before. Tears and snot mixed into a salt-flavored sap that covered his upper lip as he'd tried to tell the neighbors what had happened. "You couldn't see it from the store." Jesus, he'd been nine years old and his mom had just been killed. Did she want to know the precise number of meters he'd run?

"So the store was empty for a while?" This was the first time Gina had spoken since he'd been here. His head whipped around to look at her. She startled at his quick motion. Her eyes widened. What was she getting at?

"The neighbors put me in their car right away and we got back down there before the police arrived."

"They questioned you about what you'd seen?" Again, the older lady was talking.

He turned to her and nodded.

"Did you identify Cyrus Alexander to them by name?"

He hesitated, wondering what Suzanne was up to. Surely she'd read the file. Surely she knew he hadn't known Cyrus Alexander's name. Not then. Not before that day. Anger roiled inside him. These women were grilling *him* and they knew more than he did.

"Maybe you should tell me." He placed a hand on the folder that sat on the table between him and Gina. He slid it toward him. "Or maybe we should see what it says in your file."

~

Gina slapped her hand on the file folder as soon as Landon started sliding it toward himself. She'd seen the pictures in there. Crime scene photos she hoped Landon would never see—or had never seen—because they showed such vivid pictures of that horrible day.

A nine-year-old boy should never see his mother stabbed to death. And he shouldn't see them now.

He stared her down like a gunman from the Wild West, daring her to make the next move. She gripped the side of the folder and dragged it toward her. The tips of his fingers turned white as he pressed hard to keep her from pulling it away from her. Finally, she wrestled it from underneath his hand and tucked it into the leather portfolio on her lap.

"We'd appreciate your cooperation, Mr. Vista." Suzanne's voice was stern. Gina had never heard her talk like that.

Landon set his elbows on the table and steepled his hands in front of his face. "I didn't know Cyrus Alexander's name, but I described him to the police. Later that day, at the station, they did a lineup. I picked him out—no problem."

"What made you think it was him?"

"Because he'd been the guy I saw running from the store." Now it was Landon's turn to grind out his words.

"Your selection had nothing to do with the injury on his arm?" Cyrus's wrist had been wrapped in a blood-tinged bandage at the time of his arrest.

"I only saw the picture of his wound later. At the trial. I don't even remember seeing it in the lineup."

Gina made a mental note to look again at the photos taken at the police station.

"You're sure about that?" Suzanne asked.

Landon slapped his hands on the table and leaned toward Suzanne. "Look. I was nine years old. My mother had just been murdered. I did the best I could."

Gina's gaze shot to Landon's. *He'd done the best he could?* For the first time since she'd known Landon, he hadn't stated his testimony as a certainty. He'd left open some room for doubt.

She pulled the photograph out of her portfolio. The photograph she and Suzanne had agreed to show him. "Do you see Cyrus Alexander in this picture?"

The photo showed two rows of young men in basketball uniforms. The fronts of their jerseys each said *Wildcats*. The length of the shorts and the hairstyles indicated the picture was from a couple of decades ago.

Landon slid the picture from Gina's hand and studied it.

"That one," he said after several seconds. He pointed to one of the men in the photograph. "The tallest one in the back row."

Gina glanced at Suzanne. They'd proven their point. She pulled a printout of a screenshot from her portfolio. "His name is Caleb Bass. I saw his picture when my uncle David posted it to his Facebook page."

"The basketball team is in Eugene, Oregon," Suzanne said. "Caleb Bass has never been west of the Mississippi."

Landon jerked his head to face Gina. "You tricked me."

She hadn't prepared herself for the anger in his eyes. "I wanted to show you how people can be wrong about what they think they've seen."

"But what you've really shown me"—he stood, towering over them—"is that you'll do anything to prove your point."

Gina stood, too. "But don't you see? You could have been wrong all along."

"Yes." He slashed his hand through the air. "I could have been wrong. Is that what you want to hear?" He took a step toward her. "Is it?"

Suzanne stood and cleared her throat. "Mr. Vista."

He glared in Gina's eyes for another several seconds, then took a step back. His arms hung limp at his sides. He lowered his head. "I could have been wrong." He raised his head, his pleading eyes looked from Gina to Suzanne and back again. "I just want to be certain the right guy's in prison."

His entire body quivered, as if it had been a struggle to admit what he'd just said. Gina glanced at Suzanne. Her boss had seen it, too.

"Can we be done here?" He rubbed his fingertips on his forehead, covering his face.

Gina looked toward her boss. No way was she going to do anything that might sway Suzanne when Gina was more invested here than she should be.

"I'd like your permission to question you again," Suzanne said, "should we decide there's something more we need to ask."

Landon nodded. His normally tanned skin looked ashen against his dark hair.

Suzanne placed her hand on his arm. "You're doing the right thing here."

"Yeah," he said. "I'm willing to tell the truth." He picked up the picture of the basketball team and held it in front of Gina's face. "I don't have to trick people into it."

CHAPTER TEN

For once, Landon was happy he had to go to a fundraising event for the senator tonight. He'd do just about anything to get his mind off of what had happened this morning at Morgan's Ladder and the fact that he might have put the wrong guy in prison. He felt like even more of a fraud than usual, zipping around in a private plane while this horrible possibility roiled inside him.

They were headed to an evening soiree at a waterfront home in Naples—some hoity-toity campaign donor. Then they'd spend the night at a nearby hotel and fly back again tomorrow morning. A guy could have a worse job . . . even if he did hate this part of it.

At least he wasn't digging ditches or something like that. He liked being outdoors, but the Florida sun was unrelenting for nine months of the year, and he'd seen sixty-year-old men still toiling away in the summer heat. So he'd play nice with the rich people. And get the hell out of there as soon as he could.

He settled into his seat on the plane as Scott Meredith opened the fully stocked bar. The senator had Grey Goose on the rocks every time he drank, and the rest of the staff seemed to think that drinking the stuff was a requirement of their job descriptions, too. Scott had already fixed two of them by the time he pointed toward Landon.

"I'll grab a bottle of water in a few minutes," Landon said. It had already been a helluva day, and having a couple of drinks before they even got to Naples would only make him more tired for the long night ahead.

When the remaining staff members had their drinks in their hands, Scott settled into the seat next to him. The senator dozed in the chair facing them, on the other side of the polished built-in coffee table.

"So how's that family-impact project going?" Scott asked.

He was talking about the bios of crime victims Landon had been asked to put together for a series of television ads. "Pretty good. I have a couple more interviews and then I'll be done."

"Anything we can use?"

He shrugged. He was actually pretty proud of what he'd uncovered. For a guy who'd majored in mathematics, he'd enjoyed working with the constituents more than he'd expected. "A girl whose brother was killed by a couple of gangbangers." His interview with her had really punched him in the gut. It would make for a good story, even if it was just thirty seconds long. "Her mom never recovered from her brother's death, so the daughter was in and out of group homes until she turned eighteen." He'd admired her determination to overcome the odds against her. Had even made an anonymous donation specifically for her to the program that was helping her get her first apartment as she aged out of foster care.

"She'll let the PR firm interview her on camera?"

"She said she would."

"She black or white?" Scott was always concerned with which demographics they were appealing to.

"Latino." Like it mattered what color she was. People were people. They all needed help, regardless of their race. He hated how Scott and the senator were always so concerned with the next election.

"Then find me an old white guy who's been scammed by a Ponzi scheme and we'll have the two commercials we need."

Landon opened his mouth to speak, but the lady in charge of

logistics once they got to Naples interrupted them. "I need to ask a couple of questions about the event tonight," she said to Scott.

Landon jumped up, eager to extract himself from the conversation. "Here. Take my seat." He moved up behind the cockpit in a single seat where he could be left alone for the rest of the trip. It felt good to lay his head back and enjoy the privacy.

He closed his eyes and tried to clear his mind, but he'd been thinking about Cyrus Alexander all day. God, Gina had pissed him off this morning with that cheap-ass trick with the picture of the basketball team. And what he'd hated most of all was that she'd been right. If he couldn't even be certain that Cyrus Alexander was on a team of fifteen guys, how the hell did he know he'd been the guy running from the country store fifteen years ago?

Landon might have put the wrong guy in jail. Could he be any more of a total fuckup?

He propped his elbow on the armrest and rubbed his eyes, hoping to block out the rest of the world, but thoughts of Gina passed through his mind like marionettes on a stage. The first night they'd met. How her body had molded to his that night she'd kissed him next to her SUV. Those damn yellow shorts she'd worn that day at breakfast. Those delicate mounds of flesh he could see as she shook the ketchup bottle in front of him. And she'd known exactly what she was doing that morning at her apartment. Knew exactly where his gaze was as she leaned over the table, which made her even hotter.

His imagination created a different ending to that morning. One in which he peeled off her T-shirt and cupped those beautiful breasts on the outside of her lacy bra. He'd rub his thumbs across her nipples until she begged for more, then he'd slip off her bra and let his tongue glide across them, teasing them.

He'd slide his hands between her legs and feel her warmth—her need—before he unzipped those little yellow shorts and let them fall to her feet. She'd slide his shirt over his head before he lifted her, naked, onto her dining room table. She'd unzip his pants and touch him . . . but he couldn't make love to her then. Not yet.

He'd have to make sure it was as good for her as it was for him. He'd slide his hand between her legs and—oh, God—she would be so wet for him. So needful. So ready for him to plunge inside her.

He could feel her warm, wet walls as he slid inside her. Could feel himself pumping against her, in and out and in and out as she lay back on the table, wrapping her legs around him, making those sweet little noises he'd heard her make when they'd kissed . . .

Jesus, he got hard just thinking about it.

The sudden sound of laughter in the seats near the back made his eyes shoot open. He sat up straight, thankful he was up front, where no one else on the plane could see the huge bulge in his pants.

He rested his head against the headrest and let his eyes drift shut again, determined not to think about it anymore. Sure, she was sexy as hell, but part of what made her that way was her intelligence. Her passion for her work. The way she challenged him. All those weapons she had aimed directly at him.

But no way was he going to fall for a woman who would trick him the way she had this morning. Sure, he might fantasize about her, but that was what guys did. They got horny sometimes. He at least had the willpower not to act on it with her.

Okay, so maybe fate had sent her to Tallahassee this summer to get Cyrus Alexander out of prison. Landon could live with that. She might have even been sent to Tallahassee to help him see what he'd done wrong so many years ago.

But that was the end of his involvement with her. She'd go back to law school in a few weeks, and he'd never have to deal with her again.

Gina sat cross-legged on her couch. She finger-combed her hair as her computer pinged to indicate an incoming call. Chatting with her roommate from undergrad would be a welcome relief, especially after this morning at Morgan's Ladder. She hadn't been able to forget the look of betrayal in Landon's eyes all day.

"This is Gina," she said as the call connected.

Erica frowned from the screen. "Stop sounding like such an attorney. Hello? It's me. The one who knows what all your underwear looks like. The one who watched you throw up falafel all over our bathroom."

Ugh. During what may have been the worst case of food poisoning in US history. "I haven't eaten Greek food since then."

"Yeah. It wasn't pretty."

"So what's this big news?" Erica had texted her earlier in the day to make sure they could video-chat at a certain time right after work.

"I'm thinking of taking a semester off from grad school. Traveling through Europe. Staying in hostels. Riding the trains from country to country."

Gina smiled at Erica's exuberance. She'd always loved her energy. "Where are you going to get that kind of money?" Her friend's parents weren't wealthy. They'd struggled in low-wage jobs for years.

Erica's face grew bigger as she leaned toward the camera on her computer. Gina could see the excitement on her face.

"We'll stay in hostels," Erica said. "They don't cost much. And we'll get a job from time to time if we need to."

"We?"

"You're going with me."

Gina laughed. "Do I get a say in this?"

"We can do it next summer. You don't do an internship. I don't take classes. Like that gap year the Europeans do between high school and college."

"We've already got our undergrad degrees."

"So we're slow learners. Back then we didn't know we were supposed to do a gap year."

"I can't do it."

Erica slumped back in her chair and looked stunned. "Oh, come on. Surely there are other people who don't go through law school all at one time. Like people who get sick or have a baby or something."

"I promised my parents I'd try to get an internship in corporate law next summer." Of course, she really planned to return to Morgan's Ladder, but she'd figure all that out later.

"You'd rather be some stuck-up attorney than traveling Europe with your best friend?"

"How would I tell my parents? Who are spending a fortune on my law degree, by the way."

"'Hey, Mom and Dad, I want to go have fun for a few weeks before I settle into something that's going to be unbearably *boring* for the rest of my life?'"

Gina paused. She'd love a carefree summer with her friend. She'd love a carefree anything. But working at Morgan's Ladder was what she needed to do. "I can't."

"You're really that determined to become some corporate suit?"

Gina laughed. "You obviously haven't seen my office. There's nothing corporate about it." More like run-down and underfunded.

"How *is* the prison job going, anyway?"

Gina laughed. "It's not a prison job."

"Do you go to prisons?"

"Yes."

"Then it's a prison job."

"We're getting a guy out tomorrow. He's been in for twenty-one years for a crime he didn't commit."

"Now you're just making my summer in Europe sound frivolous."

Gina shrugged. "Maybe you'll find some hot guy between now and then to take to Europe with you."

"Speaking of hot guys . . ."

Gina smiled. This was a much safer topic. "You have a boyfriend?"

Erica scoffed. "I wish."

"So what is it?"

"I saw Christopher in Target the other day. He looked like hell."

"Oh, yeah? How?"

"Scruffy whiskers. Dirty T-shirt. Wrinkled pants. Had some skanky-looking girl with him."

"You could have stopped with the wrinkled pants." The pain of Christopher's betrayal stung in Gina's chest.

"She looked pretty nasty."

"I don't need to hear about her." Or her skankiness.

"I'm just saying . . . you should be glad you dumped him."

"He dumped me."

"Well, technically, you dumped him after . . . you know."

Yes, Gina knew exactly what Erica was talking about. The day she'd walked in and found Christopher in bed with the goth girl. "We really don't need to relive it."

"So any cute guys down there?"

Gina took a deep breath while she considered whether or not to talk to Erica about Landon. She hadn't told anyone about how she felt . . . and it might be good to talk through it. "Only one, but he's off-limits."

"Engaged?" Erica's eyebrows rose. "Or married?"

Gina laughed. "Neither."

Erica's mouth fell open. "You picked up a gay guy?"

Gina thought about the way Landon had kissed her that first night they'd met. How his big hands had fanned out across her back, molding their bodies together. How his erection had felt pressed against her. "He's definitely not gay."

"Then what's the problem?"

"I can't mix business and pleasure."

"You *work* with him?"

"He's"—Gina thought carefully how to phrase her answer—"involved with one of our cases."

"No shit?" Erica chuckled. "You're in love with a prisoner?"

Gina laughed. "No. He's involved in the case . . . in a different way."

"Is he tall enough for you? Or is it Roger Burns all over again?"

Gina cringed. Her two-week relationship with Roger Burns had been a mistake for a lot of reasons. And most of them had nothing to do with his height. "He's definitely taller than I am."

"So it's a summer job." Erica gave a dismissive wave. "Have a little fun."

"And besides, I'm pretty sure I really made him mad earlier today. I . . . kind of tricked him into realizing something he didn't want to admit."

"Does he want to see you again?"

Gina paused. She had no idea where things stood with Landon. And that was the worst part.

"Maybe you should go talk to him," Erica said, finally serious.

Gina had wondered the same thing. "Hmmm. Maybe."

"What could it hurt?"

"I don't know." If she couldn't date him, then why did she feel the need to mend their relationship? Why was it the thing she'd spent most of the day thinking about?

"Should you apologize?" Erica seemed to know not to ask about the details of the case. She waggled her eyebrows. "Maybe have a little makeup sex?"

"We're not sleeping together." Gina chuckled.

"Yeah, but do you want to?"

Of course she wanted to sleep with him, but this was more than lust. She wanted to spend Sunday mornings with him sipping coffee on a sunny back porch somewhere. To cook meals with him.

To have him around to talk to whenever she wanted. "I could get in huge trouble for having a relationship with him. It's against our code of ethics."

Erica slumped against the back of her chair. "So bad idea, huh?"

Yes. Definitely a bad idea. Gina reminded herself of that every day.

"So maybe it's a good thing you pissed him off," Erica said.

"It doesn't really matter what he thinks." Gina held her friend's gaze on the computer screen, hoping Erica wouldn't realize she was lying to both of them. "There could never be anything between us anyway."

~

Landon held back, waiting for the senator to extract himself from the first of a series of three Lincoln Town Cars that had whisked his entourage from the airport to an expansive waterfront home in Naples. This town, with its pink and tangerine-colored mansions, had been known as the place for upscale glamour and opulence on Florida's gulf coast for years.

Finally, the senator exited the car and strode up the wide stone steps. Scott Meredith, Landon, and the rest of the group followed.

A butler opened the massive front door and bowed his head in greeting. "Senator Byers. Mr. and Mrs. Winston will be glad to know you've arrived safely." He held out a hand, motioning for them to go farther down the marbled foyer. A group of people—men in sport coats and women in body-hugging dresses—were gathered in a room at the back of the house. The laughter and chatter got louder as the senator's party approached.

The foyer opened to a towering two-story living room. A wall of windows looked out over the waterway behind the house, where another equally lavish home sat on the other side of the canal. The setting sun seemed poised on the horizon solely for their benefit. Behind each mansion, an expensive vessel hung from its lift inside a boathouse, ready for another day of fun. Landon had been in homes like this before. Had mingled with their owners. Had pimped himself on behalf of the senator.

And he hated every fucking minute of it.

He felt like such a fraud. Everyone wanted to know the football star. They had no idea how he'd grown up. No idea who he was. No idea how this whole scene made him feel like such an imposter.

"Hey, hey. Senator Byers." A white-haired gentleman touched the elbow of his conversation partner, a signal to excuse himself to greet the newly arrived guests. As the man approached, his youthful face seemed incongruent with the color of his hair. Landon guessed him to be in his midforties. Not as old as he'd expected the guy to be, given his net worth and the amount of money he donated to the senator's campaign each year.

"Anton." The senator smiled as he shook the man's hand. "So wonderful of you to have us here."

"You and my fifty closest friends," he said, sweeping his arm to indicate the others in the room.

The senator laughed.

"And this guy"—Anton Winston turned to Landon—"is the staffer I wanted to meet." He held out his hand to Landon. "Happy you could make the trip."

Landon hoped his smile wasn't too stiff as he shook the man's hand. "Thank you for having me." Out of the corner of his eye, he could see Scott Meredith preening. It had been Scott's idea to bring Landon on to the senator's staff after meeting him at some booster event. And every time Landon's celebrity gained them points with the campaign donors, Scott beamed like a proud father.

"I need to find Olivia. She's been dying to meet you." Anton looked around the room, which was as long as a kid-size basketball court and towered as high as a gym. Three distinct seating areas, each with two cream-colored couches facing each other, divided the guests into elegant clusters. Others milled around fully stocked bars at each end of the room. "Oh, here she is," he said as a blonde woman stepped into the room. He pecked her cheek as she joined their group. "My wife, Olivia."

"Nice to meet you, ma'am," Landon said as he offered his hand.

The statuesque woman clasped his hand in both of hers. Her perfectly tanned skin crinkled into crow's-feet at the corners of her eyes as a smile spread across her face. "Landon Vista." Her diamond necklace glinted in the fading light. "The ladies from the club can't wait to meet you."

She whisked him away on her arm without stopping to greet the senator or anyone else in his party. Landon made the circuit of the room with her as she floated from one seating area to the other, introducing him to this person and that: the Babcocks, who wintered in Naples, but who were here in the summer because they were having some work done on their house; the Michaelsons, whose son had just finished his first year at Harvard Law; and the Drapers, who . . . Landon couldn't remember anything about them. They had blended into a sea of faces. A sea of people he didn't want to know and wouldn't remember. The only ones who caught his eye were a couple of college-age girls who leaned against the bar at the other end of the room. They were the only ones here who were even close to his age, but Olivia Winston steered him away from them.

Forty-five minutes later, he made his escape from the hostess and ducked into what looked like the kitchen. Maybe he could pretend he was looking for a bottle of water when what he really needed was a quiet spot to hide for a few minutes.

"Did you *see* Landon Vista?" a girl's voice said from around the corner before he could even rest his hips against the granite countertop. He stilled. What looked like the beginning of a breakfast nook wrapped around that corner of the kitchen.

"There aren't any guys like that at *my* college," another female voice said.

"Because you don't go to a real college."

"Too bad your parents are here. Otherwise, you could take him upstairs and . . . entertain him a bit."

"Mom would die."

"Only because *she* wants to sleep with him, too."

A potato chip bag was ripped open around the corner, where the voices were coming from. "She's like a hundred and four years old."

"That didn't keep her from sashaying around the living room with him on her arm."

"She told me to stay away from him."

He held his breath as irritation and curiosity warred inside him. "Why?"

"His family doesn't have money." A potato chip crunched. "I guess she thought I'd be slumming it."

His jaw tightened.

"Do you *care*?" the other female voice asked. "I mean, if all his body parts are as big as the ones you can see . . . I'd slum it once or twice just to see what it felt like."

"Oh, I'd definitely do him. I just wouldn't let my parents know."

The screech of a chair on the marble floor caught Landon by surprise. He quickly turned and opened a cabinet door as one of the two college-age girls he'd seen before rounded the corner.

Damn.

Plates.

"Ummm. I'm looking for a glass for some water?" he said. He hoped his face wasn't as red with anger as the blush was that crept up the girl's neck.

"Landon Vista?"

He nodded. "Yes."

"Did you . . ." She turned and pointed in the direction from which she'd come.

"Did I what?" Clearly, her friend wasn't coming to her rescue.

"How long have you been standing here?"

He shrugged. "I just walked in. I'm looking for a glass—"

Her shoulders relaxed. "They're over here." She crossed to the other side of the kitchen, opened one of the dark wooden cabinets, and got out a glass. "Ice and water in the door of the fridge. Can I get you some?"

He studied her face. Wanted to make her nervous. To maybe make her twitch a little. He'd always known he was out of his element at events like this, but he'd never had it ground into his face like that.

Slumming it.

Because Mama had been poor and his dad was a drunk. Because his parents didn't have the kind of money to build a house like this one.

He slowly reached out and took the glass from her hand. "I can get it."

"My parents were really excited when they heard you were coming."

"So this is your house?" He hated people who thought they were better than everyone else because they had money.

She nodded.

He filled his glass at the refrigerator and guzzled it down, knowing she was watching him the entire time. When he'd finished, he set his glass in the sink and turned to her. "I'd better get going." He jabbed a thumb toward the living room. "I wouldn't want your parents to think I'm *slumming* it in the kitchen."

Her eyebrows shot up and her mouth fell open. From around the corner, he heard a gasp.

Served them right.

Rich little bitches.

CHAPTER ELEVEN

Gina stood on one side of the tiny conference room in the administrative area of the prison. She felt like a latecomer, an intruder to the scene that was about to unfold. While Gina had been in her first two semesters at law school, Suzanne had fought to have Buford Monroe's conviction overturned. DNA tests hadn't been available at the time of his trial, but now proved that he hadn't committed the murder he'd been convicted of years earlier.

Her boss held the leathery hand of Ella Monroe, Buford's mother. The African American woman wore what must have been her best clothes—a flowered housedress and beat-up sneakers with laces so white they had to have been put in that morning.

"I can't believe this is finally happening." Ella's voice quavered. Her coarse, white hair swept back from her caramel-colored skin. The eagerness in her eyes seemed out of place in a face etched with time, hard work, and worry.

Suzanne patted the woman's hand and smiled. "I'll bet he'll want some of your good home cooking tonight."

"Twenty-one years," Ella said. The length of time her son had been in jail for a crime he hadn't committed.

Suzanne nodded. Her voice was grim. "Way too long."

Ella beamed. "But now he's coming home. Thank the Lord, he's coming home."

The three of them—Gina, Suzanne, and Ella—jumped like nervous rabbits when someone knocked on the conference room door.

Suzanne took a deep breath. "You ready?" she said to Ella.

The woman nodded.

Suzanne walked to the door and opened it, then stood aside as Buford rushed toward Ella, tugging her into a long, tight embrace. Gina looked away, hoping to hide her tears, thinking at that moment that nothing could be more unfair than keeping a parent from their child. Nothing she'd learned in law school—theories and definitions and precedence—could have prepared her for this moment. For the raw truth of how much a mother loves her son.

"This makes it all worthwhile," Gina whispered to her boss.

Suzanne nodded and dabbed her eyes with a tissue.

Finally, Ella and Buford parted. The big man turned toward Suzanne and took her hand in his, covering it with both of his. "Thank you." Tears trailed down his face. "I have my life back. Thank you."

Gina looked around Buford toward Ella, who smiled with trembling lips and nodded slowly to her, a silent acknowledgment of the importance of this event.

"Thank you, too." Buford moved toward Gina, embracing her hand in both of his, though they'd never met. "For everything you've done."

Gina smiled. She wasn't going to disagree with anything he said. Not on a day like today. Not when his face showed so much appreciation for work she'd never done.

"Would you like a few minutes with your mother before you go outside?" Suzanne asked. "The media's pretty thick out there."

"Five or ten? Then we'll walk out"—Buford looked toward Ella—"together?"

Ella nodded as tears streamed down her face.

Gina followed her boss into the hallway and waited. She leaned against the wall made of concrete blocks and wondered what was going on inside the conference room. Wondered what a guy said to the mother he hadn't hugged in twenty-one years. How much time it would take for them to get to know each other again. What kind of grief a mother must endure when her eighteen-year-old son is sent to prison. What it does to a mother and child who are torn apart.

What it must have done to Landon.

She pushed the thought aside, wanting to focus on the happiness of the day rather than remember the pain in Landon's eyes when they'd talked about his mother's murder. His eyes had haunted her since that first volleyball game—alternately making her want to forget she'd ever met him and wanting to learn more about him.

The click of the conference room door across the hall jarred her from her thoughts. Buford and Ella stepped into the hallway. The bevy of men who'd waited inside the warden's glass-walled office down the hall stepped out to introduce themselves to Buford— prison officials, a couple of state representatives, the state's attorney.

Then they all made their way to the front gate of the prison. To the flashing lights of cameras and TV crews jostling to get a shot of the man who'd wasted away for years, but was now thrust into the spotlight, at least for a day or two.

Gina stood back, watching as Buford and Ella waded through the crowd of reporters, mumbling answers and looking over-whelmed. Finally, they ducked their heads and got into a car that waited nearby to whisk them away.

"Not a bad day of work, huh?" Suzanne beamed at Gina.

"Beats sitting in class at law school, that's for sure." This was the kind of thing she'd dreamed about—sticking up for the people everyone else had forgotten. Struggling for those who had no one else to turn to.

"See you Friday," Suzanne said as she opened the door of her ancient Audi. "And call me tomorrow if you need me."

"I'll be fine," Gina called, proud that her boss trusted her to take care of things at work tomorrow while Suzanne visited an elderly aunt who lived in a town near the prison. She watched as Suzanne pulled out of the parking lot, off toward a well-deserved couple of days off.

Suddenly, a tiny woman in a bright red pantsuit appeared from behind an SUV parked nearby. She held a microphone in her hand. A man with a camera on his shoulder followed her. It took Gina a second to recognize Donna Crocker from the local news station. On air, the woman looked like a tall, svelte model. In person, she was the height of a middle schooler.

The light on the camera turned from red to green.

"Excuse me, Ms. Blanchard?" Donna Crocker's familiar voice left Gina no doubt as to who she was.

She instinctively glanced around for an escape, but the only other people in the parking lot were other reporters, packing their gear into news vans about a football field's length away.

"Are you in a romantic relationship with Landon Vista?" Donna Crocker shoved the microphone toward Gina's face.

Gina froze. The woman was bringing Landon into this? Today was supposed to be about Buford Monroe. She glanced at the camera with its green light aimed right at her. Anything she did—any look of surprise or feigned innocence—could appear on tonight's Tallahassee newscast. She squared her shoulders, trying to convey as much confidence as possible. "No." She congratulated herself for the simple response. Single-syllable words didn't make for good sound bites.

Donna Crocker pulled the microphone back toward herself to speak into it. "A reliable source tells us the two of you had a romantic encounter on the patio of a local tavern a couple of weeks ago."

Oh, God.

Gina glanced in the direction Suzanne's car had gone. A rush of desperation flooded her. She was in this by herself. She'd seen people in this situation on the news before—disgraced politicians and crooked businessmen—but never a twenty-two-year-old in her first weeks of an internship. What would Suzanne think? Would she lose her job? Get sent back to law school with an incomplete internship?

She hesitated. She was a smart woman. She knew they were after a sensational news story and she would do her best not to give it to them. She cocked her chin and spoke into the microphone jammed near her chin. "Today was a great day for Buford Monroe and his family."

"So you're not denying that you and Landon Vista know each other?"

"I'm saying today is about Buford Monroe reuniting with his family. About justice being served." Maybe if she refused to answer the questions, the tape they were filming would be unusable for the nightly news.

"How does Landon feel about your employer trying to get Cyrus Alexander out of jail?"

"The only case I'm focused on today is Buford Monroe."

"Given Landon Vista's past, he's perfect for Senator Byers's office. Aren't you concerned that a relationship with someone at Morgan's Ladder will hurt his career there?"

Gina glared at the newswoman. Landon was so much more than a former football star whose mother had been murdered. "He doesn't even like his role in the senator's office. He doesn't like . . . people like you . . . thinking all he is . . . you all make him out to be"—her mind searched for the right words—"some poster child for tougher sentencing laws. He's so much more than that. He's . . ." *God, what was she doing?* Her anger had hijacked her body and overtaken her brain. She needed to shut up. She took a deep breath. "I have to go." She beeped the locks on her SUV.

Donna Crocker had a look in her eyes like she was going in for the kill. "So you know more about Landon Vista than you'd initially let on." She shoved the microphone into Gina's face again.

Gina ducked inside her car, wishing the slamming of the door could block out that evil green light on the front of the camera. She'd seen the news when other people were filmed getting into their cars and driving off. They were always the guilty parties. The disgraced politicians and racketeers. The child molesters. The villains.

She cranked the key and turned to look for cars behind her as she backed from her parking space. Outside her window, the bright green light of the camera still aimed at her like a sniper's scope. Her heart pounded. Her sweaty palms slid slickly across the fake leather steering wheel. Donna Crocker stepped aside as the SUV jerked backward.

Gina yanked the gear shift into drive and barreled from the parking lot as quickly as she dared. Only when she'd pulled onto the road in the direction Suzanne had gone did she let her body fall back against the seat. Snippets of the interaction with the news crew raced through her mind like disjointed still photos strewn across a darkroom floor.

Oh, God. Oh, God. Oh, God.

The awfulness of how she might look on the news paralyzed her. What would Suzanne think of this unplanned interview?

What would *Landon* think?

She dug her phone out of her briefcase. Her thumb shook as she scrolled through her recently called numbers, looking for Suzanne's cell number.

Come on. Pick up.

Finally, the line connected. "This is Suzanne."

She swallowed. "Hey, it's Gina. I've got to tell you something."

"Go on." Suzanne's voice was wary.

"Donna Crocker from Channel Four approached me in the parking lot. She had a cameraman." The words rushed out of her mouth, almost incoherent, even to her. "I . . . I tried to handle it as best I could."

"Calm down. I'm sure you did fine."

"I kept focusing the conversation back on Buford. I think I did okay on that part."

"What else did she want to talk about?"

Gina took a deep breath. "She asked whether or not I was in a relationship with Landon Vista." She couldn't bring herself to tell her boss about the first night she'd met him at the bar. The night Donna Crocker had asked about. As much as they'd connected with each other since then, describing their actions that night to someone else would sound . . . sleazy.

A brief silence filled the air on Suzanne's end of the line. "And do you? Have a relationship with him?"

"No." The answer sounded too fast, even to her.

"Then what made Donna Crocker ask about it?"

Gina closed her eyes as long as she dared, then opened them again to watch the road. She'd always been proud of her honesty, but this time it was tougher than usual. "The first night we met . . . the night before he stormed into our office that day—"

"Please tell me you didn't sleep with him."

"No." *Why would Suzanne even think that?* "It was a kiss." *One incredible kiss.* "One stupid kiss." And one more since then, but that one wasn't currently in question.

"In front of Donna Crocker?"

"It was at a bar. On the patio. No one else was even outside." No way was she going to talk now about the other times they'd seen each other.

"Honey, you can't do anything in public with Landon Vista without half of Tallahassee knowing about it."

Hot tears of anger rushed to Gina's eyes. She knew that now, but had no idea then. She blinked back her tears, trying to keep her eyes on the road. One internship and she was already ruining her professional reputation. How could she have been so stupid? "I didn't know who he was. I mean, I knew he was Landon Vista, but I didn't know he was involved in one of our cases."

"No wonder he was so mad that day in our office. You're making out with him one day and trying to get Cyrus Alexander out of prison the next."

"So what do we do for damage control?"

"You only talked about Buford on camera?"

"I responded to one question about Landon."

Except it hadn't been a response. It had been a rant. How could she have been so stupid?

Suzanne sucked in a long breath, then let it out slowly. "Record the news so I can watch it when I get back in town. And lay low until then."

Gina hated the sound of resignation in her boss's voice. "I'm soooo sorry," she said.

"And try to be a little more discreet about your gentlemen friends while you're in town this summer."

Gina felt like she'd been slapped. She couldn't speak. Her professionalism had always been above reproach before this job.

"As a matter of fact," Suzanne continued, "that little bit of advice applies to your entire law career, wherever you are and whoever you're working for."

"Yes, ma'am," Gina said, feeling like a schoolgirl who'd been caught texting during class.

"And one more thing."

"Yes?" Gina wanted to get the conversation over for fear she was about to burst into tears.

"You'd better call Landon," Suzanne said, "and warn him about what he might see on the news tonight."

~

Gina's foot hit the brake pedal the second she passed the community clubhouse at Landon's condo complex. Even if she hadn't known what kind of vehicle he drove, the dark, curly hair and bare, broad shoulders of the man washing his truck across the parking lot from the clubhouse could only belong to Landon.

She pulled her SUV into a parking spot and got out. He seemed unaware of her presence as he took a brush out of the soapy bucket and scrubbed one of the wheels.

The bright Tallahassee sun glinted off his curls like they were polished onyx. His head beat to a rhythm she couldn't hear. The muscles in his back ebbed and flowed with the scrubbing motion of his hand—a ripple here, a bulge there. If the circumstances were different, she could certainly enjoy this sight.

He rose and turned to dip the rag into the bucket of soapy water as she approached. He saw her and straightened to his full height, tugging earbuds from his ears as he turned to face her. He didn't say a word—just stood there like the bronze statue of some mythological god of muscled, suntanned bodies.

"I've got to tell you something," she said. "I tried calling you about fifteen times." She glanced down at the earbud cords dangling from the pocket of his low-slung shorts. He nodded toward the truck. "My phone's in the console."

She swallowed and forced herself to look away from the abs that looked like they belonged in an advertisement for *Men's Health*.

"So what is it?" he said.

Her gaze returned to him. She forced herself to look at his face, but those broad shoulders still distracted her. Muscles the size of grapefruits bulged under his skin. "Can you . . . put on a shirt or something?"

He placed his hands on his hips and broadened his stance. One corner of his mouth tipped into a grin. "Can't handle looking at the goods?"

"Believe me, it was not my choice to be here." She knew after their meeting at Morgan's Ladder that he had so many reasons to dislike her.

"Then why did you come?"

She took a deep breath. How many times would she have to tell this man she was making his life more difficult? "Suzanne and

I were down at the prison in Starke today. A guy was being let out who'd been wrongly convicted of a murder twenty-one years ago."

Landon tossed the rag into the bucket. Water splashed out onto the hot pavement and immediately began to disappear. "And what's this got to do with me?"

"Channel Four was there. Donna Crocker asked if I was in a relationship with you."

He took a step forward and glared at her. "She asked you that? On camera?"

Gina nodded. She wanted to fade into the searing pavement, just as the water had done.

"And what did you say?" Landon's voice was louder, angrier.

"I kept turning the conversation back to the guy who got out today."

"And . . . ?"

How did he know there was an "and"?

"I may have said something about you not liking your job."

He glared at her. "How the hell did that even come up in the conversation?"

"She said it would ruin your career to have a relationship with me."

"Or my life." His glare intensified.

She pulled her cell phone from her pocket to check the time. "It's five fifty-two. Can we go to your place to watch the six o'clock news?"

He bent and drew the rag out of the bucket. "I learned a long time ago not to pay attention to what people are saying about me."

"But I want to see it and I don't have time to get back to my place. I want to see which parts make the newscast."

"Is that what we need here? For a news crew to see the two of us coming out of my condo? Or maybe that's what you want?" He raised his hands to frame an imaginary headline in the air. "Visiting law student tricks Landon Vista into sleeping with her while she fights to get his mom's killer out of jail."

His words stung, but she didn't want him to know that.

"You might want to work on your technique." She placed her hands on her hips. "Because if we've slept together, it was . . . unmemorable."

He smirked.

Gina pulled her cell phone from her pocket and checked the time again. "Come on. It's about to start."

He returned to the truck and bent to scrub the same wheel he'd been working on when she'd arrived. "You should have gone straight to your place."

"I thought I was being kind." Her voice was a mixture of anger and desperation. She wasn't sure which she hated worse. "I thought I was helping you."

His hand stilled on the wheel. His shoulders rose and fell as his lungs expanded with a big sigh. He stood to face her.

"I learned a long time ago to distance myself from all that crap, but you can go watch it by yourself." He opened the door to the truck and retrieved his keys. She stepped toward him and reached for them, but he quickly withdrew his arm. The action brought her closer to him. She could feel the heat radiating from his body. Smell the soapy, sweaty scent of him.

"I'm doing this under one condition: you never, ever mention my name in the media again." He held the keys above his head, exposing the trim right side of his rib cage. "Ever."

She nodded. "Agreed."

He lowered his arm and handed the keys to her. "The square silver one." He turned back toward his truck.

"You trust me in your condo? By myself?"

He turned back toward her with a glower. "I'm letting you in my condo. But I don't trust you at all."

CHAPTER TWELVE

Landon watched as Gina hurried across the parking lot toward her SUV, her hips swaying in the same skirt she'd undoubtedly worn to the prison today. The last thing some guy doing time needed was a look at that curvy ass. Hell, Landon had gotten laid on a regular basis and that ass drove him crazy.

What was he doing, giving her the keys to his condo? And why did he make such stupid decisions when it came to her? He rolled his head around, trying to release the tension in his shoulders. She did this to him. Every damn time he saw her.

Maybe he'd go for a run tonight. A nice, long, Gina-free run.

He finished washing the last wheel and returned the bucket and hose to the place the condo association kept them, then got the extra key from the glove box and started the truck.

When he arrived at his condo, Gina was out front, locking the door closed. She turned and was surprised by his presence. She looked pale. Shaken by something more significant than him startling her.

"I thought *I* had your keys," she said.

"I keep an extra one in the glove box." He took the key ring she handed him and unlocked his front door. He motioned for her to go inside.

She hesitated.

"Do you really want Donna Crocker to see us out here?" he asked.

Gina took a deep breath and stepped into his entry hall.

He followed her inside. She was uncomfortably close. "So what did they show on the news?"

"Buford Monroe's release was the top story." She looked down, but he could still see the redness that blossomed on her chest and neck. "They said Morgan's Ladder has taken on Cyrus Alexander's case." She looked up and made quotation marks in the air with her fingers. "The man convicted of murdering the mother of former FSU standout Landon Vista."

He'd heard that before. Had to live with it all through college and after.

The apologetic look on Gina's face told him she wasn't finished recapping what had been on TV. "And that you weren't happy with your job at the senator's office."

"I can't believe you'd say that."

"You *told* me you don't like being used by those people."

He swiped his hand through his hair. "Yes, but it wasn't for you to broadcast on the local news."

"Even if you hadn't told me, I've seen how you act. How you don't have that passion that you had when I saw you playing football on TV."

"You've come to this conclusion after knowing me for what, two weeks?"

"I didn't mean to say it. She kept badgering me."

He paced in front of her. "You do not have my permission to talk about me in the media. Ever."

"Okay. I deserve that." She stood taller and cocked her chin up. "But you still haven't denied you hate your job."

"That is not a topic for public discussion." What did she not get about this?

"So what's holding you here? Your father? Or maybe you like the celebrity? Otherwise you'd go somewhere people didn't know you so well. Santa Fe. Or Portland. Somewhere not as crazy about football."

He stopped his pacing and glared at her, hoping his bravado would hide the truth. No one else had even come close. No one else had seemed to care that he stayed in Tallahassee hoping his dad would one day show he gave a damn.

But Gina didn't need to know that. She'd come dangerously close to a truth no one else had ever discovered. How could she disrupt his life so completely and at the same time be the one person who actually saw him? Not the football player or the poster child for tougher sentencing laws. No. She actually saw *him*. He studied her eyes, trying to understand what she might be thinking. "Maybe you should just stick to the law. And stop trying to psychoanalyze my life."

"I should go."

He stood there, his face close to hers, for several more seconds. He felt like kissing her, though he had no idea why. This woman was like a sudden storm, with winds licking at his heels, blowing everything he'd ever known about his life into disarray.

Finally, he stepped away from her. She made her way toward the door.

"And, Gina?"

She turned to look at him.

"If we ever did sleep together . . ."

Gina's eyebrows rose. Questioning him.

"You'd definitely remember it."

~

Gina was glad her boss was out of town for the next couple of days. Maybe by the time Suzanne got back from visiting her aunt, this whole mess with Donna Crocker would have blown over. Or at least maybe another huge catastrophe would have made it seem like something other than the major screwup that it was.

She glanced toward her boss's office. Empty now, but Suzanne would be back in a couple of days and they'd talk through it. Hopefully by then, she'd have her feelings sorted through.

She wanted to call Landon, but what did you say to the guy whose life you'd messed up in so many ways? Admitting he might not have seen Cyrus Alexander running out of the country store was a major paradigm shift to begin with. But then she had to go and point out that he stayed in Tallahassee hoping his dad would eventually show he cared? And who was she to suggest that Landon needed to move on, to know he was a strong person, with or without his father's love?

She wanted to reach out and hold him. To convey to him that she understood—at least in part—how he felt. To share the wisdom she'd gained from the couple of years she'd had to digest the fact that she'd put an innocent boy in jail. To somehow show him that he was a full and vibrant man, regardless of his father's involvement in his life.

How had her life become so tangled up in his? How did he make her so angry one minute . . .

"If we ever did sleep together, you'll definitely remember it."

. . . and make her tingle with anticipation the next?

She considered calling him. To apologize? For which of the many things? For duping him with that stupid picture of the basketball team? Or to talk about damage control after her comments on the local news? To try to convince him that he'd eventually figure out how to deal with all this?

But was there anything she could say to him that would make it better? Maybe it was best if she just stayed away. It was hard to jeopardize your job by keeping your mouth shut. And she'd done enough damage already. She was even too embarrassed to call her dad, whom she could talk to about anything.

The ring of her office phone startled her. She stared at it for a couple more rings, then finally answered. "Morgan's Ladder."

"Gina Blanchard, please." The woman on the other end was all business.

"This is Gina."

"This is Mrs. Willingham from Senator Byers's office. The senator is requesting a meeting with you."

Everything in Gina's body stilled. Her heart quit beating. Her blood quit flowing. Could she turn down the request? She wouldn't even live in this state after a few more weeks. How bad would it be for her career if she dodged meetings with state senators?

"Ms. Blanchard?" The woman on the other end of the phone seemed impatient.

"Yes, I'm here." Maybe he wanted to see her for some business having to do with the task force. Maybe he knew nothing about her screwup on the evening news.

"He'd like for you to come to his office this afternoon at five p.m."

"Can I ask what this is regarding?"

The woman paused before answering. "Most people are just happy to get an audience with him." She seemed to choose her words carefully.

"Will other people be in the meeting?" Maybe that was a way to get more information.

"Ms. Blanchard." Gina knew she'd been scolded by the tone in the woman's voice. "Are you free to meet or not?"

CHAPTER THIRTEEN

Landon stood at the printer, waiting for the statistics to be included in the senator's latest presentation to finish spitting out. He'd kept his head down all day, trying to convince himself that no one watched the local news anymore anyway. But what bothered him most was how Gina saw through him. That she'd started out as the lawyer on the other side of the Cyrus Alexander case, but had somehow wormed her way into his psyche. And his life.

Scott Meredith came around the corner. "The senator would like to see you in his office."

Landon retrieved the last of the presentation from the printer's output tray and followed Scott through the door that led from the worker-bee cubicles into the upscale part of the workplace. Here, glass-walled private offices conveyed stature. Power. Prestige. This was where the decisions were made, where the deals were done, and where plans were made on how to collect more money from donors. The senator's office was at the end, protected by Mrs. Willingham, an executive assistant who guarded her boss's calendar and real estate like a pit bull.

The matronly woman normally cast her prunish smile at people when they entered her area, but she seemed to avoid looking at him and Scott. Instead, she straightened a stack of papers that didn't need straightening.

"Landon can go in?" Scott asked.

Mrs. Willingham, forced to acknowledge them, gave Landon a look that seemed intentionally blank and nodded toward the senator's office. "Go on."

Scott, too, seemed evasive. Secretive. He inclined his head toward the senator's doorway, making it clear he wouldn't be joining Landon inside.

The senator was gazing out the window, toward the capitol, when Landon entered. "You wanted to see me?" Landon asked.

The older man turned. "Shut the door, son."

Landon closed the door behind him and only then caught a small movement out of the corner of his eye. They weren't in the room alone. He turned around to see who was with them.

Gina.

She glanced at him with a worried look. He crinkled his brow, a silent question to see if she knew what this was about. She gave an almost imperceptible shrug.

"I guess the two of you know each other." The senator's voice boomed.

"Yes, sir." They answered one right after the other.

The older man glared at them. "Apparently that's a fact that all of Tallahassee knows by now." He motioned for Landon to sit in the chair next to Gina's, across from the desk. "Sit down, son."

Landon sat, though he was tempted to tell the old man to shove it.

"Did you see it on TV last night?" the senator asked.

Landon sat up straighter. "No, sir."

The senator nodded toward Gina. "She said you didn't like working here."

Landon looked over at Gina, hoping something in her countenance would help him decide what to say. Part of him wanted to tell the truth—that he hated being used for his notoriety—but the self-preservation part of his psyche took over. He decided to remain silent.

Senator Byers raised a questioning eyebrow. "What would have given her that opinion?"

"I hardly ever know what women think . . . sir." Out of the corner of his eye, he saw Gina's head turn toward him, her mouth open in shock. Or anger. Or both. But she'd gotten him into this mess, so maybe it was time for him to dish out a little trouble of his own.

The senator leaned down, placing both palms flat on his desk. "You may think this is all cutesy and fun, but let me tell you what the rules are going to be from now on. If your friend makes another comment like that. On TV. In the newspaper. On the Internet." The senator slashed his hand through the air. "To anyone, then we'll fire your ass that very same day. You got that?"

Landon swallowed and tried to see Gina in his periphery without making Senator Jackass think he wasn't focused on him. Getting reamed in front of her was embarrassing, even if all this was her fault. "Yes, sir."

"We hired you because we thought you'd be an asset," the senator continued. "Don't let yourself become a liability."

Landon's body tensed with anger. He wasn't some donor list or a trade secret. And he sure as hell didn't like being told he was a liability. Especially not in front of Gina.

The senator continued. "Reelection's going to be hard enough this time around as it is. We can't afford the negative publicity." He sat down. "And since you can't seem to keep it in your pants when you're around her, I'm pulling you off the task force. Effective immediately. You're not to see her anymore—not for work. Not after work. You understand?"

Landon's ears grew hot. His jaw tensed. He hated that the guy was talking to him like a third grader. He was a grown man. If he wanted to see Gina, then he was going to see her.

"I don't think you can do that." There was a sudden silence. Both men turned toward Gina, who'd spoken for the first time since Landon had entered the room. She leaned back, as if aware of the sudden attention. "I don't think you can tell your employees who they can date, especially if both parties don't work within your organization." Her eyes widened with realization. "Not that we're dating or anything."

"And you." Senator Jackass came around the desk to face her, aiming his venom at his new victim. "You've gone to one year of law school and now you think you're an expert on employment law?"

She held his gaze. "I didn't say that, sir." Landon was proud of the way she stood up to the bastard. He admired a person—anyone—who stood up for what they thought was right.

"You are never to mention me to the media again." The old man pronounced the words slowly, as if to make sure Gina understood. "Or Landon. Or anyone else on my staff."

"Yes, sir." Again, she held his gaze.

"Does Suzanne know you're sleeping with him? Doesn't that violate some kind of lawyer code of ethics or something?"

Landon had had it. He leapt to his feet and towered over the senator. "That's enough." His voice was stern. This might get him fired. But at this point, standing up for Gina was more important.

The senator let out a sarcastic chuckle. "So, I guess there is a relationship here."

Landon pointed to her. "She has been nothing but professional. She didn't even know who I was the night Donna Crocker was talking about. Yeah, I kissed her. But look at her. Don't tell me you wouldn't do the same thing."

The senator glanced at her face, then her breasts before he seemed to realize what he was doing. His face paled.

Landon continued. "She screwed up. She gets that." He looked at her as she stood. "You won't do it again, right?"

She shook her head as she picked up her purse.

"Is there anything else you need from us?" Landon asked the senator.

The older man regained his composure. He stood to his full height, but was still several inches shorter than Landon. "You're dangerously close to saying something you're going to regret later."

"Then we should go. You ready, Gina?" Landon heard rustling as she headed toward the door, but he held the senator's glare, challenging him.

Ten minutes ago Gina had been the enemy—the one who'd screwed up his life in yet another way—but she didn't deserve this. He felt a protectiveness toward her. Sure, she'd held her own, but this was what men did. They protected their women.

Except she wasn't his.

And he didn't think she ever would be.

~

"That wasn't much fun," Landon said as he slid into the booth at Carmine's about fifteen minutes after the senator had reprimanded them. The dark, casual atmosphere had made this one of his go-to places since his freshman year.

"Are you sure we should be seen in public together?" Gina asked, looking around the nearly empty tavern. "The senator seemed pretty serious."

Landon gave her a dismissive wave. "No one's ever in here. That's why I like it so much." Besides, he was so ticked at the senator right now that he'd love to go toe-to-toe with him on whether or not he could see Gina outside of work. He felt like seeing her just to spite the guy . . . not that he'd have to be convinced to be near her. Just watching the way her light blue shirt hugged the sides of her breasts was reason enough for any man to hang around.

He raised two fingers in the air when Carmine looked at him from behind the bar. The guy would know to bring them each a draft beer.

"I can't believe he said he'd fire you for something I might do."

Landon grunted. Yeah, the guy was an asshole.

Crimson rose on her cheeks. He wondered if that always happened when she got fired up like this. "Does he realize that men don't control the actions of women anymore?" she asked.

"He's a state senator. I'm pretty sure he's used to people doing whatever he wants, regardless of their gender."

"I think he might be stuck in the 1950s. And besides, I don't even live in this state full time." Carmine placed a beer in a frosted glass in front of her. "Thanks." She paused until the bar owner left the table. "If I'm not one of his constituents, then he can't really expect me to bow down to him like everybody else does."

He gave her a teasing grin. "I'm about to lose my job, but this is all about you?"

She smiled back. He wished he could see that smile every day. "I guess a lot of this is my fault."

Landon scoffed. "You think?"

"I'm really sorry." Her gaze held his.

"For what?" He wasn't sure he was ready to forgive her for all that, but the run-in with the senator seemed to have made them comrades for the time being.

"The picture of the basketball team. For talking to the media about you. For getting you yelled at by your boss."

He shrugged. She'd gotten chewed out, too, so he wasn't sure that one counted.

"I'll make a deal." She stretched her arms out toward him. "I'll tell you some good news I've discovered about the case. To at least start to make us even. What do you say?"

He wasn't sure what kind of good news she could have. She'd blown into his life like a maelstrom and toppled everything he'd ever known like lawn furniture in a hurricane. But maybe it was worth a shot. He still wasn't sure where their professional relationship ended and their friendship began. Assuming what they had could even be called a friendship. It was a wary one at best. "What is it?"

She leaned forward, an excited look on her face. "Your dad was a district manager for Davidson Auto Parts when you were a kid."

"*My* dad?" The company had stores all over north Florida and south Georgia.

"After what you said the other night about my dad having a steady job, I figured you didn't know."

"Was this when my mom was killed?"

She nodded. "And for a year or so before that."

He ran his fingers through his hair. "My dad wasn't drinking when it happened?" He suddenly didn't feel like having his beer. His hands shook as he pushed it farther away.

"Or he hid it pretty well."

"And he had a good job?" Even saying it out loud didn't help it seem any truer.

"That's good news, right?" She didn't seem to understand the impact the news had on him. "You can help him remember the time when he was successful. Encourage him to try to live like that again."

"He wasn't a drunk then"—he took a deep breath—"and he still didn't want us."

She touched his arm from across the table. The gentle contact was so loving, so caring, compared to the stark realization that had just plowed him over like a diesel. His dad had been a regular guy, with a job and everything.

Landon had always thought his dad loved the liquor more than anything else. But now he had a new fact. His dad just hadn't loved him. Period.

"She wouldn't have been in the store." His voice sounded hollow, like it belonged to someone else. "She wouldn't have had to work in a dive like that if we'd been a family."

"I'm . . . sorry." She slouched back against the booth. "I thought this would make you happy. I should never have told you about it."

He looked in her eyes, at that look of pity he'd gotten all his life. Saliva poured into his mouth as bile churned in his esophagus. He thought he might vomit right there in Carmine's.

He'd invited her out for a beer. Thought maybe they'd commiserate a while over what the senator had said to them. How he'd treated them. But instead she'd shown Landon—once again—how he wasn't good enough. How his dad had held a good job and still didn't want his son.

He'd thought he and Gina might be friends. That they might someday joke about what had just happened with the senator. But he wasn't sure they'd ever be friends. Because she was perfect and he was . . . not.

CHAPTER FOURTEEN

Landon stopped in the entryway of Ace's, his body rebelling against the thick smell of smoke that hit him even before he'd gotten in the door. As much as he hated this place—this icon of his father's drunkenness—he had to confront his dad. Had to find some answers to what he'd found out from Gina tonight at Carmine's.

"How's it going?" He nodded to the same bartender who'd been working the last time he'd been here.

"He's over there." The other man jabbed a thumb toward the back of the dimly lit bar. A haze gathered around the neon beer sign over the pool table where his dad was playing.

"You're becoming quite a regular around here." The cigarette in his dad's mouth bobbed as Landon approached.

"Why weren't Mama and I living with you when she was killed?"

His dad's gaze slid to Landon's, then back to the pool table where he was bent over for his next shot. He didn't say anything.

Landon felt the heat rise in his face. A table full of bikers sat in the back of the bar, but at this point, he didn't care who overheard them. "You were a district manager for Davidson Automotive."

"Yep." The cue ball smacked against the three ball, sending it ricocheting around the table.

"You could have afforded to have us with you. At least put a roof over our heads. She didn't have to be working in that place at all, raising her kid in the back room." He waved his arm behind him, as if gesturing toward the place he'd spent so many of his early years.

His dad walked toward him, the cigarette still clinging to his lips. "Where's all this coming from? You just now find this out?"

"I'm finding out a lot of things now that Morgan's Ladder is looking at the case."

"Are you going to barge in here and yell at me every time you find out something new?" His dad walked to a nearby table and chugged what was left of a mug of beer.

"So how come you didn't rescue us, Dad? Were you not paying child support? How come she had to be there?"

"Are you telling me"—he squinted as a trail of smoke snaked toward his eyes—"that if any girl you ever screwed had gotten pregnant, you'd have married her? What about that redhead I met the other night?"

"I would never *screw* her." Make love to her, sure. Revel in her soft curves. If things were different between them, he'd savor that beautiful body all day, every day. But Gina wasn't the type of girl you screwed.

His father grinned. "Hit a little nerve there, did I?"

"What do you know about me, anyway?" He charged toward Martin with his fists balled. "It's not like you were ever around to talk to me about . . . sex . . . or condoms . . . or other things dads talk to their sons about."

Martin's gaze held steady. "I wasn't going to marry a woman I wasn't in love with. That would only be piling one mistake on top of another."

"And you didn't want to talk to your son? To see if maybe you could stop him from making the same mistake you made?"

"You gotten any girls pregnant?"

Landon's shoulders dropped. The son of a bitch wasn't getting the point. "Not that I know of."

"Guess you didn't need me, then."

Landon shook his head and decided to take another approach. "What happened to you? What happened to your job?"

"That was twenty years ago. I don't see any reason to hash over old news."

Landon glared, wondering for the billionth time why he cared so much. Why he'd always had this driving need to get closer to the man who'd disowned him. "You're not going to tell me what you were like back then?"

His father's eyes challenged him. "I was the same simple guy, son. The one who's never good enough for you."

Landon stepped back from his father and thought about what his dad had said. Had he been this guy—with the scraggly hair and untucked shirt—when he'd shipped Landon off to live with his aunt and uncle? Or maybe the murder had caused him to start drinking more than he had before? On the other hand, maybe he'd been a regular, go-to-work-every-day kind of guy, who only later started the downward decline? Landon wasn't sure which was worse. All he knew was that he needed to get the hell out of there. "I'll see you later."

His dad grunted and turned to take another cigarette out of the pack on the table behind him.

Landon headed toward the front of the bar. Another thought struck him as he reached the entrance. He thrust the door open, not wanting the thought to settle in.

Maybe his dad had started drinking more because *he'd* been the murderer.

Landon stumbled out onto the sidewalk, jolted by the thought. No—his father had an alibi. He couldn't have done it.

So why was he so damned evasive?

Damn Dad.

Damn liquor.

Damn Gina.

Dealing with his dad was bad enough, but at least he'd had years to get used to being the son of a drunk.

Then she'd swept into town for the summer, just long enough to disrupt his life. To change everything he'd thought about Mama's murder case, reexposing the part of his life that he'd worked so hard to have everyone else forget. Making him contemplate things he'd never wanted to think about.

She thought she was helping him by telling him his dad had been a district manager.

But he didn't need her help. He didn't need *her*. He'd been just fine before she came along.

He walked a few feet to his truck and got in, then slammed the door shut, mad about the truth he had to admit.

She'd brought bad news and heartache into his life.

But that had nothing to do with why he couldn't get her off his mind.

～

Gina wasn't sure why Landon wanted to see her this evening. He'd called midday to ask if he could come to her apartment after work. His voice had sounded empty. Apathetic. Resigned to some fate that was out of his control.

It had been two days since she'd divulged the fact that his dad had been a district manager for Davidson Automotive at the time of the murder, and she still wished she hadn't told him.

It was the apathy that bothered her most. She'd seen the passion in his eyes on many occasions. During his playing days. That night they'd first kissed on the deck at the Twilight Pub. The day he'd barged into Morgan's Ladder because he thought she'd known who he was the night before. He was a man filled with passion, so the apathy was out of place. Like he'd given up.

Was that what she heard in Landon's voice? Was he giving up? Was she the one responsible for driving that passion from his eyes?

She busied herself straightening the apartment, glancing every few seconds out the front window to see if his truck had pulled up out front. Finally, he arrived.

She greeted him on the stoop at the top of her stairs.

"Hi," she said, trying to study the expression on his face. "Come in."

He glanced back to the road before he entered. She flinched inwardly. She was responsible for his concern. Her interview with Donna Crocker had made his life worse than it had to be.

She stood aside and he stepped into her living room. He looked more rugged today than usual, which was a hard thing to do. His dark khaki cargo shorts were wrinkled. His black T-shirt looked custom-made to perfectly encase those round, hard biceps.

"I went to see my father a couple of days ago," he said.

"And hello to you, too." She wished he hadn't gotten down to business so quickly. Wished he'd . . . what did she wish for? That he'd come to visit her on a social call? That he came to her apartment for a reason that wasn't related to the case or the task force or the senator's reprimand? That they had a relationship beyond Cyrus Alexander? A pang of regret sliced through her.

"I want to be quick. I don't want your neighbors seeing my truck out there."

She wished for the Landon who'd invited her for a beer after their meeting in the senator's office. "My neighbors have an average age of about eighty-seven and a half years old."

"So they've got nothing better to do than to peer out their windows."

"Good point." She shrugged. "So what did you and your dad talk about?"

He squared to face her, as if he wanted her full attention. "I want my DNA tested." His gaze bored into her. Resolute. Defiant.

His words drove into her like a gust of strong winter wind. "What? Why?"

"I don't trust him. He's too evasive."

"And what does that have to do with you?"

"My DNA would show we're relatives, right?"

She nodded, hesitant. Unsure of where he was headed.

"Then the DNA on my mom's clothes would say whether or not a relative of mine was the murderer."

A cold chill sliced down Gina's back. This was the first time Landon had confided this to her. "You think your dad might have done it?" Her words came out in a whisper.

He slumped against the door frame leading into her kitchen. "I think he's a son of a bitch." He scrubbed his hand down his face. "But I don't know if he's a murderer."

She reached out and took his other hand before she realized what she was doing. "But you want to find out." It wasn't a question as much as it was a statement.

"Yeah." He drew in a long breath and heaved it out. "I want to find out."

Her thumb caressed his hand where she held it. They stood there for several seconds, their eyes locked as both contemplated the weight of his decision.

"I can help you do that," she finally said.

"Any way to keep it confidential? I don't want the media to find out."

"Can I ask Suzanne about that?" Her boss would know her way around these things more than Gina would. "This must have been done before, and I bet she'll know how not to mark the specimen before it goes to the lab."

He nodded slowly.

"This must have been a tough decision to come to." She stepped closer and slid her arm up his back, offering comfort.

147

He stepped away, out of her reach. "You'll let me know what Suzanne says?" His retreat stung. All she'd wanted to do was comfort him. He was alone. He'd just taken the first step toward perhaps believing his father had committed murder, despite the alibi. He'd opened his heart to the possibility that his father might have killed his mother.

This was big stuff.

Huge.

And yet he'd stepped away from her.

He hadn't wanted her to comfort him.

He'd rather be alone than with her.

She pressed her lips together to hide her emotion and moved to open the door for him. Maybe the whole "I don't want your neighbors to see my truck" had been a setup for a quick departure.

"Let me know what you find out from your boss," he said.

She nodded. "I will." Her voice squeaked out. She wished he would leave before he realized how his retreat had hurt her.

Before he realized that he could get to her like that.

Before he realized this was about much more than the Cyrus Alexander case.

~

Stupid. Stupid. Stupid.

Landon slammed an open palm against the steering wheel as he gunned his truck away from the curb in front of Gina's apartment.

Why the hell had he stepped away when she'd tried to console him? Why did he always act like he had something to prove whenever he was around her?

He should dig his phone out of his pocket and apologize to her. He needed her help. She was the only one he knew who was plugged into people who might be able to have his DNA tested privately. The only one he felt comfortable going to about it. Sure, he could call that DA from Pascaloosa County. The guy who'd first told him that Morgan's Ladder was working on Cyrus Alexander's case. But—despite how he and Gina had started out against each other—he trusted that she wanted the same thing he did: to know who had murdered Mama.

So why had he pulled away? After all her talk about not wanting to risk her job, she'd reached out to him. She'd touched him in a way that wasn't businesslike.

Why hadn't he let her console him when every part of him had wanted to receive her comfort? He'd seen the hurt in her eyes when he'd stepped away. Knew that his action had hurt her.

And yet he'd done nothing to mend it.

He pulled his phone from his pocket and scrolled to her number. Should he call her to apologize? What would he say? What if he'd read her actions wrong and she really didn't care about him?

He set the phone on the seat beside him, not sure what he should do. He picked it up again, thought about it, then stuffed it back into his pocket.

He turned onto Apalachee Parkway, toward Boomer's house. He could go there and watch a little ESPN. They could shoot some shit and he could pretend none of this was going on.

There, he could forget what an ass he'd been to Gina. He could forget about her and the DNA and the media and the senator and all the other crap having to do with the case.

But was that really what he wanted? He pulled into the parking lot of a fast-food restaurant, not sure if going to Boomer's was what he needed right now.

Sure, he'd like to forget about the case. Would like—for one night—to forget that he might have put an innocent guy in prison and that his own father might be a murderer. But he didn't want to forget about Gina. He didn't want to forget her soft skin or her determined eyes or the way she made him think that maybe—just maybe—she understood what he was going through.

He watched as a couple of college students got out of a beat-up Chevy and walked, arm in arm, toward the restaurant. The girl laughed at something the guy said. He pecked her cheek as they stepped onto the curb, then held the door open for her.

An unexpected jealousy welled inside Landon's chest at the sight of them. He wondered if he and Gina could ever be that close. That carefree.

And then it hit him. These were the thoughts that scared him. This is why he had pulled away from her. Because he wanted to have a real relationship with the woman who was causing such chaos in his life.

And that terrified the hell out of him.

CHAPTER FIFTEEN

Landon told himself he was here on Gina's doorstep to apologize for pulling away from her last night. That, and to return the terrible sweatpants he'd worn home after breakfast at her house a few mornings ago. He'd done laundry last night when he'd gotten home and figured tonight was as good as any to return them.

The door to her upstairs apartment swung open. An older man with salt-and-pepper hair and a middle-aged paunch stood where Landon had expected Gina. The man stepped closer and cocked his head in Landon's direction, scrutinizing him.

A smile spread across the man's face. "Hey, hey. Landon Vista. Come on in." The man grasped his elbow and tugged him inside. "Look, Terri, it's Landon Vista."

A delicious smell filled the apartment—something with tomato sauce and garlic. Something that made it smell like a home.

A tall woman with the same strawberry-blonde hair as Gina's rushed from the kitchen. Laugh lines in the shape of parentheses framed her mouth, the only visible wrinkles on her otherwise flawless skin.

"The football player you told me about?" She grasped his hand in both of hers. "And such a handsome man."

"Nice to meet you, ma'am." He dipped his head toward her, then scanned the apartment. *Where the hell was Gina?*

The man stuck out his hand. "Ted Blanchard. Gina's father."

"She should be home any minute." Her mom leaned closer, as if she didn't want anyone to hear. "They had to go to the prison today," she whispered.

Landon froze. Was Gina visiting Cyrus Alexander? Last Landon knew, Cyrus was at the state prison in Starke, a couple of hours away. Were they there swabbing his mouth, testing for DNA that might exonerate him?

Landon had gone through the same humiliating test the day before. Yet another time his dad's actions had made Landon feel low-class. Like in fifth grade when Martin had shown up drunk at Landon's school. Or in ninth grade when Matthew Cunningham had shown everyone Martin's drunken mug shot in the local newspaper.

Yes, all the unpleasant memories had come flooding back, all because of a swab in his mouth and what it might prove about his father.

"Have a seat." Ted stood aside and motioned toward the couch. "I can't believe I'm in the same room as the guy I used to curse at on TV."

"He doesn't really need to know that, Ted," Gina's mom said.

The older man gestured toward the couch. "Terri promised Gina she'd make her favorite meal while we were in town. Homemade lasagna. You can stay, can't you?"

"It makes enough to feed half of Tallahassee," her mom said. "I'll get you two a glass of sweet tea. You can sit down and relax while I make the salad."

Ted raised his eyebrows as if seeking Landon's response to their invitation.

"I guess I can stay a minute," Landon said. Stick around long enough to see if Gina learned anything new about the case.

Terri headed for the kitchen with that same self-assured gait her daughter had.

"Gina told me you two had met," Ted said.

Landon nodded. "There's a volleyball league for people who work near the capitol. She's on one of the opposing teams." Her dad didn't need to know that she'd blocked all his shots that first night they'd met.

"No rec football?"

"I play that in the fall."

Ted's eyebrow crooked up. "Tackle?"

"Flag. Fewer injuries that way." He hoped Gina's father didn't ask him about the NFL. Most people did when they talked sports with him—wanted his take on why he hadn't gone on to the next level, even though the local media had analyzed the hell out of it a couple of years ago. "He doesn't play an offense that works well in the NFL" or "Too slow off the line" were the usual culprits.

He looked around the room, grasping for another topic. "I didn't realize Gina had company." *Where was it she'd said she'd been raised before heading off to college? Georgia somewhere? Maybe Savannah?*

Ted grinned as his wife returned with two glasses. "We're on our way to St. Pete Beach. The Don CeSar."

"That's where we went on our honeymoon." She smiled as she handed Landon one of the drinks.

Landon tried to smile, but it felt fake. He wasn't good at sharing in other people's happiness, especially when it came to happy couples. But he was pretty sure the Don CeSar was that pink beachfront hotel where the senator had held a fundraiser the year before. At least he knew that much.

Gina's mom returned to the kitchen. Her dad sat on the edge of the chair opposite him, leaning toward him. Landon felt like a teenager about to be quizzed by the father of a girl he was taking to prom.

"Gina told me you still live in Tallahassee." Ted said. "Work at the capitol? You write speeches or something?"

"I work for a state senator." So, Gina'd been talking to her dad about him. He wasn't sure if that was good or bad. "Research mainly. Statistical analysis. Put data together for hearings. That sort of thing."

"Like how taxes are going to be spent? How much money's going toward education?"

Landon shot him a sideways glance, trying to figure out if the man knew where the conversation was headed. "Crime related, mostly. Tougher sentencing guidelines. Harsher sentences for repeat offenders."

Ted nodded. "I understand you and Gina"—the slow pace of her dad's words told Landon he was choosing his words carefully—"may be on opposite sides of the crime issues."

He swallowed. "Yes, sir." Good. A short answer with no implications. No voice inflection.

Ted's eyes bored into his. "I admire a man who stands for something."

"Yes, sir." *So what was the guy trying to tell him?*

"A man who's had a tough life"—he tapped Landon's knee where it jutted into the space between them—"is a man with a lot of character."

So he did know Landon's story, either from Gina or from having heard it on TV during his playing days.

"My Gina's a stubborn one." A look of pride warmed the man's face. "I wouldn't want her on the opposite side of anything. Gets that from her mama."

Landon's stomach muscles tensed as footsteps sounded on the stairs that hugged the side of the detached garage leading to Gina's apartment. His mind raced. What would he say to Gina when she found him all chummy with her dad, chatting over glasses of sweet tea like they were old friends?

The door opened.

"Landon?" A confused look crossed her face. "What are you doing here?"

~

Gina had noticed a truck like Landon's in front of the house next door, but this was the South. *Lots of guys drive trucks like that,* she'd reassured herself. All she wanted to do was to go inside and rid herself of all the remnants of the prison she'd visited today. The lonely sound of the prison doors closing still hung in her clothes. She wanted to change into a pair of sweats and sit down at the table, to enjoy her mom's homemade lasagna. To forget about the wasted years and wasted lives she'd seen today.

What she didn't want—and hadn't prepared for—was to see Landon. What she didn't expect was him sitting in her living room, drinking iced tea with her dad. Not today. Probably not any day.

"Is that any kind of way to treat your dinner guest?" her dad said, rising to greet her.

Landon hustled off the couch. "I'm not staying." His gaze met hers, as if trying to convince her he didn't want to be here with her family any more than she wanted him to be here.

"Oh, come on," her dad said. "You've got to try Terri's lasagna. Best pasta I've had since I went to Little Italy in New York."

"Is that Gina?" Her mom came around the corner from the kitchen. "How was your day, honey?"

"We"—her gaze slid to Landon—"should probably talk about that later, Mom."

His eyes searched hers, as if asking if she'd found out anything new about the case today. She hadn't learned anything, but this wasn't the time to talk about that. Her parents already hated what she was doing this summer. They wanted her to go into real estate law or tax law. Something without prisons and rapists and murders.

"We'll talk football." Her dad slapped Landon on the back. "Remember that game against Auburn? Must have been your sopho- more, maybe junior, year?"

"I'm going to change clothes," Gina said as she set her briefcase down and headed for her bedroom. Her dad could talk to anyone. Make anyone feel like a long-lost buddy, no matter how short a time he'd known them. She knew Landon would soon be seated at their dinner table, eating her mother's lasagna like he belonged there. Like it was the most natural thing in the world for him to share a meal with them.

Her dad would want to talk football, but her mom might ask about her job or her day at the prison or—God forbid—how long Gina and Landon had been dating.

Gina stripped her suit off and pulled on the first pair of shorts and T-shirt that she ran across. She'd done enough damage to Landon on her own. She didn't need her mother causing more.

CHAPTER SIXTEEN

Landon had offered twice to help with the dishes, but her mom had refused.

"You two go sit in the living room," Terri said as she shooed Landon and Ted out of the kitchen. "We'll have pie and ice cream as soon as we get this mess cleaned up."

Landon tried to figure out if now was an appropriate time for him to make his exit. He glanced toward Gina as he left the kitchen, but she seemed more interested in checking for his reaction than in revealing her own.

"You see what we brought for Gina?" Her dad pulled a picture frame off the bookshelf as the two men entered the living room. "Has one of those little memory cards in back. Keeps rotating the pictures."

In the frame, one digital family photo dissolved while another one took its place. Landon chuckled at the strawberry-blonde little girl who stood in a leotard, her arms proudly stretched over her head, marking the end of her gymnastics routine.

Ted shook his head. "She practiced and practiced those flips until she could do them. Had more chutzpah than anyone I've ever seen."

"Still does," Landon said, thinking about how she'd stood up to the senator the other day in his office. How she'd gotten under his own skin, even when he'd been so certain a girl like her would never have anything to do with a guy like him. "Wasn't she kind of tall for a gymnast?"

Ted chuckled. "She found her niche with volleyball, that's for sure."

The picture faded and another one took its place. In it, a dark-haired boy held a tiny kitten in his arms.

"She told me about her brother."

Ted's gaze stayed on the picture, his face grim. "That's why she does it, you know. Because of what happened after Tommy's death."

"Why she's out to save the world?"

The life returned to Ted's eyes. "You noticed, too, huh? She's become more . . . focused, more determined since all that happened. But I guess I don't have to tell you how a single event can change a life so much, huh?"

"No." Landon looked again at the little boy in the picture. "You don't."

Ted motioned toward the kitchen with his head. "Must have been a surprise when she and her boss brought your mom's case up again."

"I had no idea it would ever happen."

"So is Gina the ally?" Ted cocked an eyebrow. "Or the enemy?"

Landon took a deep breath. "I just want to find out the truth." He wanted to know who'd murdered his mother. He wanted to know if his dad really had an alibi. He wanted to know what might happen between him and Gina once all this was over.

"Just remember—she's been through tough times, too. She knows how hard this is for you. It took a lot to get her through what she's been through."

Landon's chest ached. The family gathering, the soft clinking of dishes in the kitchen, the gentle laughter of Gina's mother, the home-cooked meal, the man-to-man chat—it all reminded him of what he'd missed. Of what he'd longed for all his life. Of what he could have had with his own father if Martin had been a different man or if Landon had a different set of life circumstances.

Gina might have been through something tough. Through something horrific. But at least she'd had her family. She'd had someone to care for her. To guide her through it.

She'd had them. And he'd had no one.

~

Thirty minutes later, Landon followed Gina down the steps outside her apartment, hating himself for enjoying the way her butt looked in the little khaki shorts she'd put on when she changed out of her suit. He wondered how many other guys had joined her family for dinner over the years. How many had been important enough in her life to meet her parents.

How many she'd slept with. *Why was he thinking about that?* He didn't want to think about her gorgeous thighs wrapped around some other guy's hips. Some guy who didn't deserve her, or he'd still be around.

"I don't know anything about the DNA yet," she said as they reached the bottom of the staircase. "I assume that's why you came over?"

"I thought I owed you an apology." God, this was harder to say than he thought it would be. "You tried to be there for me and I . . . was kind of an ass."

One of her eyebrows quirked upward. "You think?"

"But I had dinner with your parents, so now we're even."

"You were a good sport in there, letting them rope you into staying."

He'd actually had a good time listening the details of her father's work, her mom's real estate company, the goings-on of their small-town neighbors. They'd even asked about his life since football. They were people who laughed and hugged and teased. People who cared about each other.

People who made him feel like he belonged, even though he didn't.

"It wasn't so bad," he said.

"You're lucky you escaped before Daddy got too wound up talking football."

"Football's easy." Other topics, he wasn't so sure about. Had never been sure he knew how to act, how to joke, when to hug. "It's the get-togethers with Mom and Dad that are scary."

She laughed. "My parents aren't scary."

"They are when you don't have a lot of experience with normal family life."

"I'm not sure there is such a thing. And mine wouldn't qualify even if there was." A look of sadness crossed her face. "You lived with your aunt's family," she said. "Weren't they normal?"

He leaned against the wall of the house and thought about how to answer. How to explain that he'd always felt like an outsider, brought there out of a sense of obligation when Mama was killed, but never quite fitting in. "Their entire lives revolved around their little girl, my cousin. Dance classes, cheerleader tryouts. They even took her to Orlando for some modeling work. They thought she was perfect . . . until the preacher's son got her pregnant at sixteen."

Gina's eyebrows rose. "Puts a crimp in the modeling at least."

"They shipped her off to some home for unwed mothers so nobody else would know."

"I didn't know they even had those anymore."

"Wouldn't even tell me why she was going away until I asked them point-blank the day she was leaving, like they were afraid I would tell someone their precious little angel had gotten knocked up."

"Your cousin didn't tell you?"

Landon shook his head. "I guess she was too ashamed. They'd raised her to be their little princess and"—he thought about it for a second—"she fell off the throne."

"Surely they were proud of you." She stood in front of him, close enough for him to reach out and touch.

But he didn't.

He couldn't.

As badly as he wanted to.

"You played football for a Division I school," she said.

His laugh sounded bitter, even to him. "They were happy college was paid for."

"Well, my parents loved you. You can borrow them any time you want."

Okay, so "loved him" was a figure of speech. They'd only known him a couple of hours, but already he felt more comfortable here than he'd felt in most places throughout his life. The bittersweet feeling socked him in the gut—made him long for the family he hadn't had since Mama had died.

Would he have grown up a different person, given a family like Gina's? Would he have her confidence? Her insistence that she could change the world? Her parents seemed relatively well-off, but they had a richness that had nothing to do with money—a quiet grace that showed they knew their value in the world. A concept that had always escaped him.

"Must be nice to know"—Landon couldn't believe he was saying this out loud, especially to her; not something this close to his heart—"that they'd drop what they were doing and come take care of you if you were in trouble somehow." He'd never had that security. And he wasn't even sure he could understand it completely.

She cocked her head to one side. "Wouldn't Calvin do that for you?"

Landon shrugged. He'd mentioned Calvin to her a couple of times the other day.

She ran her hand down his arm. He liked that she did that sometimes. That she felt like she could. "A family doesn't have to mean a dad and a mom and the kids. Sometimes it's a neighbor or a teacher." She cocked her head to look him straight in the eye. "Or a coach."

Of course she was right. He was lucky to have Calvin. And somehow he felt lucky to know her, though he still hadn't figured out why. The only certainty was that she would be the woman who breezed in and out of Tallahassee one summer, changing him forever. He wanted to change the subject. Wanted to stop thinking about the fact that he'd never had a real family.

"You visited the prison today," he said.

She nodded slowly, as if switching gears from the friendly chatter to the reason for the chasm between them. "We did."

"No news at all on the DNA?"

She shook her head. "I know it's hard." The grief in her eyes told him she really did understand.

"Seems like a waste of time to visit him when you'll know in a day or two whether he really did it or not." The waiting must be even worse for Cyrus Alexander.

"We've still got work to do."

"Yeah? Like what?"

She gave him a you-know-better-than-to-ask-that look. "I can't tell you about meetings with our clients."

"That's right. Attorney-client privilege." Landon would be a happy man if he never heard that phrase again in his lifetime.

"I can tell you that Cyrus has a son."

His head whipped up. "What?"

"A sophomore in high school."

He didn't want to believe it. "The math doesn't work. He's been in prison for fifteen years and—"

Her steady gaze caught his. "Tim was born just before the sentencing. Days before. Cyrus has missed the kid's entire life."

Landon felt like he'd been punched in the gut. He might have done that to the kid. And if Cyrus was innocent . . . God, this made a wrongful conviction so much worse. "How long have you known this?" He pushed away from the wall and glared at her. "Why didn't you tell me before?" This changed everything. "Why are you telling me now?"

"I thought you might have a little sympathy for the kid. You both—"

He felt the defensiveness inside him click on. The same defensiveness that had been lurking there since elementary school, just under the surface. "We both what? Came from loser families?" He motioned up toward her apartment. "Because we didn't have a dad bringing home a paycheck and a mom cooking us lasagna every night?"

Her face paled. "Because you both grew up without your dads. You're anything but a loser."

A humorless laugh escaped from his throat. "That's not what it felt like when every kid in fourth grade looked at you like you were damaged goods. The only freak in the whole school whose mom had been murdered. I can still see the kids staring at me when I walked into my new classroom, knowing they'd been told about my mom."

"Just think how he must feel, being the only kid in class whose dad is in prison for murder."

But the DNA test could show that his own father was the murderer, which would make him even more of an outcast. "I've got to go." He yanked the keys from his pocket and stalked toward his truck as a maze of emotions swirled inside him.

How stupid could he have been? He'd actually thought that coming here to see her was the right thing to do. He'd thought it might make him feel less alone.

Then, lulled by the ambience of a quiet family dinner, he'd actually felt good for a while. Comfortable. Like maybe he could have this one day. How stupid could he have been?

He cranked the ignition and jerked the truck into reverse. In front of him, Gina waved. He cocked his chin; the subtle motion was the only good-bye he was willing to give.

What had he been thinking, anyway? He'd actually thought they might be together one day, after the whole Cyrus Alexander business was over. But now, reality hit him smack in the chest, like a barbell dropped on a weight bench.

He could never be with her. Not when her entire life was built on the safety of family. The comfort of home. It was all so foreign to him, like a language he didn't understand.

Yes, he was drawn to her, but he'd have to get over that. He'd been alone for years. And he was going to have to stay that way.

CHAPTER SEVENTEEN

"You two sure make a nice-looking couple," Terri said once Gina got back into her apartment and carried the pie plates into the kitchen.

She spun to look at her mom. "Me and Landon?" No way could Terri know how much time she spent thinking about him. "You're the one who invited him to dinner."

"It's not a problem between the two of you?" Her mom scraped some leftover crust into the trash can. "The man you're trying to get out of prison?"

"It's not like we're dating or anything. For God's sake, I'm pretty much the enemy." She didn't want to be, but that's what it felt like most of the time.

"He wore your pants home the other morning." A hint of crimson crept up her mom's neck as she nodded toward the sweatpants Landon had apparently brought with him tonight. "That's how you treat your enemies?"

Gina's eyes widened. Her own mother—the woman who'd stammered through "the talk"—assumed they were sleeping together? All they'd had were a couple of fantastic kisses. Sure, she'd thought about more—his hands gliding over her body, his lips exploring her collarbone, her breasts. The hard parts of his body touching the soft parts of hers. The scent of him as she held him close, her hands greedily caressing those rounded shoulders. That strong neck. That gorgeous stomach.

But each time she thought about that, reality set in—that she'd thrust his life into shambles. He'd gone from certainty about his testimony to uncertainty. From a sad but predictable relationship with his father to practically accusing the guy of murder. And Gina was in the middle of it all. "We're not dating. Or . . . that." She followed her mom's lead, referring to sex in vague, delicate terms. "Not now. Probably not ever."

Terri gave her a knowing smile. "I've seen the way he looks at you."

"With hatred and contempt?"

"He couldn't keep his eyes off you during dinner."

Gina shook her head. "He doesn't want to date me." As hard as it was to admit, his retreat the other night had convinced her of it. "He wants my help with his mom's murder case, but that's all."

"You never know." Her mom wiped the kitchen counter. "If it was meant to be, it will happen between the two of you. Your father and I . . . had an obstacle when we first met. He was engaged to marry someone else." The crimson rose again on her neck.

"Really?" Gina tried to imagine a younger version of her mom stealing a guy from another girl.

"I knew the minute I saw him in economics class that he was going to be someone special in my life." Her mom got a dreamy look on her face. "Did you ever get that feeling?"

Gina thought about the way the crime scene photos had haunted her. The way her own eyes had been drawn to Landon's haunting gaze, despite everything else going on in the pictures around him. "Yeah," she said. "I think I have."

"Then something will happen between you."

"That's what you said with Christopher."

"He never looked at you the way Landon does." Her mother folded the dish towel and placed it on the counter.

"You only met him once." Granted, it was two weeks before Gina had caught him sleeping with another girl, but she'd never told her mother that. It was just too embarrassing.

"You give it time." Her mom patted her hand. "I think something will happen between the two of you."

"I'm only in Tallahassee for a couple more weeks."

And that's when it hit her. In two short weeks, she wouldn't see him again.

As quickly as he'd entered her life, he'd be gone from it.

And nothing in law school had prepared her for that.

~

Gina sat at her desk at Morgan's Ladder and tapped the down arrow on her keyboard, moving from one e-mail to another. She should be working, but couldn't concentrate on anything. She'd stayed up late with her parents last night, trying to enjoy their company before they left this morning. But she'd had a hard time thinking about anything except the Barbara Landon case. Any day now, they'd have the results of the DNA—Landon's, Cyrus's, and from the crime scene. A sudden noise, a spilled cup of coffee, an angry word might send her into a nervous breakdown, whatever that looked like. Maybe she was already there. Or at least at the tipping point.

And to make matters worse, Suzanne had been in her office for fifteen minutes on the phone. With the door shut.

And Suzanne rarely shut her door.

Finally, her boss opened her office door and called Gina inside.

Gina took a deep breath as she took in Suzanne's drained, pale expression. She sank into the chair across from Suzanne's desk. She wanted to scream at her boss to speak, to blurt out whatever she'd found out from the lab. But Gina's sudden nausea told her she didn't want to know the answer. Her eyes darted around the room, looking for a trash can. She was going to need it if her belly didn't stop rumbling.

Finally, Suzanne spoke. "They don't know if Cyrus is the killer or not."

A cold chill swept down Gina's body, like an elevator plummeting down its shaft. "What?" This was the day they were supposed to get answers, not more questions. The day that was supposed to clear everything up.

"The DNA from the crime scene is too deteriorated. The results were inconclusive."

Gina closed her eyes and swallowed, willing herself not to throw up. This wasn't an answer she'd even contemplated. What did it mean? For Cyrus, it meant more prison time. For Landon, it meant no answers. This was the worst possible scenario. It didn't help anyone.

She opened her eyes. "So they'll never be able to use it? They'll never be able to compare it to anyone else's DNA? It will never tell them who the real killer was?"

Suzanne shook her head. "Not with the current technology."

"So we accomplished nothing." The second the words escaped her mouth, she wished she could take them back. The look on Suzanne's face must mirror her own—disbelief, sorrow, defeat. She would never want her boss to think she thought badly of her. "I . . . I didn't mean we didn't try. I meant that . . ."

Suzanne held her hand up to interrupt her. "It's disappointing."

"Yes." Disappointing. A huge understatement. "So what do we do now?"

"We continue to look for other evidence. Eventually, we decide if it's worth pursuing."

Gina's head whipped up. "We would drop the case?" Panic surged through her body. She'd expected a conclusion, but now it felt like she'd been thrown into a tumultuous ocean of doubt.

And she was quickly drowning.

They couldn't just give up on Cyrus.

They couldn't give up on Landon.

"We've got limited resources," Suzanne said. "We'll eventually have to weigh whether or not it makes sense to keep this one going if we're never going to find any exculpatory evidence. There are too many others out there who need our help." She stood.

"But we're his only hope." Gina wasn't sure if she was talking about Cyrus or Landon.

"I'm as committed to this case as you are, but there are dozens of prisoners who want our services. People we might be able to help."

"Unlike Cyrus" was the implication. But Gina would have to worry about this another day, once she'd had a chance to think everything through. "I need to go talk to Landon."

Any other day, she'd be concerned with what her boss thought about her relationship with him, but today transcended that. This news had so many implications. She needed to be with him.

"Take the rest of the day off." She motioned toward the door. "Go help him get through this."

Gina moved to her desk and turned off her computer, but it felt like someone else was in control of her body. She knew what she had to do, but the news was so overwhelming that nothing beyond rote motion was possible for her.

As her computer powered down, she remembered that she had forgotten to turn on her out-of-office message, but what did it really matter? It all seemed futile now. Yes, she felt this way because of the blow she'd just taken, but if justice couldn't be served—if an innocent man really was in prison—then the back-and-forth e-mails with attorneys and crime labs—the minutia of every day seemed so . . . trivial. So unnecessary. So unimportant.

As she pulled her phone from her pocket to call Landon, it struck her that his was the only number from one of her cases that she stored in her personal cell phone. Yes, she'd met him before she knew he was part of one of her cases, but his involvement in her life transcended the case.

She sat back in her chair as the phone dialed his number. If Morgan's Ladder ever did drop the case, would he still be a part of her life? She didn't want to think about that possibility.

Landon's voice on the phone interrupted her thoughts. "Hey," he said, sounding rushed and harried.

"You busy?"

He scoffed. "You don't even know."

"I need to talk to you."

"Can it wait 'til tonight?"

"I think this is something you'll want to know."

He hesitated. "About . . . you know?"

She was pretty sure he hadn't told anyone at work about the DNA tests, so she understood his not wanting to say the words in an open workspace. "Yes."

The silence on the other end of the phone told her that, he, too, knew this was important information. A game-changer.

A *life*-changer.

Finally, he spoke. "Tell me where to meet you."

CHAPTER EIGHTEEN

Landon glanced toward the entrance of the park. Again. He couldn't stand still. Not with everything at stake. Not with his entire life about to change. He pushed himself off the side of his truck and paced to the other side of the parking lot. He checked the time on his cell phone. Twenty minutes since Gina had called him to say she had the results of the DNA testing.

Where the hell was she?

He should have made her tell him right then and there, over the phone. No, he wouldn't have wanted to get the news in the office—not with the open workspaces that offered no privacy. Not with all those people around. He wasn't sure how he'd react, depending on what the news ended up being.

If Cyrus was guilty, he'd feel a huge sense of relief. The right man had been in prison the entire time and Landon's eyewitness testimony had helped put him there. That would be the best outcome. To know his mom's murder had been vindicated all those years ago. But if the DNA showed that Cyrus didn't do it . . .

That was the outcome Landon dreaded. That the wrong man had been in prison all those years.

Or, worse yet—if Landon's own DNA closely matched the DNA on his mother's clothes. He closed his eyes as the possibility flooded his mind. The same one that had kept him awake the last several nights—that the DNA could show a close relative of his had committed the murder.

And everything in his life would change.

He opened his eyes and kicked a rock beneath his feet. It ricocheted off the tire of his truck and slammed against the curb. If his dad was guilty, then he'd lose him. Not that he'd ever really had him. But the pain, the hatred, the feelings of not belonging would be immediately surrounded by a hard outer shell that would likely never go away.

You killed my mother, you son of a bitch.

He could see himself looking his old man in the face, his own eyes filled with contempt, telling him once and for all he was finished with him.

But then what would he say to Cyrus? How do you apologize to a man who'd spent fifteen years in prison for a crime he didn't commit? A man you helped convict? Could Cyrus file a civil suit against him? And was that what Landon deserved after putting an innocent guy in jail?

The crunching of tires on gravel came up over the ridge as Gina's SUV turned onto the road and into the park. He stood, waiting for her to pull up beside him and get out. Glad this was one of the days he'd been able to wear a golf shirt to work, since the Tallahassee heat bore down on him. He wiped his hand across his forehead and rubbed the sweat off on the pants fabric at his hip.

"So?" he said the second she got out of the car.

She motioned to a picnic table under a live oak. "Let's go over in the shade."

"Can you just tell me?" But she'd already taken off, striding in front of him toward the tree. He followed, his eagerness to hear her news rising with each step he took. He wanted to grab her shoulder, twirl her around, and demand that she tell him the results of the test.

She reached the picnic table, brushed her hand across the end of it, and sat down, facing him. One sandal-covered foot rested on the seat below her. Somehow he knew he'd remember that toenail polish for the rest of his life. Dark red. Like the blood on the floor of the country store. That color would always haunt him.

"So what'd you find out?" He paced in front of her, unable to rein in his nervous energy.

"It's . . . not what we expected."

He stopped midstride and spun to study her face. "What does that mean?"

"The DNA is too deteriorated." He hated that goddamn look of pity on her face. "They can't use it."

"Mine? I'll give them another sample."

She shook her head. "Not yours. The DNA on your mom's clothes. They can't use it."

The tremor in his jaw seemed like a harbinger of things to come. "What do you mean, they can't use it? It'll never be able to tell us who did it?"

"That's what the lab said."

The tremor spread to his shoulders, which now shook so much he was sure Gina could see it. "But the science. You just don't understand the science."

She reached for his hand and held it. "Suzanne got the head of the lab on the phone to make sure he agreed. He'd already verified it. He explained everything to her."

Landon sank onto the bench of the picnic table next to Gina's foot. His entire body trembled.

"Suzanne's seen this a couple of times before." She wrapped her arms around his shoulders. "Where the DNA is inconclusive. I wish . . . I wish I had known it was a possibility. I would have at least told you this could happen. So you might . . . be prepared."

Landon couldn't respond. He just shook. His world was upended, yet again. The oppressive heat intertwined with Gina's news, and he knew what purgatory must be like. It was as if he'd done something to deserve this. To be forever condemned to the madness created by this confluence of events.

"I wish I had something different to tell you." Gina rubbed his back with the palm of her hand. "I didn't want you to be in the office when you got the news."

"So what happens to Cyrus Alexander?" His words were barely a whisper, but it was all the energy he could muster. His throat was so dry he could barely swallow.

"He was convicted of the crime. The DNA didn't exonerate him . . ."

Her voice trailed off. She didn't have to say it. He knew. Cyrus Alexander would stay in prison. Landon hoped to God the right guy was sitting in that cell.

He sat back against the table, his shoulders resting on Gina's leg. The connection with her comforted him. She ran a hand through his curls, just like Mama had done when he was little. Did she know what she was doing? How significant the gesture was on today of all days?

"What can I do to help you?" she said as her fingers wove through his hair again.

"Nothing." He didn't want her to know how much the gesture shook him.

"Why don't you come over tonight? I don't want you to be alone."

He shook his head.

"Dinner. A couple of beers. We can talk about anything you want to talk about. Or nothing at all."

He ignored her invitation. He took a deep breath and his chest shuddered involuntarily. "Are you going back to work?" he asked.

He wasn't facing her, but somehow he felt closer to her than he'd felt to anyone in a long time. Maybe in his entire life.

"No." The word was unsteady.

So the news had jarred her, too. Probably not as much as it had him, but he heard the pain in her voice and knew that she, too, needed some time alone. He turned to face her. "Does it ever get any easier?"

Tears glistened in her eyes. "I'm not sure. It hasn't yet."

He rested his arm on the table, running it the length of her thigh. His fingertips brushed the fabric of her pants near her butt. Any other time, it would have seemed too familiar, too intimate. But now, it was comforting.

"That really wasn't the answer I was looking for," he said. Maybe someday he'd ask her the details about the guy she'd sent to prison, but not now. Not today. Maybe not ever. All he knew was that he couldn't talk about any of it today.

"If you do get some answers," she said, "be sure to let me know." She brushed a hair from her face. "Because I sure as hell don't have any, either."

He wasn't sure if she was talking about Cyrus Alexander or the guy she sent to prison. Hell, she might have been talking about how she felt about Landon himself. Regardless, he knew how she felt. Because he didn't have any answers, either.

All he had was confusion. And frustration.

And emptiness.

CHAPTER NINETEEN

Landon's lungs screamed for air. His calves burned. It had been three years since he'd done fifteen miles in one run, but tiring his body to the point of exhaustion seemed like the only way to escape now. The only way he'd ever sleep again. *If* he ever slept again. He still hadn't completely absorbed the news about the inconclusive DNA, and that had been two days ago.

There would always be questions about Mama's murder, yet she deserved so much more than that.

He'd never know if his testimony had put the right man in prison.

He'd never know the truth.

He slipped the key from on top of the window frame and unlocked the door. Compared to outside, his air-conditioned condo felt like a walk-in freezer, but he welcomed the chill. No one sweated like a man running in the heat and humidity of a Tallahassee summer, even though the hottest part of the day had been hours ago.

He braced his hands on the breakfast bar and extended one leg behind him, stretching one calf, then the other. He took deep, deliberate breaths until his inhalations returned to normal.

His cell phone rang as he was grabbing a towel to get in the shower.

"Mr. Vista?" the male voice on the other end of the line sounded official.

"Yes." He reached into the shower to turn on the water.

"This is Sergeant Hernandez of the Tallahassee Police Department."

He froze. Law enforcement officers translated to death and tragedy in his life.

"Son, your father's been picked up on a drunk-and-disorderly."

Of course he has. Landon stepped out of the bathroom to get away from the noise of the running water. "What'd he do?"

"Kept hassling another patron at the bar he was in. Refused to leave when the manager asked him to. Urinated on the bouncer's shoe when he finally kicked him out."

It was seven thirty at night. Who got shit-faced by seven thirty on a Sunday night? Moot point. He already knew the answer to that question.

"Why are *you* calling me?" Landon asked. "I thought the guy arrested got to make the phone call."

"The doc's stitching his head up now. The bouncer didn't take too kindly to his shoe being pissed on."

Landon emptied the contents of his pockets, preparing for the shower. "Let him stay there. It'll be good for him."

"Can't keep him here. He's already paid bail."

"My dad doesn't have enough money for bail." The sarcasm in his voice sounded biting, even to him.

"Desk lieutenant said he paid it in cash. Your dad wants you to come get him. Keeps bragging about his son being Landon Vista and how we'd better treat him right."

"I'm not coming to get him."

"Doc'll be done with him in a couple of minutes."

"I'm not coming to get him." *What did the guy not understand about that?*

"You want me to tell him that?" the sergeant said.

"I don't care what you tell him. Tell him anything you want."

Landon punched the button to end the call, then yanked his tank top over his head. He needed a shower even worse now that his damn father had tainted the evening with yet another embarrassing stunt. He rolled his head from side to side, determined not to let the anger at his father camp out with that burn at the base of his neck, at the same place it always did.

The time Landon had spent with Gina's parents made him realize how nice it might have been to have a father who held down a job, slept in the same bed every night, provided a house for his kids to live in. *To hell with him.* Landon wasn't going to be a part of his dad's drama anymore, just like his dad hadn't been a part of Landon's life growing up.

He was still seething an hour later, after he'd showered and discovered that the strange smell in his kitchen came from the week-old shrimp pasta he'd thrown away last night. He took his trash bag to the dumpster off to the side of his condo complex and heaved it into the rusted, smelly drum, then headed back inside.

"What the hell do you think you're doing?"

He turned to see his father, his forehead covered by a white bandage, standing under the streetlight. One sleeve of his faded plaid shirt was torn, and the knees of his pants looked as if he'd been crawling around on the floor at the local Jiffy Lube. A taxi pulled away from the curb in the background.

"Not getting you out of jail." Landon brushed past his father, not sure where the smell of the dumpster ended and his dad's odor started.

"Obviously." His dad hustled after him. "And why the hell not?"

Landon turned to face him, his fists clenched by his side. "I am not going to clean up your mess every time you make it."

"You just wait 'til you're thrown in jail." His dad's smirk bared his yellow teeth. "See if I come help you out."

"I *have* been thrown in jail. And you know who I called?" He swept his arm through the air. "It sure as hell wasn't you."

His dad grinned, looking absurdly pleased that his son had been in jail, as if it were a proud family tradition. Something to talk about over holiday meals. "What'd you get arrested for?"

Landon walked up the sidewalk again. "It was a while ago." Calvin had been there for him. "It doesn't matter now."

"Why didn't you call me?" his dad said behind him.

Landon waved a dismissive hand and walked toward his condo.

"You don't think I'd have your back?" his dad repeated as he dashed in front of Landon. "Don't you think I would have picked you up?"

Landon opened his front door and walked into the living room. His dad followed him inside.

A crush of childhood feelings swirled inside him. Landon closed his eyes for a minute. "Why would I think you'd be there for me," he said, "when you were never there any of the other times?" He might as well get all his feelings out before he confronted his father about the sawmill alibi, which now seemed lame, even for his father.

"Name one time I wasn't there for you." His dad plopped down in the leather recliner. Landon wondered if he could hose the thing off in the morning.

"How about when I played Little League and you were never in the stands? Or when I broke my arm in eighth grade? Did you stay up worrying about me when I was seventeen years old and out getting drunk off my ass with my buddies? Where were you during all those times?"

His father's face paled. "Aunt Marilyn and Uncle Bob were there."

"They aren't my parents."

"They were better parents than I would have been."

"You only started to care when I started to make the newspapers, the all-conference teams. Then all of a sudden—poof!—you're back in my life. When it became convenient for you and when you might get something out of it."

179

"If I needed to be preached to"—his dad's eyes narrowed—"I'd go to church."

"Where'd you get the money to post bail?"

His dad seemed offended. "I been working a little bit."

"You have a little bit of money? An opportunity to get ahead?" Landon paced around the room, anger seeping from his pores. "And you spend it on bail? Or some stupid bait shop?"

His father's eyes nailed him. "My money is none of your business."

"Okay, then let's switch to something that *is* my business." He lunged toward his father, stopping just short of bumping him with his chest. "Where were you the day Mama was killed?" If the DNA wasn't going to give him any answers, then maybe he'd finally badger his father enough to learn the truth.

Martin waved a dismissive hand. "This is all old news."

"You and Grady Buchanan were delivering a load of lumber to the North Carolina mountains. Or don't you remember?"

"That girlfriend of yours has you all messed up in the head," Martin said. "You shoulda been over this shit a long time ago."

"Where were you that day?" Landed repeated.

"I was with Grady Buchanan. We delivered some wood in North Carolina, then went to the casino in Cherokee."

So the old man was sticking with his story. Landon had given him one final chance to come clean and the guy had blown it.

He was never going to get any answers. He picked up his car keys. "I was just going out for the night," he lied. "Where do you want me to drop you off?"

～

Landon felt like he might bust down Gina's door if she didn't answer soon. His adrenaline was still pumping from the run-in he'd had with his dad, and besides, her SUV was parked on the street, so why wasn't she answering? He needed to talk to her. Needed to hold her. Needed the grounding her presence gave him.

Finally, he saw her silhouette come down the short hallway. Her hand went to the inside of the wall in the breakfast nook, and the light in the kitchen came on around the corner. She squinted toward the door, then walked to it and flipped on the outside light before she unlocked the deadbolt.

"You look like hell," she said as she opened the door.

He stormed in—his body still pumped with adrenaline—and tried to calm himself down. He didn't want to scare her. And he would never, ever hurt her. He leaned on the wall just inside the door and shoved his hands in the pockets of his jeans. "I had a fight with my dad."

Worry settled into Gina's brow. "An argument? Or like a fistfight?"

He must look as wild as his emotions made him feel. "An argument." Though come to think of it, Landon wished he would have punched him.

"Okay," she said slowly, as if trying to gauge what might come next. "You want to talk about it?"

He felt his heart still racing, his mind still whirling from the argument. He nodded. He glanced down her body as she stood in front of him and took in her outfit—a long, yellow T-shirt shirt hung to her knees. It was looser at the bottom than it was on top, where it cradled her round, ample breasts.

She reached for his hand and led him to the couch, then sat next to him, pulling her knees up to her chin and tucking the long T-shirt over them. Her bloodred toenail polish had been replaced with a sexy-as-hell pale pink that almost matched the smooth skin of her ankle as it peeked out from under the fabric.

He breathed slowly, trying to calm down, trying not to scare her with his wild anger.

"What did he do?" she asked quietly, brushing one of his curls from his forehead.

"He actually thinks he was a good dad. Like he did me a favor by not being around. 'Aunt Marilyn and Uncle Bob were there,' he said. Like that was going to take the place of a dad." Landon couldn't sit still. He got up and paced the living room, his emotions still in control of his body.

"What brought all this on? Why tonight?"

"He was mad that I didn't come get him out of jail. Some stupid drunk-and-disorderly charge." He paced some more, then ended up with his back to her, facing the picture of her family skiing.

"If he's treated you so badly all these years"—her voice was almost a whisper, floating from behind him like a voice from the heavens—"why is he so important to you?"

His back stiffened. She didn't understand. And probably never would. Not with parents who loved her and raised her. Parents who were always there for her.

"I just wanted him to care." His voice came out in shudders.

He couldn't face her, even if it meant looking at the damn picture of everything he never had. At least this way, he wouldn't be able to see her face as she cowered away, frightened by the depth of his anger.

The couch rustled behind him, and seconds later, she slid her arms around his waist and rested her head on his back between his shoulder blades. Even if she didn't understand, her touch made it seem like she did. Even though he would never be good enough for her, he'd savor the few moments when she acted like she cared.

"You know what I think?" she whispered in the darkness. Her voice came from behind, just below his ear.

He didn't say anything. Didn't want to do anything that might bring this moment to an end.

"I think you're witty and caring and . . . that you've got a lot to add to this world. And none of those things has anything to do with your dad. They have everything to do with you. The fact that you're as strong as you are . . . and that you've lived with this . . . makes you way more of a man than he is. Makes you way better than just about any man I've ever met."

His breath caught in his chest. No one, including his mother, had ever said anything so kind to him. So meaningful. He closed his eyes, wondering if he'd imagined her words, but the feel of her head on his back confirmed it was real.

He wanted his body to soak in the memories of having her near. Of having someone care, not because he was the nephew or because he could throw a pigskin farther downfield than anyone else. But care about *him*.

His dad had forced him to face one of the worst truths of his life, but he was also facing the fact that someone cared about him. Wanted to listen to his stories. Everything he wanted was right here, in this room. The soft touch. The sweet smells. The caring.

She lifted her head from his back as he slowly turned to face her. He looked into her eyes and saw a pool of understanding.

"You . . ." She touched her hand to his chest. "Are one of the most amazing people I've ever met."

And somehow he knew she believed it. The conviction in her gaze gave him a power, a knowledge, his father could never take away.

He lowered his head, brushing his lips slowly across the softness of her mouth. The tumult of emotions crashing inside his body changed from anger at his father to a passion he'd never known. He cupped her face in his hands, kissing her—gently at first, then pulling her tightly against him while he tried to drink in every facet of her.

He felt like he was put on earth to kiss her. To hold her. To lie beside her.

And he hoped to God she felt the same way.

CHAPTER TWENTY

Gina closed her eyes as Landon's lips brushed hers. She knew the unmistakable energy that crackled between them. Felt the urgency of his kiss the second his lips settled on hers.

Theirs was a passion that had been denied too long. A force that drove his body to hers, and hers to him. His tongue claimed hers in a way that hadn't been present in their earlier kisses—a confidence, a certainty that this was meant to be.

One of his big hands splayed across her back, pulling her to him until she felt each sculpted muscle on his chest and stomach. She raised her hands to his waistline and slipped them inside his untucked shirt. She was rewarded by a barely audible moan as she feathered her fingertips across his sides.

His lips left hers, tracing a line down her neck to her collarbone while his hands glided across her shoulders. He cupped her breasts on the outside of her shirt, his thumbs tracing circles against her hardened nipples.

Everything in her head screamed "Stop." Yes, the DNA had been inconclusive, but she still planned to work to get Cyrus Alexander out of prison. She had to find an answer, for both Cyrus and Landon. Professional duties and the sting of Christopher's betrayal wove together in her consciousness, only to be swept away by how right it felt to be here with Landon. How nothing else in the world seemed to matter. How she could sort out her feelings tomorrow, once he'd glided his eager hands over her body.

As she surrendered to the war inside her, he slipped her top over her head, dropping it to the floor. His gaze and his hands followed the curves of her breasts like they were a priceless treasure.

His chest rose and fell twice before his eyes met hers. "You . . . are . . . so . . . beautiful," he said, then lowered his mouth to her breast, stroking it with his tongue while his other hand caressed its mate.

She arched her back, offering herself to him as if no pain, no sorrow could come from tonight. The need that burned inside her didn't know tomorrow, but only the urgency of the moment. The need to touch him, to feel his skin on hers. She raised the fabric of his shirt to feel the striated muscles of his stomach beneath her fingers. He pulled away long enough to yank the shirt over his head, leaving her to marvel at the chest that resembled a work of art as much as it did a living man.

Her hands explored the roundness of his biceps, the softness of his hair where it curled at his neck, the feeling of solidness that only Landon gave her.

Finally, her fingers traveled to the front of his shorts, outlining the hardened ridge beneath the fabric. She could tell by the way he touched her that he needed her as badly as she needed him. She used both hands to unbuckle his belt and ease down the zipper.

"Make love to me," she whispered as he kissed the nape of her neck.

A slow, shuddering breath heated the sensitive spot behind her ear. "Bedroom," he said, as if he couldn't say any more.

He followed her there and glided his hands over her hips and backside as she bent over the bed to move the book she'd been reading before she fell asleep. When she turned to face him, those green eyes she would never forget were clouded with emotion, darker than she'd ever seen them.

He gently pushed her panties down, then stopped her arm as she reached to turn off the bedside lamp. "I . . . want to see . . . everything," he said, his voice shuddering with passion.

She dropped her hand, leaving the faint light on to illuminate them. All the better to see his wonderful body as it joined with hers. Since they could have only one night together, at least her mind would be imprinted with memories of it. She slid her hands inside the waistband of his shorts and pushed them down, marveling at the sight of his strong body. His muscular hips and thighs. The erection that showed her so clearly how much he wanted her.

He guided her to lie on the bed and resumed his exploration as their bodies twined together. Again, his mouth covered her breast. His hand slowly skimmed her rib cage, her stomach, the outside of her thigh.

When his gentle touch slid up the inside of her legs, she parted them, opening herself to him. He slid a finger inside, then bathed her in the wetness, stroking her to a level of desire she wasn't sure she could maintain. Never before had a man been as concerned with her pleasure as he had been with his own. Never before had sleeping with someone felt like such an act of sharing.

She ran her hands along his spine, beckoning him. Knowing the level of pleasure they'd both get when they joined together.

He rolled away from her and fumbled with his wallet before donning a condom. His face was filled with need as he settled himself on top of her and—with his green eyes never leaving hers—slid himself inside with one motion, gentle but firm.

He touched her in places she'd never been touched before. Drowned her with emotion she didn't want to have. Gave her more pleasure than she'd ever imagined possible. She closed her eyes, every cell in her body attuned to the uncontrolled passion between them. Her fingers wrapped around his straining biceps, feeling the strength he shared with her.

Three breathless moans escaped her as she came. He thrust two more times, then released himself inside her. When their hips stilled, they lay there, spent, as if neither wanted the moment to end.

Finally, he raised his head. His gaze returned to hers.

And she feared she was lost forever.

~

Landon's fingers toyed with the ends of Gina's strawberry-blonde hair as her soft breath warmed his chest. Now *that* had been the best, most mind-blowing sex of his life. He wouldn't even put it in the same category with the times he'd slept with other women.

He still couldn't believe he'd actually gotten to touch her, to push himself inside her, especially when he'd spent so many days convincing himself he wasn't attracted to her.

Yeah, right.

Like he'd ever really believed that line of BS he'd told himself.

But he hadn't stopped long enough to evaluate all the reasons he shouldn't sleep with her. Not when she was standing in her living room, the outline of her nipples piercing her T-shirt.

There'd been obvious attraction from the first time they'd met, but was she lying there, with her head on his chest, regretting what she'd done? She'd known about his loser dad before she'd slept with him. Known that most people wanted him only for who he'd been on the football field.

And still, she'd let him touch her in all the ways he'd lain awake thinking about on so many other nights. She'd actually been the one, in the darkened living room, to say the words. *"Make love to me."* He got hard just thinking about it.

The tips of her fingers feathered down his side. She seemed to have a particular fondness for his hip, tracing the curve of his bone with her forefinger. She raised her head, kissed the line of his jaw, found his mouth with hers. Pressed her soft, supple body to his more muscular one. Wrapped her fingers around his already-swelling cock.

And soon, he donned a condom and sank into her warm wetness again, marveling at the feel of her around him. Her pelvis moved with a perfect rhythm as she straddled him, pushing him farther inside her with each slow, seductive movement. He lifted his head to take one breast in his mouth, suckling it, tracing her nipple with his tongue, tasting the sweetness that belonged only to her.

Then his hands moved to her hips, holding them still as he exploded inside her.

Just as her moans of ecstasy echoed in his ears.

CHAPTER TWENTY-ONE

A peace more complete than Gina had felt in a long time settled over her like a warm blanket being tucked around her on a cold winter's night. The quiet strength of Landon beside her. The gentle rise and fall of his chest while he lay next to her. The moonbeam cast across his long, muscular body.

"So what are you thinking about?" she asked, somewhat afraid to know the answer.

She felt, rather than heard, the soft chuckle in his chest. "That I hadn't really planned on this to happen today."

She rolled onto her side to face him. "Not *today*? Had you thought it would happen . . . ever?" She'd fought an attraction to him every day. Did he fight the same battle?

He grinned as he tucked her hair behind her ear. "I knew you couldn't keep your hands off me forever."

"So you come over here when I'm in my pajamas? To tempt me?"

"It was nine o'clock at night. Who goes to bed at nine o'clock at night? I mean, besides your grandma."

She settled her head on his chest. "It's been a long day." She hadn't slept much since the DNA from Barbara Landon's clothes had come back inconclusive.

"Hmmm," he grunted in agreement as he wrapped his arm around her shoulders and caressed her upper arm with his thumb. "Tell me about it."

Her mind replayed the evening as they lay in silence for several minutes. How troubled Landon had looked when he'd shown up at her house. How puzzled she still was by the fact that he didn't seem to think he was good enough. The way that humbleness only made him more attractive. More human.

"What are you thinking about?" Landon's deep voice rumbled in his chest next to her ear.

She hesitated. Yes, she'd slept with the guy. Twice. But was his relationship with his father any of her business? Might it be her business someday?

She'd always felt like it was everyone's responsibility to make other people feel better about themselves. To take every opportunity to share a kindness in the world.

"I'm glad you came to me tonight." She waited for a response, but none came, so she continued. "I know it really bothers you about your dad."

Still no response. Was this conversation too deep for him? Too deep for this situation? But, again, she wanted him to know what a wonderful man he was. "I really want you to understand . . . you're not whatever your dad thinks of you." She rose to look at him. "Whatever you've made of yourself—and that's a lot—you've made on your own. Not because of him."

A sadness spread through his green eyes. "That isn't why I came here tonight."

Gina didn't believe that. She wasn't stupid enough to think that Landon would have come to her apartment if he hadn't had the run-in with his father. Yes, she was glad they'd shared tonight, but she knew that something else had driven him to her.

"I wish you'd stop waiting for him."

His mouth tipped into a teasing grin. "Are you going to psycho-analyze me every time we sleep together?"

Her heart skipped a few beats, but she tried to be coy. "You're pretty cocky, thinking you get to sleep with me again."

He chuckled. "Are you saying it's not going to happen?"

Of course she wanted it to happen again. And although her heart had recovered from Christopher's betrayal, the experience had taught her to be wary. And—after all—this was Landon Vista. The man all of Tallahassee fawned over. The man who could sleep with any woman in Leon County he wanted to. Yes, she'd have to be care-ful. "I'm saying you'd better be on your best behavior."

His breath warmed her ear as he pulled her toward him even more. "I'm pretty sure you just saw my best behavior."

~

Landon could see the slate-gray dawn through the curtains of Gina's bedroom. She slept in the crook of his arm, one of her long legs draped over his. Warm. Content. As beautiful a woman as he'd ever seen. And certainly the most desirable he'd ever held. Maybe what she said about him last night was true. Certainly no one else had ever made him feel as . . . worthy as she had. Not the football boosters or the coaches or the scouts or the other girls he'd slept with. He looked at her, wondering how a single human being could challenge him so much—his notion of right and wrong, guilt and innocence. His perception of who he was. Of who he might be one day.

He slid back the sheet and slipped his leg out from under hers. He hated to wake her, but he had to go pee. She stirred, turning over in the bed. He stilled and waited for her to settle back in.

Finally, he slipped out of bed, eager to return to her warm cocoon as soon as he could. The kitchen light was still on—the one that had barely lit them last night in the living room. He checked the lock on the front door. All was good. Life, for at least tonight's brief interlude, was going well.

He walked to the kitchen to turn off the light; a stack of Gina's files and work papers was strewn across the table in the small breakfast nook. He quickly scanned the labels on the files. All names he didn't recognize. Were they convicts? Or victims?

Then the sheet of paper on a pile of loose notes caught his eye. Notes to the file on Cyrus Alexander. The first entry—a punch to the gut—had some scientific mumbo jumbo about the lab, then concluded in plain English that the results of the DNA from his mother's clothes were inconclusive. That the DNA was unusable. He already had the news, but seeing it here, in black and white, was like having it branded into his soul.

His gaze shifted to the next entry.

Due to limited resources, Morgan's Ladder dropping the case.

His back stiffened. His forehead and scalp chilled with a cold sweat. They were dropping the case? They brought all this up in his life and were now going to leave him hanging? With no answers about who'd killed his mother? With the wrong guy maybe sitting in a prison cell? When he could be out raising his son?

Landon looked at the closed door of Gina's bedroom. He'd walked out of there just seconds ago satisfied. Content. Maybe even in love.

But now white-hot anger simmered in his chest. She'd slept with him. Not once, but twice. She'd talked to him about his father. They'd stayed awake until 2 a.m. talking and cuddling—her strong, soft body pressed against his. Her head resting on his shoulder. His arm wrapped around her shoulders possessively. And she hadn't told him about this?

She'd used him, just like everyone else had. She'd writhed and moaned underneath him, enjoying the sex as much as he had. That's all it was for her.

He rubbed the back of his neck, willing the tension away that gathered there. Disappointment and anger roiled in his belly. Last night, as they'd lain beside each other, he'd thought they might have a future together, but she'd betrayed him. She hadn't told him the truth. And that was something he couldn't handle. Not from her. Not from anyone.

He went to the bedroom and peered through the darkness to locate his shorts, then quietly pulled them on.

Maybe one day he would understand what last night meant. Maybe as an old man, he'd look back and realize that she was the one who made him see things differently.

But for now, all he knew was that she'd hidden something important from him. Sure, they'd been consensual adults having sex, but she should have told him that Morgan's Ladder was dropping the case. Something of this magnitude wasn't a topic you withheld because you had a chance to sleep with someone you'd been lusting over for weeks.

He was sick and damn tired of being used.

And he was sure as hell going to leave before she had a chance to use him again.

~

Gina felt a warm glow cascading down her body. A glow only Landon could provide. For the second or third time that night, she scooted toward him, unconsciously seeking his warmth, the pleasure of knowing he was near.

Her eyes shot open at a sound across the room, behind her. The soft clinking of a belt buckle?

She rolled to face him. "Landon?"

His head came up, a surprised look on his face. Or was it guilt?

"You're leaving?" She tried to hide the fact that a predawn departure hurt her. She would have liked more class, more respect, than what looked like sneaking out once the handiwork was done.

But most of all, it wasn't how she wanted her evening with him to end.

He jabbed a thumb in the direction of the front door. "I've . . . ummm . . . got to go."

She sat up and pulled the sheet across her naked bosom. "Is something wrong?" She turned on the lamp beside her bed. He'd talked about making love to her again in the future, and now he was walking out? "I mean, I thought last night was . . ." *Great. Fantastic.*

He nodded, as if he could read her mind. "Yeah. It was." But the tone in his voice didn't match the words in her head. His green eyes bored into hers, saying far more than he was apparently willing to share out loud. Confusion and regret roiled inside the olive green.

"But you're leaving." She felt as if their intimacy had been siphoned out of the room, replaced with a negativity so thick she could feel it crawling across her skin.

"We're two consenting adults who should know better than to get involved."

"And what we did last night"—she hated the sound of disappointment in her voice—"is how you don't get involved?"

"You asked me to make love to you. We . . ." He couldn't seem to find the words to describe what had been between them.

But Gina could think of several options to finish his sentence.

We connected.

We shared our souls.

We may be falling in love.

"We shouldn't get involved." His voice had a tone of resignation to it.

"If that's how you feel"—she swallowed, but her throat remained dry—"then you're right. You should go."

Their gazes locked for another moment, then he retrieved his keys from her dresser and left her apartment without another word.

CHAPTER TWENTY-TWO

Gina stood from her desk as her boss unlocked the front door of Morgan's Ladder and pushed the door open.

Suzanne let out a startled scream when she realized another person was in the room. Her hand flattened on her chest. The rasping of her quick breaths filled the room. "Oh, my God. If you're in here"—she looked toward the front of the office—"why was the door locked?"

"I've been here since five a.m." Gina worked hard to control her anger. It wasn't going to do either of them any good if she yelled at her boss. "It was still dark outside when I got here."

Suzanne moved toward her office, but Gina stepped away from her desk and into the center of the main work area—not really blocking her boss's way, but pretty close to it.

Suzanne's eyebrows rose with a questioning look. "Can I help you with something?"

"We're dropping the case?"

Suzanne took a deep breath, as if steeling herself for the conversation. She let her worn messenger bag fall onto a nearby stack of file boxes. "I assume you're talking about Cyrus Alexander?"

"It didn't even take you forty-eight hours to come to that conclusion? You couldn't even wait until Monday to enter the notes in the file?" Gina motioned to her computer.

Realization spread across Suzanne's face. Her skin paled. "I was working on some cases Saturday night. I didn't think you'd see the notes before I had a chance to tell you this morning."

"So you let me find out by *reading* about it on the computer?" She'd even printed them out, ready to have the hard-copy proof in her hands when she confronted her boss on Monday morning.

What she hadn't planned was for Landon to find the paper in her breakfast nook before she got Suzanne to change her mind. She couldn't think of any other reason why he'd left the way he did.

Gina wasn't sure who had been more callous—Suzanne for not telling her, or herself for letting Landon discover it before she'd had a chance to change Suzanne's mind. She still wasn't sure how she was going to approach this with him.

"We can't drop the case." Gina's voice was forceful, unwavering.

"You leave in a couple of weeks and then it's just me. I don't have the manpower to work a case if the DNA isn't going to help me."

"So you just leave him there?" Gina held her hands in the air, begging. "Rotting in jail?"

Suzanne's lip quivered. Gina could tell this upset her, too. "There are many others who need my help," the older woman said, as if trying to convince herself as much as Gina. "Men and women I haven't even met yet."

"But Cyrus . . . and Landon . . ."

Suzanne's chin came up. "So now we get to the crux of the matter."

"I can't let him not know who killed his mother. He deserves to know the truth."

"They *all* deserve the truth." Suzanne's gaze was steady. "Not just the ones who"—she cocked her head—"get your attention for other reasons."

Gina sank into her chair. She'd slept with someone involved in one of their cases. She'd own up to that fact. She'd figure out how to reconcile that at a later date, but for now she needed to figure out how to find Landon some peace.

She rested her elbows on her desk and braced her forehead on the heels of her hands, her head down. She heard Suzanne move to the little sink in one corner of the office and start a pot of coffee. The older woman then returned to where she'd once been and stood there silently, waiting.

Finally, Gina spoke, her head still down. Her anger had eased, leaving her in a pit of quicksand filled with sadness and loss. A pit she didn't think she'd ever escape. "What made you take on Cyrus's case to begin with? What made you think he was telling the truth?"

"Sometimes I can see how sloppy the work was done the first time around. Sometimes the facts don't add up. But with Cyrus, it was like . . . a feeling I got when I looked in his eyes."

Gina raised her head to look at her boss. "I thought the same thing, but I tried to ignore it. Lawyers are trained to look at the facts, not to feelings."

"One of the many crocks of shit they teach you in law school." Suzanne leaned against a filing cabinet on the other side of the room. "Or just about any school you go to."

"Do you ever get used to this . . . futility? To this . . . up and down of emotions?"

Gina wasn't sure she could handle knowing how much was at stake and not always being able to help. Maybe the party they'd attend this weekend to celebrate Buford Monroe's release would restore her confidence in their ability to change people's lives.

"I haven't been through what you've been through." Suzanne knew all about Gina's testimony helping send Nick Varnadore to juvi. She'd said it was part of why she'd selected Gina for the internship. "And I've never been in love with someone who had anything to do with one of my cases."

Gina reached for the bottle of water on her desk and twisted the cap off. She took a drink, contemplating what her boss had said. "Why do you think I'm in love with him?"

"Are you saying you're not?" Suzanne moved back to the coffeemaker and poured herself a cup.

"I don't know." Gina wasn't prepared to answer the question. Not to herself. Not to anyone. "Have you ever been in love?"

Suzanne took a long breath, then smiled. "Rodrigo Martino Gonzalez."

Gina grinned at her boss's obvious pleasure at remembering him. "That's quite a name."

"He was quite a guy." Suzanne opened an individual container of creamer and poured it into her cup. "We lived on Key Biscayne together for about a year and a half. In a little hut right on the beach."

That explained a lot about Suzanne's choice in footwear. "You were married?" For some reason, she'd never imagined her boss as anything other than single, like she was now.

Suzanne shook her head. "Living in sin." She chortled. "At least that's what they called it back then."

"What happened?"

Suzanne seemed lost in the circles of her coffee as she stirred. "I said I was in love with him. I never said he was in love with me."

So Rodrigo had been her boss's equivalent of Christopher—a guy she'd thought she was in love with, but who'd broken her heart.

"How do you know when it's the real thing?" This wasn't exactly the kind of conversation one was supposed to have with their boss, but then she and Suzanne faced life-and-death issues that regular office workers didn't face.

"When it's the stupidest, most difficult thing that could happen"—Suzanne looked up, mist glistening in her eyes—"and you still want to do it. Then you know it's really love."

Sleeping with Landon had certainly been stupid, especially with the case at such a critical juncture. Suzanne wanted to drop it from

Morgan's Ladder and Gina had slept with a key witness. She couldn't have screwed up much worse than that.

So why did she think she was in love with him? Or, like Suzanne, might she end up middle-aged and alone? Not that her boss wasn't an admirable woman. Gina had grown to respect her as much as anyone she'd ever known, but she wondered how her boss's life might have been different if she were still on the shores of the ocean with Rodrigo Martino Gonzalez.

Suzanne picked up her messenger bag and moved toward her office. "We can't stand here all morning wishing we were back in the Keys."

"Will you tell me about him sometime?" Gina asked.

Suzanne laughed. "I don't know. That was a long time ago."

"Oh, come on." The half smile on her boss's face told Gina that at least some of the memories were pleasant. "Key Biscayne. Sounds exotic."

Suzanne scoffed. "If you like being dirt poor and having to fish for your dinner every day." She stopped in the doorway to her office and turned. "And Gina?"

Gina looked up.

"This is why you don't get into a relationship with someone who's involved in one of your cases. It doesn't work here. It doesn't work in a law firm. It doesn't work if you work in a corporation."

"You think I'm no longer objective?" That was the worst criticism an attorney could receive.

"I think you stopped being objective on this one a long time ago." Suzanne walked into her office and shut the door.

Gina closed her eyes. She prided herself on her professionalism. On being above reproach. She'd done the worst thing she could have done this summer.

She'd fallen in love with Landon Vista.

$\approx$

Gina hopped from her SUV and looked toward the gathering of people who milled outside the white clapboard house where Buford Monroe grew up. An old abandoned chicken coop stood behind the house; weeds licked at the bumper of a faded red truck that looked like it hadn't moved in years. A gaggle of children played in the water of an old hand pump.

This part of her job—the celebration of Buford's release—made her proud of her work, but it also shone a bright, glaring light on their failure in the Barbara Landon case. It had been a week since Landon had discovered that Morgan's Ladder was dropping Cyrus Alexander's case.

She'd tried texting and calling Landon at first, but her attempts had gone unanswered. Finally, he'd texted back and said he was on some kind of business trip with the senator and had been really busy.

She shook her hair back and raised her head high. Today, she would concentrate on Buford and try to hide the gaping wound in her psyche from Landon and Cyrus Alexander.

She walked toward the gathering of people, knowing she'd be seen as a friend of the family, but it still felt funny when she realized she'd be the only white person in a crowd full of African Americans. Maybe this was how Lisa Pinkney, the one black girl in her graduating class, felt during high school. Like an outsider. A person who didn't quite fit in. Someone whose life experiences had shaped them into a different person than those standing before her.

She knew her support of Buford and Ella Monroe would propel her forward. That there were many more similarities between her and these people than there were differences. They, too, had suffered grief and happiness. Victory and sadness.

"Hey, hey, Gina," Buford called as he rounded the corner from the back of the house. His booming bass voice filled the air like the noise from a freight train. "Come on over to meet everybody."

A sea of faces turned toward her. She jumped across the narrow ditch separating the yard from the roadway and was immediately engulfed in Buford's burly arms. Men in seersucker suits and women in cotton dresses surged toward her.

"My redheaded angel," Buford repeated as he introduced her to aunts, uncles, cousins, and friends. One by one, they thanked her for helping to free Buford from prison.

"After all these years, you brought our Buford home," an elderly uncle said as he held both of Gina's hands in his.

An older woman placed her warm, leathery palm on Gina's cheek. "I haven't seen Miss Ella look so good in years," she said. "Thank you, honey."

"Where is Miss Ella?" Gina asked, looking over the woman's head for Buford's mother.

"Honey, she in the house checking on those pies o' hers," one of the older women chuckled. "Miss Ella's pies are world famous."

A burly man the size of Buford wrapped an arm around the former prisoner's shoulder. "Buford thinks this party is for him, but it's really about Miss Ella's pies."

Buford chortled. "Just ignore them, Miss Gina. They forgot their manners, anyway. You want a glass o' sweet tea?"

"I'd love some unsweet, if you've got it."

"Let me go find out." The big man turned to go into the house. Gina followed. She had been inspired by Miss Ella's quiet strength and wanted to greet the woman with the level of respect she deserved.

"Mama." Buford lowered his head as he crossed into the house through the back door. "I got someone here to see you."

Two other women and a man turned in the crowded kitchen as Miss Ella set a ladle in the spoon rest near the stove and turned. Her eyes lit up as a smile slid across her weather-beaten face. "Gina." She held her arms wide. "Now the party is ready to start."

Gina laughed. "What about Suzanne? She's the one who did all the work."

Miss Ella patted her on the arm. "Now you know I'm gonna say the same thing when she gets here, too."

Buford chuckled. "She the boss. You gotta make her think she's the most important one."

Miss Ella motioned toward the others who stood in the kitchen, smiling at them. "Let me introduce you to some of our church family. We been going to church together since before Buford was born."

Gina smiled and greeted each person one by one, shaking their hand as Miss Ella introduced them. She wondered how the older woman—and the rest of them, for that matter—had kept their faith while Buford spent time in prison. Had they trusted that he was innocent? Had Miss Ella known her child would come back to her one day? Had their faith ever wavered during this whole ordeal? Gina had so many reasons to admire this woman. Her hardships and character were as much a part of her as the wrinkles that dug deep lines into the beautiful caramel-colored skin of her face.

One of the uncles Gina had met in the yard stuck his head in the kitchen door. "Come on out, y'all. The band's about to start."

Buford offered his arm to escort Gina. She looped her arm through his and let him lead her outside, where Suzanne had arrived and was engulfed by the same sea of appreciative faces Gina had met when she'd first arrived.

A trombone player led a makeshift band of four musicians in a John Philip Sousa march around the yard. The crowd cheered. Someone blew a loud noisemaker. A couple of preteen boys exploded party poppers full of confetti.

The revelry and camaraderie continued through the afternoon. Besides a couple of old men toweling their foreheads with handkerchiefs, no one seemed to notice the heat. They ate and reminisced and hugged until the sun was setting in the western sky.

Gina had escaped to the front steps of the house, where she sat scrolling through the pictures of the party she'd taken on her smartphone, deciding which ones to text to her law school friends who'd been asking about her work this summer.

She smiled to herself. Just a few weeks ago, she'd slouched, half-asleep, listening to Dr. Ramesh drone on about torts. Today, she'd celebrated getting a wrongly convicted man out of prison. It felt good. Purposeful. She wanted to share that joy with the world.

Buford rounded the corner. "Miss Ella's gonna be mad if you don't try a piece of her famous pecan pie." He offered a plate with a slice of pie the size of Rhode Island.

"I don't know how a woman her age has made it through the day," Gina said as she accepted the plate from him. Suzanne had left a long time ago. "I need about a two-day nap."

"It was a long time coming for her." He settled on the step next to Gina. "I guess she been saving up all her energy for this."

"I thought I'd stick around and help her clean up." She took her first bite of pie and immediately understood why Miss Ella was famous for it. She crunched through the crisp outer shell of pecans and was rewarded by the sweet, gooey mixture inside. She wasn't sure what all it was made of, but she was fairly certain it was a mixture of sugar and heaven. "Oh, my God. This is delicious."

Buford laughed at her surprise. "You didn't believe me? And her peach cobbler's even better."

"You must have missed it a lot." Something about the quiet of the evening magnified the importance of the event. "The cooking. The laughter. The hugs."

"The pie."

She put a hand on his thick, meaty shoulder. "You're a good man, Buford Monroe."

He smiled and rested his hand on top of hers. "A good man with a couple of angels watching over him."

They sat in silence as the night air filled with the sound of croaking frogs. Gina hadn't even seen a pond, but the noise seemed like it was within yards of her.

A whirring sound joined the chorus of frogs, like a motor coming to life. A few seconds later, a high-pitched buzz cut through the air. The frogs fell silent as quickly as their chorus had come to life.

"What's that noise?" Gina asked.

Buford motioned with his head toward the property to the north of them. "Old Man Summers don't like to cut his wood in the heat of the day. He fires that thing up when it starts to cool off at night. Mama can't sleep for the noise and all the lights he has shining over there."

"A sawmill?" Gina was surprised at how quickly the word popped into her mind. The man who lived next to the country store where Barbara Landon was murdered had operated a sawmill. She read that fact each time she studied the file. But he'd been out of town at the time of the murder.

Buford nodded.

"Are there a lot of them in Florida?" The place Landon had lived was three counties—more than a hundred miles—from where they sat now.

"I ain't been many places, but there's a lot of them in this part of Florida, anyway. Cypress has natural oils that keeps the bugs away. Ain't nothin' like it for buildin' log cabins and decks and such."

"Aren't those the trees that grow in the swamps?" She'd seen pictures of them plenty of times. "The ones with those big"—she arched the back of one hand and pointed to her protruding knuckles—"those big things growing up out of the water?"

Buford laughed. "They're called knees."

"They look more like knuckles." She stuck another piece of the delicious pie into her mouth.

Buford once again nodded toward the property to the north. "Mama gonna get her shotgun after him if he keeps that thing running all summer long."

Gina grinned. She was glad Buford could joke about Miss Ella getting a shotgun after someone. Seemed like a healthy state of mind for someone who'd spent twenty-one years in prison for a crime he hadn't committed. "He runs the place all by himself?"

Buford scoffed. "Won't even let his own sons run the mill. Does it all himself, like he's afraid one of them is gonna cut their arm off or something. They're forty-five or fifty years old now. When he gonna let 'em do it?"

Gina stopped chewing. The bite of pie in her mouth suddenly had no flavor. Martin Vista's alibi had been that he and Grady Buchanan, the mill owner next door, were delivering a load of wood to North Carolina at the time of Barbara Landon's murder. Only Maggie Buchanan, Grady's college-age daughter, had been home, napping at the time of the murder. Yet Landon's testimony a few days ago had been that he'd heard a buzzing noise a little while before he'd seen Cyrus Alexander run from the back of the store.

She shot up from the porch steps. Her fork clattered down the stairs. "I've got to go see if Miss Ella needs help cleaning up."

Buford looked up at her, startled. "You okay?" he asked as he unfolded his big body to a stance.

"I'm fine." She bent to pick up the fork. "I just . . . I just realized I need to go back to the office tonight."

~

Landon stood at the point, dribbling the basketball just outside Calvin's reach. The big, sweaty coach stood vigil, ready to pounce the second Landon made a move toward the net.

"I hate to see you lose this game, too," Landon taunted.

Calvin swatted at the ball. "I'm six inches shorter and about a decade older than you are."

"Do you even remember the last time you beat me?"

"Last time we played."

"I don't think so." Landon dropped back and launched the ball in a perfect arc toward the basket. It swooshed through. "And you're not going to win this time, either."

Calvin walked to the back of his car and picked up the towel he'd left there. He wiped off his bald head and took a swig from a bottle of water. "When I'm old and crippled, are you still going to challenge me to a game of one-on-one every time you want to talk about something?"

Landon tugged at the lid of his water bottle. "Who says I have something to talk to you about?"

Calvin chuckled. "That's the only time you ever ask me to play basketball."

Landon thought a minute, looking out onto Calvin's street. There didn't seem to be any way to get out of this one. Calvin had nailed him.

"So, 'fess up," Calvin said. "It's the redhead, isn't it?" He pointed his finger at Landon as he remembered her name. "Gina."

Calvin had always known him well. "I've seen her a lot because of the case." Okay—not completely true, but he was just introducing the topic at this point.

"And?"

"I keep learning new things about it." He wasn't ready to talk about his latest discovery at Gina's a few nights ago, but that was just the latest example of what he was talking about. "It drives me crazy."

"Because it's your mom's case?" Calvin took a swig from his water bottle. "Or because it's Gina?"

Landon grunted. "Both."

"What would you and Gina be doing if this case hadn't been between you?"

Landon slid his mentor a sideways glance. "The same thing we did already."

Calvin's mouth fell open. "You slept with her?"

He didn't answer. There was too much emotion swirling in his mind about her for him to treat it like a conquest to brag about.

Calvin's face softened into a look of understanding. "So what's the problem?"

Landon was still too hurt about Morgan's Ladder dropping the case to talk about it, but Calvin had been around long enough to know his relationship with his father. "She thinks I stay in Tallahassee because my dad is here."

"And this comes as a surprise to you?"

"This is where I live. This is where my job is."

The coach took the ball from underneath Landon's arm and dribbled it. "This is where your father is."

He grabbed the ball back. "She just doesn't need to be in my business."

"Then stop seeing her. Is that what you want?"

Landon hurled the ball toward the basket. It bounced off the backboard, way too forceful to have made it in. "I'm not sure what I want." He'd wanted to go to her in the last couple of days, but couldn't forgive her for withholding such an important bit of news.

Calvin chased after the ball and returned it to Landon. "Then this doesn't seem like her problem. It seems like yours."

Landon glared at him. The son of a bitch was right. Until Landon figured out what he wanted from Gina, he'd continue to be frustrated and confused. "She's going away at the end of the summer."

"So is that what pisses you off about her?"

"Who said I'm pissed off?"

The coach pointed to the basketball goal. "You almost knocked my backboard right off the pole."

"Never mind. I don't even know why I brought it up." He took his keys off the back of Calvin's car. He hadn't planned to talk about Gina's leaving in days, but there it was, slipping off the tip of his tongue like it had been lurking there all along. Was he really worried about her leaving? Or would he be happy to see her gone? Could he go back to the life he'd had before she came to Tallahassee and stirred up all this trouble?

Or was it even possible for him to go back to being the guy he'd been before she came along?

CHAPTER TWENTY-THREE

Landon thought it was pretty damn ballsy of Gina to show up at his condo, but here she was, parked right out front when he got home from playing hoops with Calvin.

Of course, she'd been ballsy since the first night they'd met. She'd been ballsy when he'd stormed into her office at Morgan's Ladder and accused her of knowing that Barbara Landon was his mom.

It wasn't that he hadn't *wanted* to see her in the week since they'd slept together. But he didn't know what he'd say to her. How he felt about her not telling him that Morgan's Ladder was dropping the case. Why she made him feel like he had a big ball of spaghetti stuck in his sternum.

She got out of her SUV when he pulled in beside her. "I know you don't want to see me, but I've learned something you need to know."

"Yeah?' He grabbed the gym bag out of the bed of the truck. He tried to ignore the way his body hummed every time she was near. "What's that?" Some other bit of news that would make his life even worse? That had been her M.O. all summer.

"First, I know what you saw on the table at my house the other night."

He held her gaze. Granted, he'd been pissed as hell the night he'd seen it, but this was Gina. The girl who'd made him think that maybe—just maybe—he was as good as people like her. But he still didn't understand why she hadn't told him. "Seems like that might have been a bit of information you would have shared with me before . . ."

She crossed her arms and waited, as if wanting to see how he characterized their night together.

He finally gave up. "You want to come in?"

She nodded and followed him up the sidewalk.

"I didn't know. I found out about it by accident," she said behind him as he unlocked the front door. "I planned to talk Suzanne out of dropping the case. There wasn't going to be any reason for you to know."

"You've had a week to come up with that story." He wasn't going to let her off that easy. He stood aside and let her enter the condo first. God, she smelled good.

"It's not a *story*." She turned in the foyer to face him. "It's the truth."

He kicked the door shut behind him. "Your boss made that decision and told you nothing about it?" Sarcasm dripped from his voice.

"She said she planned to tell me Monday. She didn't think I'd see the notes over the weekend." Gina seemed flustered. "Look, I don't care if you believe me or not." She paused. "Well, I do care, but—"

"Is Morgan's Ladder on the case or not?"

Her shoulders fell. "I don't know."

Damn it. He would never know the answers to all the questions that had haunted him this summer. All the questions that her arrival in Tallahassee had forced to the forefront. Maybe he could hire a private investigator or . . .

"I'm still trying to talk her out of it, but if the DNA isn't going to help us prove it, she thinks there are others she could help more."

Landon's jaw tightened. He wished he'd met her at a different time, in a different context. Not one that was laced with so much pain and confusion.

She held her hands in the air—a victory stance. Her eyes lit up. "But I have bigger news."

He doubted that, but he liked her being here, so he'd listen. Despite his anger the other night, he'd caught himself every day wishing she was nearby. He had things to tell her, experiences to share with her, moments when he wished she was near for no reason in particular.

"I was in Macclenny today," she continued. "West of Jacksonville. There was a party to celebrate the guy who got out on the day that Donna Crocker . . . well, you know." She clearly didn't want to relive the mistake she'd made in the media. "I heard a whirring sound. A buzzing like you said you heard the day of your mom's murder."

Landon held his breath. He braced himself for this new bit of information to have the same disastrous consequences as the others.

"Your dad's alibi was that he'd been out of town for a couple of days." She hesitated. He purposefully kept his face blank, not offering any kind of reaction. "Delivering a load of wood with Grady Buchanan, the guy next door."

"And?"

"Grady Buchanan had a one-man shop. If you heard a sawmill that morning"—she looked him straight in the eye—"then who was running it?"

≈

Gina followed Suzanne over the threshold of the ramshackle cottage and immediately felt like something was out of place. The forty-ish woman before them seemed too polished, too sophisticated, for the worn furnishings that surrounded her. She smoothed the crease of her tailored tweed pants as Gina and Suzanne stepped into an L-shaped room that was a living room in one portion and a dining room in the other.

This was Gina's last hope. She'd convinced Suzanne to come talk to Grady Buchanan's daughter before notifying the prison system and Cyrus Alexander that Morgan's Ladder would no longer be representing him.

"Please. Have a seat." The woman motioned with a manicured hand toward a sagging couch. A burgundy-colored afghan with several big snags in it covered the sofa.

"Thank you for agreeing to see us, Mrs. Rowling," Suzanne said as she sat.

"Ms. Buchanan," the woman said.

Suzanne's eyebrows rose.

"I petitioned to have my name changed back to Buchanan after Seth died. It became final a couple of weeks ago."

Gina settled into an old wooden rocker on the other side of the room. She wondered what kind of a woman didn't want to keep her husband's name after his death.

What had happened between them?

"But, please, call me Maggie."

Gina felt like she needed to enter the conversation—not be some gawking onlooker. "We were sorry to hear about your husband's death. And your father's."

Maggie opened her mouth to say something, then stopped herself. Instead, she cast an obligatory, appreciative smile. "Thank you."

Suzanne opened her notebook. "Do you mind if we get started?"

"Seems like the thing to do, since that's why you're here." The look in Maggie's eyes matched her cool demeanor.

Suzanne studied the woman's face for a few seconds, then thumbed through her notebook. Gina knew her boss didn't need to review the contents. They'd talked about them during their drive from Tallahassee to Pensacola, where Maggie had lived for years. "The file indicates you were home from college when Barbara Landon was murdered."

Maggie nodded.

"You were home for the summer?"

"In between summer and fall semesters. Only a couple of weeks." She twisted the ring on her right hand. "Maybe three."

"You went to school here in Pensacola?" The University of West Florida was a small state university in town.

Maggie's smile seemed real this time. "The first in my family."

"Congratulations," Gina said.

Maggie tipped her head in acknowledgment.

"Where were you at the time of Barbara Landon's murder?" Suzanne asked.

"At my dad's house. Next to the store." According to the file, Maggie's mother had passed away when she was twelve.

"The store where the murder took place?"

Some of these questions seemed basic, but Suzanne had said earlier how sometimes the simplest things were overlooked. Things that could help determine a man's innocence or guilt. Like the whir-ring of a sawmill blade.

"Yes," Maggie said.

"And where was your father?"

"He'd gone to deliver a load of wood up to the mountains in North Carolina."

"This was a normal occurrence?"

Maggie nodded. "It's what my father did for a living. He har-vested cypress trees from the marshes and delivered them for build-ing log cabins."

"He would deliver logs to a lumberyard?" Gina asked. Maybe there would be a record of the delivery to verify this.

"Not a lumberyard." Maggie shook her head. "A building site. And by that time they weren't logs. He milled them behind the house. Cut them to spec for each cabin. They arrived on-site ready to build. Like Lincoln Logs."

"The file indicates that Martin Vista was with him on the trip."

Maggie nodded.

"Can you be certain of that?"

Maggie stilled for a moment and raised her chin, as if pondering the question. "Martin always went with him. Dad would cut the wood and Martin would go up there to help him unload it."

But Landon's father had been a regional manager for Davidson Automotive. "Martin Vista had a full-time job working for someone else," Gina said.

Maggie turned toward her. "Daddy made friends with anyone who liked to gamble. He and Martin would take a load up, then go to the casino in Cherokee, North Carolina. It was like their weekend getaway." She looked down at her hands. "I think Daddy spent most of the money he made on gambling."

"And you're certain Martin Vista was with him that weekend?" Suzanne asked.

Maggie thought for a moment. "His truck was at our house the whole time." Her shoulders rose. "I guess they were together."

"Did you see them leave together? Come back together?"

Maggie's chin rose in defiance. "No."

"A witness says they heard the sawmill running that day." Suzanne spoke slowly. Cautiously. "Did your father have other employees?"

Maggie glanced at Gina, then back to Suzanne. She toyed with the collar on her crisp, white blouse. "No."

"Who would have been running the sawmill?" Gina scooted to the edge of her seat. "In your father's absence?"

Maggie's eyes widened. "I . . . don't know."

"Was there anyone else at the house with you that weekend?" Suzanne's voice was tinged with sternness. Apparently she, too, felt like Maggie had information she hadn't yet shared.

"Seth . . ." The word barely squeaked out of Maggie's mouth. She cleared her throat. "Seth came to visit me that weekend." She looked down at her hands crossed on her lap. "Daddy didn't know. He wouldn't have approved."

"You're saying Seth Rowling was at your house that weekend?" Suzanne's voice was calm.

But this was new information. Had no one asked Maggie Buchanan that question before? Had she not offered that information, knowing a murder had taken place next door? Gina wanted to jump up and shake the woman by her collar until she gave them all the information she had.

Maggie looked up. Her nod was barely perceptible. "Yes."

"Did the police know that?" Gina asked.

"Daddy was good friends with Buster McCauley."

Buster McCauley, the chief of police in the small, rural county at the time of the murder.

Suzanne seemed to know exactly what had happened. "You didn't tell the police that Seth Rowling was staying with you because you didn't want Buster McCauley to tell your father?"

"I was a college girl. Unmarried." Maggie got up and paced the living room. "Daddy would have been ashamed. Embarrassed. I didn't want him to know."

Suzanne leaned forward. "Did Seth Rowling stay within your sight at all times? Was he ever away from you?"

Maggie stopped with her back toward them. "I mean, I . . . took a shower every morning." She turned to face them. "And a nap one day."

"Do you have a picture of your husband, Ms. Buchanan? One from when you were in college?"

"I . . . I'd have to dig to find a picture from back then." She opened a drawer in an old buffet near the dining table. "But here's our church directory." She opened the booklet to a specific page while she walked it over to Suzanne.

The older woman swallowed and quietly passed the book to Gina.

The picture above Seth and Maggie Rowling's name showed Maggie with a fortysomething man with closely cropped hair. The gray in his hair blended with what appeared to be a lighter color.

Gina's heart quickened. "What color was his hair? Before it turned gray?"

"Kind of a dark dishwater blond."

Suzanne had apparently seen the same thing Gina had. "And when he was in college?"

"It was a lot lighter then. Almost white blond."

For the first time that afternoon, Suzanne slid a sideways glance in Gina's direction.

Gina shot up, unable to control her energy. "How tall was he? What was his build?"

Maggie face paled. "You"—her voice was weak—"you don't think he had anything to do with that woman's murder, do you?"

CHAPTER TWENTY-FOUR

How tall was he?" Suzanne's voice was stern as she repeated Gina's question to Maggie Buchanan. "What was his build?"

Maggie placed her hands on her hips as she stood in the living room. "Should I get a lawyer?"

"Only if you killed Barbara Landon," Gina said.

"Or have withheld evidence," Suzanne added.

Maggie looked out the side window for several seconds. "He was six feet two." Her gaze fell to the floor. "Very muscular." Her voice cracked. "But long and wiry."

Just like Cyrus Alexander.

"Barbara Landon was murdered that Saturday afternoon," Suzanne said. "Where was Seth Rowling that day?"

Maggie's pacing started again. "He was with me all day. At Daddy's house."

"Doing . . . ?"

Maggie stopped and faced Suzanne. She gave her a you've-got-to-be-kidding look. "We had a house alone to ourselves. We were kids in college. We made out. Watched movies. Smoked some pot."

"Had sex?" Suzanne asked.

Maggie's gaze fell to the floor. "I was on my period." She paused. "Seth wasn't very happy about that." She ran her right hand down the side of her face. "That was the first time he ever hit me."

"Because you wouldn't have sex with him?" Gina tried to hide the surprise in her voice.

"Yes."

"Did the violence continue?" Suzanne asked.

Maggie's eyes seemed to glaze over. "Yes."

"And still you married him." Suzanne didn't ask a question. She already knew the answer.

Maggie's face showed no emotion. "Seems pretty stupid, doesn't it?"

Now Gina understood why Maggie had reverted to her maiden name after his death.

"It happens to the best of us," Suzanne said, comforting Maggie.

Gina's gaze shot to her boss. She never would have imagined such a strong, independent woman would allow herself to get into a relationship like that. Had it been her Key Biscayne lover who had abused her?

"He . . ." Maggie continued. "He said he'd come all the way from Pensacola thinking we'd have sex and I was wrong to lead him on like that. I had thought it would be nice just to . . . to spend time together."

Gina knew how strong the need for sexual release could be in a college-age man. She'd grown up being taught to never leave her drink unattended, to never get in the car with a boy she didn't know. Twitter was filled with news of sexual abuse in high school, in college, from professional athletes. The whole notion sickened her. Still, she was eager to steer the conversation back to Barbara Landon's murder.

"You were with Seth Rowling that entire afternoon?"

Maggie's hand flattened on her sternum. "Yes."

"But the sawmill. Lan—" Gina stopped herself. "A witness heard the sawmill running the day of the murder."

"Seth said he knew how to run it. There was some scrap wood. He'd been asking me if he could cut some for bookshelves at his apartment back in Pensacola."

"Were you with him when he ran the sawmill?" Suzanne asked.

Maggie shook her head. "That was . . . right after he hit me. I wanted to get away from him. I went up to my room. That's when I took my nap."

"With the noise of the sawmill?" Gina remembered Buford Monroe saying his mother hated that noise. "You took a nap?"

"My bedroom was on the other side of the house," Maggie said. "And when your daddy runs a sawmill for a living, you learn to sleep through it."

Suzanne jotted something in her notebook, then looked up. "How did you learn of the murder at the store next door?"

"The police came the next day to ask me about it. I didn't know until they told me."

"Did they question Seth, too?" Suzanne asked.

Maggie stilled. Her eyes widened.

Suzanne leaned forward. "Maggie?"

"Seth was really drunk when I woke up from my nap, but he just kept drinking and drinking. Finally, he passed out." Maggie looked down at her hands. "He was a violent drunk, even back then."

Gina and Suzanne exchanged a worried look.

Maggie continued. "When I woke up the next morning, he was gone."

"So the police never questioned him?" Suzanne asked.

Maggie's gaze rose, meeting Suzanne's. "By the time the police got there, Seth was gone."

~

Landon sat in the bleachers of the small-town gym, wondering how the teenage players could run up and down the basketball court in such stifling heat. Though the school was air-conditioned, the old units seemed to be losing the battle against the brutal Florida summer. He pulled his T-shirt away from his chest, hoping at least one molecule of cool air might find its way to his skin.

Once he'd set his mind to it, it hadn't been hard to track down Tim Alexander, Cyrus's son. Not when the local newspaper covered high school sports like it was the only thing going on in this tiny little town. Probably because it was.

He'd thought coming here today might be a good way to clear his brain, which still clung to memories of his night with Gina like it had happened five minutes ago. How the hell did someone have sex like that, then just walk away? For the first time, his heart had been part of the equation, too. At least until he'd found the file notes in her apartment.

He ran his hands through his hair as the fortysomething woman sitting next to him glanced sideways at him for about the tenth time since he'd sat down. He wished he could tell her to stop staring, to leave him the hell alone. But he'd learned long ago that he was expected to be a nice guy. Accessible to the masses, even when he'd rather not be. So instead, he tried to ignore her, which became increasing difficult when she nudged the guy on her other side and whispered in his ear. The guy, presumably her husband, leaned forward to look at him. She leaned backward, giving him a better view, then the two shared another whispered conversation.

Landon tried to watch the basketball game, sensing that his private afternoon was about to be violated.

"You're Landon Vista, aren't you?" The woman interrupted his thoughts about Gina. She laid her hand on his arm, like she had some right to touch him because of who he was.

An older man in front of her turned around and looked at him, too.

Landon gave a slight nod, then returned his gaze to the basketball court in front of them. Tim pulled down a rebound and shot it out of the lane to the point guard.

"My Randall has been best friends with Tim since kindergarten." She pointed to the guard taking the ball down the court. He had the same orange-red hair as her husband. She shook her head. "It's a lot for a boy to go through."

"Yes, ma'am," he said. *Would she not shut up?* The old man in front of her turned around to look for the second time.

She touched Landon's arm again. "Kind of funny how the best-behaved, most respectful kid in the class is the one whose dad is in prison for murder."

Landon didn't say anything, but he knew how the kid felt. Like he always had something to prove. But for now, he wanted the woman to shut up before the entire section of bleachers heard her. The news of Cyrus's case being reopened had to be huge news in a tiny town like this one. And he certainly knew what it was like to be a boy awash in the middle of a murder case. How people stared. Assumed you weren't as good as they were because of something that had happened beyond your control.

"I thank the Lord every day that John's here to help me." She motioned toward the man with orange-red hair who listened to their conversation. "Raising boys is hard work."

"Is Tim's mom here?" Landon asked, looking around for someone who might look like the boy.

The woman jabbed a thumb toward the wall behind her. "She had the morning shift out at the plant. We brought Tim with us." The woman smiled and held out her hand. "Patti McIntire." She leaned back. "And this is John."

Landon shook hands with them both, then returned his attention to the game. Patti spoke on and off throughout both halves, asking about his football days, sharing tidbits about Tim's life.

"The boys would like meeting you some day," Patti said when the game was over and the hometown team had won handily. "A real college football player and all. Most of 'em play in the fall. Of course, the school only has a hundred and thirty kids, so pretty much everyone makes the team."

"I . . ." Landon grasped at words. Was she talking about her own boys? Or Tim Alexander? Did Landon want to meet Cyrus's son? Would it do the kid any good? It would likely mess with Landon's head, so what would it do to a sixteen-year-old? "I don't know if that would do them any good."

Patti opened her purse and fished around inside. "Well, let me give you one of my business cards." She pulled a dog-eared card from the depths of the bag. "I do hair. Women's," she clarified. "Not men's. Except my boys."

He glanced down at the phone number and logo for Patti's Shear Designs as she leaned toward him. When her closeness made him look up, she gave him a death stare that she'd undoubtedly perfected on her own kids. "You wouldn't have come here if you didn't want to meet him."

"I . . . I don't want him to know I was here today." Landon wasn't sure what he thought. He wanted to sort out his feelings before he involved a kid who'd already had a tough sixteen years. "I . . . don't want to upset him."

Patti laughed. "You're a stranger here. Well, I mean you don't live here. And you're Landon Vista. The whole town knows you're here today. Everybody who's not here has already heard about it by now."

"If he and I do meet"—Landon wasn't sure what he was saying—"it should be private."

"That's why you have my card, honey." She picked up her bag and motioned to her husband that she was ready to go. "And don't you ever think I'd do anything that might hurt Tim. That child deserves all the kindness anyone can give him."

Landon placed his hand on her arm to stop her. "You won't tell anybody about our conversation?"

"I'll give you a while to get in touch with him." She winked. "And after that, it's the best story anyone's ever told at bunco night."

He stood motionless as she clattered down the bleachers, greeting other parents as she went. Probably the same parents she'd gossip with about him when the time was right. But he did trust that she'd look out for Tim's best interests. She'd had that motherly look in her eye when she talked about him. The one that would turn to fierce protection if anyone tried to harm him.

Landon sat back down, waiting for the crowd to clear out of the gym. A few people paused to look up at him as they walked out or stood, chatting with friends.

So why *had* he come here? It was like Gina's presence had caused him to stretch the boundaries of his life. Two months ago, there had been Boomer and Ricardo, his work for the senator's office. The volleyball league and the Twilight Pub. But she made him look at his life differently. Like the borders were different. Like there were different possibilities.

But that didn't mean he needed to disrupt Tim's life. Like Landon at that age, the poor kid probably just wanted to be left alone.

But how long did he have before Patti McIntire, or any other person in town, told Tim that Landon had been here today?

If Cyrus Alexander really was innocent, then Landon had already messed this kid's life up about as bad as anyone could. Had Patti been right? Had Landon really come here because he wanted to meet Tim?

He stood and clambered down the metal bleacher before he had to think about that too much.

CHAPTER TWENTY-FIVE

Gina tried to concentrate on the guy serving the volleyball on the other side of the net, but she hadn't been able to think of anything other than Landon in the few minutes since he'd walked into the gym. She'd known from the league schedule that his team had the game after hers, but she hadn't expected to feel like a confused teenager when he arrived.

The ball sailed over the net. Gina cupped her hands to come under it with a dig—a move she'd made thousands of times over the last few years. What should have been a perfect set for her teammate to spike over the net instead glanced off her fingertips with a flat thud. Game point for the other team. She looked straight ahead, rotated one position, and got ready for the next serve. She didn't want to see her teammates' surprised looks at her screwup. And she certainly didn't want Landon to know how much his presence bothered her.

The next serve blooped over the net. Gina dove, raising it with a one-handed hit to save it from landing on the floor. That was the level of play they expected from her—and that she expected from herself. She rolled into a standing position just as her teammate's spike bounced out of the net. The other team cheered and traded high fives. Gina's team grumbled. But she'd played Division I volleyball. And this was a recreational league. The loss meant far less to her than Landon waiting on the sidelines.

She raised a hand to acknowledge him and walked nervously to the row of folding chairs where her gym bag sat. She tugged her kneepads down to her ankles and gathered the bag, ready to go.

A pair of big hands came to rest on the back of the folding chair. "Mind if I follow you out?"

She jumped. She'd assumed Landon was out on the court, warming up with his team for the next game. "You don't have to . . . ?" She jabbed a thumb to indicate his teammates behind her.

"I don't need to do any drills." He grinned. "I'm already the best player on the team."

She chuckled and headed toward the door of the gym. Once they got outside, he gently grasped her wrist and pulled her around the corner, out of the path of the players who'd just finished their game and were headed to their cars.

"So what have you been up to?" he asked as he leaned against the brick exterior of the building.

She shrugged. "Work, mainly." She wanted to scream *I have two more weeks here*. But she had more pride than that. If he didn't feel the same magnetic pull that she felt, then he wasn't going to develop it during her last few days in town.

"Any new developments in the case?" he asked.

She shook her head. She'd already decided she wasn't going to get his hopes up on anything having to do with the case until they were dead sure about it. And while Maggie Buchanan's information was a substantial new twist, it wasn't something Gina was willing to share with him. Not yet, anyway.

"Did you figure out if it was the sawmill I heard?"

"We're working on it." She hated to withhold what she knew about Seth Rowling having been next door at the time of the murder, but this summer had taught her to keep her personal and professional lives completely separate. And she wasn't going to risk hurting Landon again.

He reached up and pulled on the front of her jersey, beckoning her toward him. She took a tentative step. And then another. His masculine scent made her want to move even closer.

"I've missed you." His voice was tender, almost reverent.

She smiled, but for some reason she had to fight back tears. For God's sake—she wasn't a crier. Well, except when she got mad, but she wasn't angry now.

Was he really getting to her so much that she couldn't even be near him without being overwhelmed with emotion?

"I've got to drive to Orlando after the game tonight." He raised his hand to stroke her jaw with his fingertips. "The senator's got an all-day event down there tomorrow. They all drove down earlier today." He motioned with his head toward the gym. "But we would have been short a player if I hadn't come." He rolled his eyes. "And believe it or not, I'm the breakfast speaker at seven a.m."

"Wow. Tough gig." She could handle a light conversation. Teasing him was not a problem. It was the relationship part she wasn't sure about. "Good thing you're in good shape for such a grueling schedule." She squeezed one of his biceps. She'd forgotten how hard they were. Last time she'd been this close to them, they were on either side of her head as Landon made love to her. She took a deep breath and closed her eyes. She wanted to remember everything about him. His touch. His scent. His voice.

"I don't know how to do this," he whispered.

She opened her eyes. "Do what?" Her voice was filled with emotion, but she wasn't going to spill her heart out between them without knowing for sure what he was talking about.

His fingers dipped to run along her collarbone. "There can't be any secrets between us."

Like the fact that Seth Rowling had been next door on the day of his mom's murder? But Landon didn't know anything about that. Was he talking about the file notes he'd seen on the table in her breakfast nook? That seemed like eons ago. She needed to slow down her reaction until she could think straight.

"Maybe we should talk about this when you're back from Orlando," she said. Yes. She liked that idea. That would mean she'd get to see him at least one more time before she left Tallahassee.

He leaned toward her, his cheek brushing hers. "I've got to get inside for my game."

The intimacy of his breath on her neck gave her chills. When he stepped away from her, she wanted to reach out and pull him back.

"I'll text you when I know for sure when I'll be back in town," he said.

She nodded, and he disappeared around the corner. She heard the heavy metal door to the gym open and close. He was gone.

She slouched against the brick wall of the building. She hadn't expected that tonight.

He'd missed her.

She reached up to where his cheek had touched hers, as if he might still be there.

But a sudden thought stopped her dreamy reaction. If he really did miss her, then why hadn't he called for days? Why hadn't he given her an opportunity to explain the file notes he'd seen at her house?

And how was she going to keep from feeling guilty about hiding another important fact from him?

~

Last night's conversation with Landon at the gym was pretty much all Gina had thought about for most of the morning, but at least now it was lunchtime. Maybe she'd go for a walk down to the park and back after she ate so she could clear her mind.

She pulled her lunch box from underneath her desk and unzipped it. Today's lunch—store-bought chicken salad and some carrot sticks—was the same as yesterday's lunch. And lunch from the day before that. But Suzanne—always a frugal one—brought her lunch every day, so Gina had learned to shop at the grocery store for things she could bring to work.

Suzanne's office door burst open. The strap of her worn leather messenger bag crisscrossed her body. "Pack that back up and bring it with you."

Gina complied, stuffing the contents back into the plastic lunch box. "Where are we going?"

"Pensacola."

"Right now?" That was a three-hour drive. Six hours round-trip. To get there and back would mean they'd be gone well into the evening. That was fine with Gina, just . . . unprecedented since she'd worked at Morgan's Ladder.

"Yes, Pensacola. Right now." Suzanne armed the security system using the panel near the front door. "Come on."

Gina grabbed her purse and scampered to the door, knowing she had only thirty seconds before the system was set. "Why are we going there?"

Both women stepped out onto the sidewalk, and Suzanne pulled the door shut behind them.

She turned to Gina, a solemn look on her face. "Maggie Buchanan has something she wants to show us."

CHAPTER TWENTY-SIX

Suzanne's old Audi pulled into the driveway of Maggie Buchanan's run-down cottage, and again, Gina was reminded of how the woman inside didn't match the character of the house. "Maggie seems so . . . put together," she said. "And the house isn't." The white paint faded to gray in some spots, peeled at the corners, and the front porch drooped on one end.

"When you live with an abuser, it's often about hiding the truth." Suzanne turned the car off and opened her door. "As long as the people at work or at church or wherever don't suspect anything or say anything outright, then a woman can go on not admitting how bad it is, but it seeps out in other ways."

Gina was eager to go inside, to see what it was that Maggie Buchanan wanted to show them, but the dichotomy between the woman's public life and private life intrigued her. "What did Seth do for a living?" The psychology of an abused woman was foreign to her. Did Maggie pour all their money into tailored clothes and expensive manicures?

Suzanne twisted toward the backseat to get her messenger bag. "I'm not sure he ever really had a profession. My guess is Maggie made most of the money."

Gina knew that Maggie had been a branch manager at a locally owned bank and held a board position on the Pensacola Chamber of

Commerce. But thinking about what made a woman put up with abuse was something she'd consider at another time. For now, she wanted to get inside to see what Maggie Buchanan had to show them.

Maggie stepped out onto the front porch as Gina and Suzanne approached. She looked more haggard than before. It was more than just her attire—her tailored pants had been replaced by trim-fitting jeans, and she wore a knit top instead of a crisply starched oxford. Rather, it was the gaunt look of her face. Dark circles rimmed her eyes, making them seem sunken into her head. Her lips pinched more tightly than before. Her hair—neatly coiffed when they'd met the first time—was pulled back into a messy ponytail.

"Your questions the other day got me thinking." Maggie skipped any pleasantries as Gina and Suzanne climbed the few steps to her front porch.

"About . . . ?" Suzanne asked.

Maggie looked up and down the desolate road, as if she didn't want anyone else to know her visitors were here. "Please, come in."

She turned to face them as soon as all three were inside the living room. "I thought Seth left early that weekend because I couldn't have sex with him. I thought he was mad about that."

Gina's pulse quickened. She ran her palms down the front of her navy dress pants. Suzanne leaned toward the other woman.

"But I got to thinking," Maggie continued. "After you all were here. What if he murdered Barbara Landon?" Her eyes grew larger. "What if that's why he left so quickly?" She paced to the other side of the room. "I mean, I thought his behavior was a little odd, but he'd just slapped me that morning. I was happy to see him go."

Suzanne was apparently as eager as Gina to know what Maggie had found. "You said you had something to show us."

"Yes." Maggie seemed distant. Like her body was here, but her mind wanted to take her elsewhere. Someplace far away. Her hand rose slowly as she pointed down the hallway of the old farmhouse. "In the attic."

Suzanne pulled two pairs of latex gloves from her messenger bag, then dropped it on the floor. She had come prepared for evidence. "Can we go look at it?"

Maggie nodded slowly but didn't move.

"You'll take us there now?" Adrenaline rushed through Gina's body.

Maggie blinked and shook her head as if waking from a slumber. "Yes. This way."

She led them down the hallway to a doorway tucked beyond the last bedroom. She opened the door to a set of narrow, winding steps leading to the attic. Though it looked like she was poised to lead them upstairs, she hesitated. She took a deep breath. Then another.

Gina's heart raced as she willed Maggie to hurry. Yes, it could be because it was Gina's first time actually helping to build the case to set a man free, but this was also Landon's life. Today could mean the difference between Landon knowing who killed his mother and not knowing. It could mean he might learn his testimony had helped send an innocent man to prison. She knew how that felt. And she knew she'd never get over it.

Finally, Maggie placed her foot on the first step, then stopped. Suzanne bumped into Gina and Gina almost ran into the back of Maggie as the somber procession came to an abrupt halt.

"We need to go up there, Maggie," Suzanne said from behind Gina. "I know this is difficult."

Maggie hung her head, but then took another step up. And another.

Gina followed her. Her heart raced. Her legs felt shakier than when she'd run that half marathon in college. She had to concentrate in order to put one foot in front of the other. Thank God there was a wall to hold on to. It felt warm on her fingertips. Though she'd been invited, she felt like a burglar. An intruder who had no idea what secrets lay ahead of her. She hoped to God whatever Maggie had found would help determine the truth. Something that would help Landon find the peace he deserved.

The air inside the attic got hotter and staler as they climbed. When they finally reached the top of the stairs, Maggie pulled a yellowed string to turn on a bare light bulb above their heads. She turned to face Gina and Suzanne. "There were some boxes up here that were taped shut. Seth had told me they were none of my business and told me to stay away from them. But after your visit the other day, I"—Maggie looked down to the floor—"I decided to look inside." She raised her head. A single tear trickled down one cheek.

Suzanne slipped on a pair of the latex gloves and handed the other pair to Gina before walking over to two copy-paper boxes. Wide tape that had once been clear but was now a sickly yellow color wound around both ends of each. Beside them, a pair of kitchen shears lay on the attic floor.

"Are those the boxes?" Suzanne's voice was quiet, almost reverent. As if she knew the importance of this moment to Maggie. And to Cyrus. And to Landon.

Maggie nodded.

Gina rushed over to the boxes and peered inside as she slid on her gloves. She lifted out each item and held each up for Suzanne to see.

A couple of high school yearbooks.

A family Bible.

A framed cross-stitch sampler with the words *Harold and Elizabeth, March 8, 1957.*

"Seth's parents," Maggie said. "That hung at their house. Their wedding date."

Next, there were two black-and-white pictures and a color photograph. The color picture showed a high school track team, posed in rows for what looked like a yearbook photograph. The other two showed a tall, gangly teenager with white-blond hair. In each, he was skateboarding.

"This is Seth?" Gina asked, holding up one of the black-and-whites.

Maggie nodded.

Gina held up the picture for Suzanne to see. The two exchanged a grim glance. He could have been Cyrus Alexander's twin.

Gina set the pictures aside and reached into the box again. The last item, nestled in the bottom, among packing peanuts, was a tattered envelope. The kind they'd used when she'd worked one summer in the administrative offices at the hospital her father managed. The kind that would hold an 8½" x 11" sheet of paper and that was used to send things interoffice, with the little button and string on the back to keep it closed en route to its destination.

Slowly, she unwound the string from the button.

A weak whimper escaped from Maggie's throat.

Gina looked up. Her hand stilled. Maggie's face was pale and her lip quivered.

"Keep going," Suzanne instructed.

Gina unwound the string two more times. It pulled free from the button. She felt dizzy. She took a deep breath and let it out.

Finally, she peered inside. Several yellowed newspaper clippings were tucked inside. She pulled the pile of them out and set the envelope on the dusty floor. She gently lowered the fragile newspaper clippings back into the box, then took them out, one by one, and unfolded them.

Each one featured Barbara Landon's murder.

One from the day of the murder.

Several from the trial.

As soon as she looked at each one, she passed the clippings on to Suzanne.

"Why would he have been so interested in her murder?" Maggie's voice shook as she watched them.

Suzanne took the last one as Gina handed it to her. "I think we all know the answer to that question."

CHAPTER TWENTY-SEVEN

Gina cringed as she thought of the way Cyrus's eyes had begged her and Suzanne for help when they'd met with him at the prison. She'd tried to steel herself against their silent plea, knowing that so many people in prison claimed to be innocent.

But now she understood why his eyes had been so convincing.

He'd been innocent the entire time.

Maggie sank to the floor as if she couldn't hold herself up anymore. "Does this prove he killed her?"

"It doesn't look good." Suzanne took the last article from Gina. "But it also doesn't prove anything beyond the shadow of a doubt."

"Will I be in trouble? For having this in my attic all these years?" Maggie's hand covered her mouth. "And not knowing?"

"The authorities won't be happy that you hid the fact that Seth was there that weekend." Suzanne placed her hand on Maggie's knee. "But we'll help you as best we can."

Gina, too, believed that Maggie hadn't known. That she'd been in a violent relationship in which she would have been afraid to question her husband. Not in her own mind and certainly not out loud to her abuser. But she knew that Suzanne couldn't promise a free ride to Maggie Buchanan. Not with so many parts of the legal system outside her control.

"Why would he do that?" Maggie's questioning gaze begged the other women for an answer. "He'd never even been to my house before."

Gina knew the crime scene had revealed no indications of robbery or attempted rape.

"You told us he'd just hit you. That he was mad you couldn't have sex with him," Suzanne said. "So he went next door. Men hurting women is all about establishing power."

Gina lowered her head in an unspoken tribute to Barbara Landon. The other two women fell silent, too, each with her own thoughts.

After several seconds of quiet, Gina looked around the attic, wondering if there might be more evidence here. An old living room chair with a leg broken off sat in one corner. An artificial Christmas tree was bursting from its torn box. The handlebars of an exercise bike held a string of holiday lights.

She rose and looked behind an armoire that had been partially refinished, to the only place in the attic that wasn't visible from the top of the staircase.

Behind it, a rusty, green metal tackle box like Gina's grandfather had owned was tucked under the rafters. But unlike Gina's grandfather's, the lid was bolted shut with a thick lock.

"There's something back here," Gina called back to Maggie. "Do you mind if I get it out?"

Maggie's shrugged approval looked like that of a woman defeated.

Gina closed the sagging door of the armoire to give herself more room. She knelt and twisted until she could get both of her hands behind it. She pulled out the tackle box and set it in the ring formed by the three women.

"Seth was a fisherman?" Suzanne asked.

"Not"—Maggie swallowed—"for years. I haven't seen that thing . . ."

"Since?" Suzanne prodded her.

"I don't know."

"How do we get the lock off?" Gina asked, looking around for those big pincher things they used on cop shows. But, no, that would be wishing for too much to have a pair of those handy.

"Bring it downstairs," Suzanne said. "Out to the yard."

Gina's eyes questioned her. Suzanne nodded toward the staircase.

Gina lifted the green metal box and scrambled downstairs, glad to get out of the stuffy attic. Her lungs gasped for the cool air of the hallway. She forced her legs to carry her through the living room and out the front door into the yard. Suzanne's and Maggie's footsteps followed behind her.

When she turned around, she saw that Suzanne had picked up her messenger bag as they passed through the living room.

"Set it on the ground," Suzanne said as she pulled a small pistol from her pouch. "And stand back."

Gina's eyes widened. She'd never known her boss carried a gun. It hadn't been in there during their visits to prisons because—surely—the guards would have confiscated it before letting her in to visit their clients. Their clients who were *convicted murderers*.

She set the box on the ground and backed away, as her boss had instructed.

A single shot rang through the air. The lock spun on the latch and fell to the ground.

Gina looked at Suzanne in awe. She was a crusader, a role model, and Annie Oakley all wrapped into one.

"So open it," Suzanne said impatiently. "See what's inside."

Gina knelt on the ground and unfastened the big, rusted silver latch. The lid squeaked open. Inside, two trays attached to the lid rose as the cover fell open. The little bins in the trays held rusty fishhooks and a couple of tiny bobbers. A dirty rag was bunched up in the bottom well, covering anything else in the tackle box.

She pinched the rag between one finger and her thumb and gently moved it aside. Underneath sat one item. An ornate wooden box.

Gina gently lifted the wooden box from Seth Rowling's tackle box. Her heart beat faster, as if it knew what was in the box. Maybe, just maybe, the contents of the box would help them prove it was Seth Rowling and not Cyrus Alexander who had killed Landon's mother.

She took a step, holding it out to Maggie.

"I don't want it." Maggie held her hands in front of her and backed away. "You open it."

Gina looked down at the intricately carved box. She had visions of unleashing something evil, like Indiana Jones had done when he released those melting faces from the Lost Ark of the Covenant. She suddenly wasn't sure she wanted to know what was inside.

"Go ahead," Suzanne said.

Gina swallowed and looked down at the box, unable to make any other move.

"For Landon," Suzanne said. "And for Cyrus."

Gina's hand shook as she slowly lifted the ornately carved lid. There were four objects inside.

A smooth, flat rock the color of butterscotch.

A folded-up slip of paper.

A tangle of bright purple yarn.

And a silver charm bracelet containing one tarnished charm—the silhouette of a little boy's head.

Gina gently pulled the bracelet out of the box and turned her head to read the inscription.

L . . .

The charm spun a quarter turn on the end of the chain. Frustrated, Gina knelt to set the box down inside the tackle box. She laid the charm across her other palm so she could read it.

Landon.

A chill ran up Gina's spine and spread like a lightening bolt across the back of her scalp.

She looked up at the curious face of her boss. Her scalp tickled with beads of sweat. "The charm. It says 'Landon' on it."

Suzanne's expression was grim. "A souvenir."

If Suzanne was right, Seth had taken it when he'd murdered Barbara Landon. Gina tried to imagine what it must have been like for a young single mother to know she was about to be stabbed to death, leaving a young son alone with a killer.

Maggie turned away from them. She braced one hand on a tree next to her and threw up.

"What else is in the box?" Suzanne said, nodding toward it.

Gina knelt to set it on the ground in front of her. Her hands shook as she took the slip of paper from it. She eased it open, not wanting to damage it. Sloppy handwriting, slanted at a harsher angle than Gina had ever seen, was written in blue ink pen.

Dear Lord,

Please forgive me.

Seth Atchison Rowling

She handed the note to Suzanne, who read it quickly, then looked up at Maggie. "Seth was a religious man?"

Maggie was still bent over, wiping her mouth with the back of her hand. She scoffed. "Does a religious man beat his wife? Does he kill people?"

Suzanne read the note aloud to her.

Maggie rose and stilled for several seconds, as if she was soaking it in. Finally, she spoke, her voice tinged with hatred. "I guess if he'd felt really bad about it, he would have come forward while he was still alive."

A wave of anger roiled inside Gina as she thought of Cyrus Alexander, sitting in prison for fifteen years while Seth Rowling's tackle box held his ticket to freedom.

"This was here the entire time," she said. "You could have gotten Cyrus Alexander out of prison at any time."

"I . . . I didn't know."

"But you had suspicions. You said so yourself."

Maggie fixed her gaze on Gina's and held it for several seconds. "Have you ever done anything you regretted?" Maggie's voice filled with venom. "Or are you too young and perfect for that?"

Gina took a step back as if Maggie's words had lashed out like a viper's tongue in her direction. Of course Gina had done something she regretted. She'd done the exact thing Maggie had done. She'd allowed an innocent person to go to prison. Maybe it didn't show on the outside, but Gina had done plenty that she regretted.

"You could have called the police," Suzanne said.

Maggie turned, her anger aimed at Gina's boss. "The same police who didn't take Seth away when he broke my jaw? The same ones who acted like it was 'my duty' to have sex with him when he raped me? Are those the police you're talking about?"

Suzanne spread her hands in front of her as if to diffuse the situation. She took three long, slow breaths while Maggie glared at her. "We're in this together," Suzanne said. "If an innocent man is in prison, we all want to get him out."

A profound sadness settled over Gina like a fog settling into the valleys of a mountain range. Her body was suddenly very tired. Her brain was tired. Even her heart was tired. She didn't have the energy for anything else today. "What do we do now?"

Suzanne knelt to place the slip of paper back inside the box. "We need to let the police know what we've found."

Of course. They needed to act on the news that Gina was still absorbing.

Suzanne placed the lid on the box and tucked it under her arm. "The world needs to know what a bastard Seth Rowling was."

CHAPTER TWENTY-EIGHT

Landon still couldn't figure out why Gina insisted on meeting him at his condo when he was getting back from Orlando at eleven o'clock at night. He'd have much rather swung by her place, crawled into bed with her, and made the world disappear as he lost himself in her soft, silky body.

"Hey," she said as they both got out of their cars at the same time. He hated the tentativeness in her voice. It was so anti-Gina. So opposite of the confidence that made her so attractive. "Do you mind if I come in?"

Actually, he'd mind if she *didn't* come in. He'd been thinking about her for the last twenty-four hours. Hell, he'd been thinking about her for the last week. He was still mad as hell that she hadn't told him Morgan's Ladder was dropping the case, but the more he thought about it, the more he believed that she'd planned to try to talk her boss out of it. He motioned for her to follow him.

As he led the way up the sidewalk, his stomach flip-flopped. He never got nervous around girls, but she was different. She made him feel things no one else made him feel.

He unlocked the door and stepped inside to turn off the alarm, then stood aside to let her in. He followed her down the front hall toward the living room. A quick glance at the living room told him he hadn't put his laundry away a couple of nights ago. He hadn't really felt like doing much the last few days. But she wasn't here to judge him on his housekeeping skills.

He tossed his keys in the wooden bowl on the counter that separated the kitchen from the living room. "I would have been happy to come to your place."

She ignored his comment. "We talked to Grady Buchanan's daughter."

His stomach clenched. His breath grew shallow. "And?"

"She confirmed your father and her father were out of town when your mom was murdered."

He frowned. How was this news?

"But the thing is"—she hesitated, as if she didn't know how to say whatever came next—"she had a boyfriend there with her that weekend. A boyfriend who fit Cyrus Alexander's description."

She paused. Landon sucked in a big, gulping breath. He searched her face for clues. For more information than she'd already shared. Was this the news he'd expected to hear these past few weeks? That he'd sent an innocent man to prison? But they'd been certain of the killer once. How could they be certain again? And know for sure? "You and Suzanne think he did it?"

She nodded slowly. "Do you remember a bracelet your mom used to have? One with a little charm on it?"

Hot tears sprang up, right behind his eyes. He hadn't thought about that bracelet in years. One hand went to his other wrist, as if touching the inexpensive piece of jewelry. "The outline of a little boy's head. With my name on it. Her girlfriends had all chipped in to buy it for her when I was born." He panicked. How could he not have remembered it?

"Maggie Buchanan's husband had it hidden in his tackle box."

Landon lowered himself onto one of the stools at the breakfast bar. Like always, Gina was sending his life into a tailspin. Nothing in his head seemed to make sense. "Where did he get it?"

"He took it from your mother." Her words came out slowly, as if she didn't want to hurt him with their sharpness. "When he killed her."

Landon searched her eyes. He didn't understand what she was saying. How could the police not have questioned the boyfriend before? If he and Cyrus Alexander looked alike, how could the police have not seen the resemblance? "But why did he do it? Did he have an alibi?"

Gina shook her head. "Maggie Buchanan didn't tell the police he was there. She was afraid the sheriff would tell her father he'd been at the house with her. No one even knew he was in town."

"But why? Why would he do it?"

"We'll never know for sure, but he had a history of beating up women, especially when he was drunk. And apparently he drank a lot."

Landon couldn't take a breath deep enough to fill his lungs. If the authorities didn't know the boyfriend was in town, they never questioned him. They never would have known there was another tall, blond man who looked like Cyrus Alexander. "This means Cyrus Alexander has been in prison this entire time . . . ?" He couldn't finish his sentence. He couldn't think about what he'd done to that man. To his son, Tim. To their family.

She nodded. "And he's innocent." But unlike the other times they'd discussed the case, she didn't act like she had something to prove. She, of all people, knew what he was going through. She knew what it was like to send an innocent person to prison.

He turned his chair toward the counter and rested his head on his arms. He needed to think. To absorb the news. His chest heaved, gasping for breath. Though his eyes were open, all he saw was spinning rings of light where his arms and kitchen counter should be. His foot slipped off the rung of the chair and hung loose, without foundation, much like Landon felt right now.

She laid her hand on his back and rubbed silently for several minutes. She seemed to understand that he couldn't talk. That he didn't know how to feel or what to say.

Finally, he raised his head. Her eyes were rimmed in tears.

"I did all this," he said. "I made this happen."

She held his face between her palms. "You were nine years old."

"How soon can they get Cyrus out?"

"A few days maybe."

He reached for her, overwhelmed by the feelings of guilt and shame and remorse crashing inside him. He pulled her to him and they clung to each other.

Then he realized that she might go. That she'd shared her news and might leave him now.

He raised his head to look at her. "I know I left your house in the middle of the night. And we have a lot of things to talk about."

She bit her lip and nodded. He could see in her eyes how much he'd hurt her.

"But would you stay here tonight? If I asked you to?"

～

A ball of anger and empathy tossed around inside Gina's chest like a tumbleweed. She understood why Landon didn't want to be alone tonight. She'd been through the guilt of finding out that the person she'd helped convict hadn't really committed the crime. But—damn it—Landon hadn't let her explain the other night. He'd made love to her—twice—then walked out without giving her a chance to clarify the note he'd seen in her breakfast nook. She'd thought a lot about him since their meeting at the gym. A man who let his anger and emotion get the best of him, a man who wouldn't talk things out with her, was not a man she wanted to sleep with again.

Or maybe he'd just used finding the file notes as an excuse to leave. He'd gotten what he wanted and used the notes as a convenient reason to escape. Men did a lot of things to get laid. They lied. They cheated. She'd learned that lesson loud and clear from

Christopher, who hadn't been able to resist sleeping with someone else, even when he and Gina had had a healthy sex life.

But either way, Landon's emotions tonight were real. And she'd been through it. She owed it to him—as one of the few people who understood what he was going through—to stay with him. She wanted to help him get through this.

"I'll stay for a little while." She set her purse on a nearby chair. "But I'm not committing to anything longer than a couple of hours."

He heaved a sigh of relief. "Thank you."

"And I'm not sleeping in your bed with you."

"I didn't mean that—"

Gina held up her hand to stop him. She was here to help him work through his emotions, but her heart wasn't ready to talk about what had gone on between them the other night.

"I just"—he ran his fingers through his hair—"want you to stay."

She took his hand and led him to the couch, where they sat side by side. He leaned down to take off his tennis shoes and socks. She kicked off her flip-flops and placed her newly pedicured feet on the edge of the coffee table.

"Did you guys win your game tonight?" There would be plenty of time to talk about Cyrus Alexander.

Landon ran his hands up and down both thighs like he was having trouble sitting still. He nodded. "Beat that team from the Department of Insurance."

"The one with the twins?"

"Yeah. Except one of them broke his ankle falling out of a golf cart the other day."

She chuckled and placed a hand on his to still it.

He stopped for a second, then turned his palm over until his fingers intertwined with hers.

She took a deep breath, hoping she knew what he needed to hear. "This is going to be tough to get over. You know that, right?"

"How will I ever repay him?" His voice shook.

They both knew he was talking about Cyrus Alexander. Tears welled in her eyes as she thought of Nick Varnadore and the harm she'd done to him. "The sad thing is—I don't know that you can ever repay someone for something like that."

"Can he file a civil suit against me? For having him locked up all those years?"

"First of all, it wasn't you who locked him up." She ran her fingers across the back of his hand. "And I asked Suzanne about that the other day. She said most civil cases are against prosecutors who hid evidence to win their case."

"I want to apologize to his son."

Gina turned to look at him. "Really?"

" There's not a worse thing that you can do to a kid than take his dad away." He swallowed. Gina could tell how much it hurt him to talk about a kid without a dad. "You don't think I should?"

She thought about it for several long seconds. "I think it's about the toughest thing anyone could ever do. And I think you'd be a brave man to walk into a conversation like that."

"I wouldn't be any braver than a kid growing up with a dad in prison."

"What would you say to him?"

"I believe in owning up to my mistakes. And helping to convict his dad was a helluva mistake."

She couldn't argue with him there, so she settled herself against the back of the couch. One of her shoulders touched his. Their thighs ran side by side, ending with suntanned feet on the coffee table.

They sat in silence for several minutes. A siren blared somewhere in the distance. The short chime of a text came through on Landon's phone. He pulled it from his pocket and turned it off without looking at the message. He tossed the phone onto the coffee table and leaned against the back of the couch, returning to his spot next to her. Again, silence filled the space between them.

"I barely remember Grady Buchanan's daughter," Landon finally said. "And I had no idea she was even there that weekend."

Gina considered sharing that Seth Rowling had beat Maggie, but she decided against it. It would only make Landon angrier that the bastard hadn't been in jail long before the murder.

No, this was Landon's internal struggle to work through. Just as no one was able to help her work through her maze of emotions, no one would be able to help him, either. All she could do was be there with him.

They continued through the night with little bits of conversation interspersed with long periods of quiet contemplation. When she woke the next morning, she found herself on the couch, covered with a plush blanket. A pillow—presumably from Landon's bed—had been tucked under her head.

She gathered her purse, peeked in to see Landon asleep in his bed, and quietly let herself out the front door.

She pulled her cell phone out of her purse to check the time as she walked toward her car. Five missed calls from her parents' house. Three from her mom's cell phone and six from her dad's. Darn it. She hated to make her parents worry. She hit the call back icon to dial their number. Her dad had been waking up at dawn for as long as she could remember.

"Daddy?" she said as soon as he answered the phone.

"Gina? Thank God." The relief in his voice turned to anger. "Where are you?"

Her eyebrows rose, even though her father couldn't see her through the phone. "In Tallahassee . . . ?" Where else would she be? And what was he so freaked out about?

"We called you all night last night."

She checked the little switch on the side of her phone. It was on vibrate. She flipped the ringer on and put the phone back to her ear. "Why all the calls?" Anxiety rose in her chest. "Is Mom okay?"

"Yes, yes. Everything's fine. It's just when you didn't call us back, we started to worry."

"I'm sorry. I forgot to switch my phone off of vibrate after a meeting."

"I even tried to reach your landlord to see if she could check your apartment."

"I wasn't there."

"Honey, I know you're an adult now, but when you were in college you had roommates and sorority sisters and whatnot—people who knew where you were supposed to be. Down there, with you all alone, I worry about—"

"I was with Landon."

"At his house?" The anger in her father's voice gave way to a protective, more fatherly tone.

"It's not what you think, Dad."

"You're an adult, Gina. It doesn't matter what I think." She knew it had taken a lot for him to say that.

She wasn't ready to talk about the case and how the latest developments had affected Landon. She was too worn out by it all to verbalize the facts around another innocent person having spent time in prison. "I slept on the couch." She knew that answer would make her dad happy.

"So, you're not"—she could tell this was making him uncomfortable—"you're not a couple?"

"No, Daddy." And given how he'd walked out on her the other night, she knew that wasn't ever likely. "We're not a couple."

CHAPTER TWENTY-NINE

L andon took the last turn Gina had read aloud to him from the GPS in her phone. His truck bounced through the potholes on the old country road. They'd eventually have to talk about what the last few weeks meant between them—and what kind of relationship, if any, they had—but for now all he could focus on was the fact that he'd put an innocent man in prison.

"You're sure you want to do this?" she asked.

No, he wasn't sure. In fact, he was nervous as hell. But he'd already spoken to Tim Alexander's mom and asked if he could see her son. She'd been leery at first, but now here he was, pulling into their gravel driveway in rural Pascaloosa County.

In front of him, a small gray house stood alone on a tiny patch of hardened earth. Waist-high grasses surrounded the brown yard, as if waiting for a breeze that would never come in the middle of a Florida summer. At least not this far inland.

He parked his truck next to an old Dodge Dart, and both he and Gina stepped out into the yard.

The sound of a TV blared from the front of the shack, through the dilapidated screens that covered the window and the door.

"No air-conditioning?" Gina whispered. "In this heat?"

He'd come to the same conclusion she had. No one deserved to live like that. Not in the clutches of the humidity that gripped this part of the state eight or nine months out of the year.

Inside, the sound from the TV silenced, then footsteps clunked across a wooden floor.

By the time Landon had reached the porch, a tall, thin figure shadowed the inside of the screen door.

"Tim." Landon recognized the boy from the basketball game.

"Yeah." The screen door creaked open and the boy stepped outside. He wore nylon gym shorts and a red T-shirt. A tuft of yellow whiskers that looked like rug fuzz clung to his chin.

"I'm Landon." He offered his hand, but the boy didn't shake it.

"Mama said you were coming by."

"She's not here? She told me to come by sometime after three."

Tim nodded toward the driveway. "Car wouldn't start this morning. She has to wait for her friend, Carol, to bring her home from work."

Landon tried to imagine what Tim must be going through. He'd had just twenty-four hours to think about meeting Landon. And now his mother wasn't here for him to lean on, to rely on. "You okay to talk a minute? I mean, without her here?" Must seem crazy—and a little dangerous—for a high school kid to meet with him, given the fact that his dad had been convicted of killing Landon's mom.

Tim studied the horizon, not looking at Landon. "They think my dad may be innocent. This group called Morgan's Ladder— they're trying to help him."

"I know." Landon motioned toward Gina. "Gina, here, works for Morgan's Ladder." They'd agreed before they came here not to tell Tim about the latest developments about Seth Rowling. No use stirring up the kid's hope if for some reason all this fell through.

Tim's eyes darted to her, then back to him, then to Gina again, as if he wasn't sure what to say. His gaze finally rested on Landon. "I heard you came to my game the other day."

Landon nodded. "You pretty much dominated under the boards." Maybe the kid would warm up to him if they talked sports. "But your point guard needs to pass the ball more."

"Coach yells at him about that all the time."

Landon chuckled. "I can see why." He avoided looking at Gina. Maybe she thought he should stop with the small talk and get on with the real conversation. Maybe he shouldn't have brought her here.

"So, why are you here?" Tim tucked a stringy, blond strand of hair behind his ear.

"Because I know what it's like to grow up without a dad."

The boy's eyes narrowed. "What do you know about having a dad in prison?"

"Mine chose not to see me much." Landon's voice cracked. "I'm not sure which is worse."

"And you didn't have a mom." The boy's gaze met Landon's.

"Not since I was nine."

"But my dad didn't do it. He tells me that every time I see him."

Landon nodded. How did you tell a kid you were sorry for taking his dad away from him? But Cyrus's release wasn't Landon's decision and he wasn't about to say anything that could give the kid false hopes. "I hope he gets out. I hope they determine he didn't do it." He took a deep breath. "And assuming he's innocent . . ."

"He is." Tim's voice had more authority, more conviction in it than anything he'd said to this point. He turned to Gina. "Tell him my dad is innocent."

"We—"

Landon put a hand on her arm to stop her. "I came to say I'm sorry."

Tim kicked at a loose piece of wood on the porch floor. "I could never watch FSU games with other people when you were playing.

The announcers would talk about your mom. And everyone would stare at me."

"I know how it goes. I'm still the only guy I ever met whose mom had been killed." Landon sucked in a deep breath, willing himself to go on. "Add in a dad who's a drunk . . . and you're never convinced your family is as good as anyone else's." In a way, he was glad Gina was here, but he wasn't sure how he felt about baring his soul in front of her.

Tim's head whipped up, again studying the horizon, as if he didn't want to acknowledge that Landon was talking about both of them.

"Maybe we shouldn't be here without your mom home," Landon said. He took the piece of paper he'd prepared at home from his pocket. "Here's my cell number. Call me anytime, if I can help with anything."

"Why are you doing this?"

Landon had wondered that same thing many times and always came down to the same conclusion: One afternoon. Two lives altered forever. Two little boys who grew up thinking they weren't as good as everybody else. "Because your life could have been a lot different. Just like mine."

"Mama said other people lied to put my dad in prison." The boy eyed the slip of paper, but didn't take it. "If it's their fault, too, then why are you so worried about apologizing to me?"

Landon paused. How could he convey that he felt forever linked to the boy? That their lives were so similar, yet so different? "Maybe I can help with something. Maybe you'll need someone to talk to." Like Calvin had always been there for him, Landon wanted to be there for Tim.

The boy finally took the paper from his hand. Landon stepped off the porch and toward the driveway. Gina followed.

"Hey, miss," Tim called after her.

She turned toward him. "Yes?"

"Thanks for trying to get my dad out."

She cast a worried look in Landon's direction before answering. "We're doing the best we can."

"It's gonna suck if he has to stay in there."

Gina opened her mouth, then closed it again, as if she wasn't sure what to say.

"Yeah." Landon jumped in to save her. "It's gonna suck big-time."

He got in the truck and watched as Tim walked back into the house. Gina got in beside him and buckled her seat belt.

He draped both arms over the steering wheel and took a long, deep breath. "You were right."

"About what?"

"That was a really hard conversation."

She placed a hand on his thigh. "You handled it well."

He started the truck. "He needs to know he's a good kid, regardless of where his dad has been."

"Does that apply to everyone?"

He glanced at her as he turned to look behind him to back up. "Why wouldn't it?"

"'He needs to know he's a good kid, regardless of where his dad has been.'" She repeated his exact words. "Seems like it should apply to you, too."

He turned up the radio, purposefully ignoring her. He wanted to believe her, but he couldn't get into it. To begin thinking that maybe he—like Tim—was a person separate and apart from his past. Besides, his dad hadn't been locked away—without cause—in some prison for fifteen years. No, Martin had been free to roam wherever he pleased. To be a part of Landon's life or not. And he'd chosen not to. At least not until Landon's football career had heated up. At least not until the day he'd shown up drunk at Landon's high school practice, bragging to everyone that Landon was his son.

But, as tempting as it was to talk to Gina about it, he wasn't going to do it. It had been hidden away far too long. His old rule had served him well: don't talk to anyone.

～

Suzanne looked uncomfortable in her trim business suit—the same one she'd worn the day Buford Monroe had been let out of prison. Gina wondered if her boss wore that same outfit every time one of their clients was exonerated. Every other day, she was a throwback to the sixties, but when an innocent prisoner was about to be freed, she was all business.

They'd had a flurry of activity at Morgan's Ladder these last few days, all culminating with today's scheduled release of Cyrus Alexander.

Suzanne leaned toward Gina so that their conversation could be private. "You asked Landon if he wanted to be here today?"

Gina waited to answer while another Tallahassee news crew passed them, moving into position in the administrative area of the prison to capture Cyrus Alexander's release for the evening news. "He left town for a couple of days."

"He's going to have to answer the questions eventually. They're going to find him."

Gina nodded. "I know. We practiced what he was going to say. He hates all this." She waved her hand to indicate the bevy of camera crews assembled not far from them. "All the notoriety."

Suzanne scoffed. "Then he's living in the wrong town."

"I know." He was in the wrong town for a lot of reasons.

"You've been a good friend to him."

Gina let the hint of a smile cross her face. "Thanks."

"Too bad you have to leave so quickly. I think the two of you might have something between you."

She was convinced her boss was making idle chatter because she was nervous about speaking to the press. "Shouldn't you be thinking about Cyrus Alexander?"

"Ms. Holmes?" A loud male voice boomed from the doorway of one of the offices that lined the corridor. The two women turned. "We're ready for you now."

Gina followed her boss into the room where they would have a few minutes of privacy with Cyrus and his family before he was released. They were introduced to Tim's mother and a couple of aunts. Then they came to Tim.

Suzanne offered a handshake.

The boy awkwardly took Suzanne's hand in his and shook it. "Thank you." The boy's voice was thick with emotion. "For everything."

Suzanne beamed. Gina had never seen her so happy. "I'm glad we could help," Suzanne said as she turned to introduce Gina.

Tim's eyes lit up as he stepped forward, and Gina automatically wrapped her arms around the boy's scrawny body. "Tim." She wanted to make him less nervous. To somehow convey that everything was going to be okay. That his father would meld into the family like he'd never been gone. Of course, she couldn't guarantee any of those things, but she could hope.

She closed her eyes as the boy hugged her tight for several seconds. "I'm glad you're here," he said.

When they parted, Gina grabbed his hand and held it as she stood next to him.

Gina loved the surprised look on her boss's face. There wasn't much Gina could do that Suzanne didn't already know about.

Suzanne leaned toward her. "You two have met?" she asked.

"Landon went to see him a few days ago," Gina whispered. "I tagged along."

Suzanne smiled. "I knew I liked that man."

A back door to the office opened, and Cyrus Alexander, his hair cut and his civilian clothes pressed, walked in. Tim's grip on Gina's hand tightened to the point of pain, but she knew the boy was nervous. The least she could do was to live through a few excruciating seconds while the boy's world changed forever.

Cyrus's eyes glistened as he looked around the room and smiled at each person. When he got to Tim, he rushed forward. Tim dropped his grasp of Gina's hand and stood completely still, waiting for his father to cross the small room.

Cyrus wrapped his arm around his son and held tight. Tears streamed down his face. "I can't believe I get to hug you," he said.

Gina's eyes burned as she fought back her own tears. She was happy for Cyrus and for Tim, but she also imagined Nick Varnadore's family gathered in a room like this one, reuniting with the son who'd missed his high school graduation while he was behind bars. Yes, justice was important, but justice gone awry was just so . . . damn unfair.

Cyrus separated from his son and hugged the boy's mother. He kissed her on the lips—the first real kiss they'd shared in years. "You've done a good job with our boy."

She smiled at Tim and then at Cyrus. "I know," she said.

The group let out a burst of nervous laughter.

"Are we ready?" the prison official asked.

Suzanne looked to Cyrus for an answer.

He gave one quick nod of his head. "I been in here too damn long to wait any longer."

As they'd planned, Suzanne led the group out of the office and toward the camera crews that clamored for a glimpse of Cyrus. Bright lights flicked on, and news reporters, previously lounging about the corridor, straightened their jackets and tamed their hair.

Suzanne walked to the podium and cleared her throat. "It is an honor for Morgan's Ladder to be involved in the release of another innocent man from prison." She paused. "As with many such cases, Cyrus Alexander was a victim of witness misidentification, prosecutorial incompetence, and subpar police work. The killer—in this case, Mr. Seth Rowling, now deceased—hadn't been questioned by police at the time of the murder. And the only eyewitness was a nine-year-old boy."

"Where is Landon Vista today?" The reporter's voice was loud and clear. Every camera on the scene undoubtedly captured the question.

"Mr. Vista is not a part of this group." Suzanne motioned to the relatives and prison officials gathered around her.

"So where is he?" the same reporter asked.

Don't look at me. Don't look at me. Don't look at me.

Gina willed her boss not to give any nonverbal cues that Gina might know where Landon had gone. All she knew was that he'd left town. He hadn't given her any indication where he might be going or how long he'd be gone. And for that, she was grateful. If she didn't know the answers, there was no way she could give them away.

And Suzanne was too smart to give Gina away as anything other than an attorney on the team at Morgan's Ladder. "Mr. Vista is obviously remorseful that his testimony helped convict an innocent man."

Gina wondered where Landon was. How he was feeling tonight. And if Cyrus Alexander's release from prison would be an ending.

Or a beginning.

CHAPTER THIRTY

L andon stood back and watched as Calvin swatted spiderwebs away from the door of the cabin. It was pretty damn funny to watch a two-hundred-thirty-pound man afraid of a few little bugs.

Calvin called this trip to a state park on a lake in the North Georgia mountains a "guys' getaway," but Landon knew his friend had invited him as a convenient excuse to get him out of town.

Finally, his former coach wrestled the door open and they stepped over the threshold. Inside, a tiny kitchenette with an ancient gas stove took up one corner of the midsize room. A round dining table with mismatched chairs looked perfect for a game of poker, had there been more than just him and Calvin on the trip. A sliding glass door in the small living area looked out over a weathered wooden porch.

Calvin walked into the single bedroom and threw his duffle bag onto the bed. "Dibs on this room," he said.

"Dibs? What are you, ten years old?" The apartment-size couch was way too small for someone Landon's size, not that Calvin would fit on it any better.

Calvin pointed above them. "There's supposed to be a bed in the loft."

It was the least Landon could do since his friend had planned this excursion on his behalf. He climbed the rough-hewn staircase to an area just large enough for the king-size bed. A single window looked out into the tops of the trees. Exactly the kind of place that would help him relax while avoiding the chaos of the Tallahassee news media. And it felt kind of like a tree house. "It's pretty cool up here," he called down to Calvin.

"Good. 'Cuz you're not sleeping with me."

Landon dropped his bag onto the floor next to the bed and went back down the stairs, where Calvin was sliding open the back door. They stepped out onto the porch and looked over the edge of the railing. The sharp incline of the mountain meant that the porch was twenty or thirty feet off the ground, supported by stilts. Two rocking chairs looked out over the forest.

"Rachel would love this place," Calvin said.

Landon looked over the edge of the porch again. The height gave him the heebie-jeebies, which was stupid, so he challenged himself to lean out over the edge even farther. "You should have brought her with us."

"Nah. Guys' weekend away. No girls allowed."

"I know what you're doing."

Calvin lifted the lid to inspect the grill that sat behind the rocking chairs. "Yeah? What's that?"

"You're getting me out of town while the whole Cyrus Alexander thing goes down." Landon wasn't sure what he'd have done otherwise, but he sure as hell didn't want to be in Tallahassee while the media focused on it.

"Maybe." Calvin closed the lid and dusted his hands on his shorts. "Would that be such a bad thing?"

"I owe you one."

Calvin laughed. "No, bud. I've known you for a long time. You owe me several." He disappeared back inside the cabin.

Within minutes, Calvin produced a cooler filled with thick steaks and a casserole dish of Rachel's homemade scalloped potatoes.

Landon turned on the oven and finished unpacking the car while Calvin lit the grill on the cabin's elevated back porch.

An hour later they were in the rocking chairs, each with a cigar and a cold beer, as the sun lowered toward a distant mountaintop. Landon knew he didn't deserve this peacefulness.

"What do you suppose Cyrus Alexander's doing right now?" He exhaled a cloud of smoke into the treetops, trying to feel as relaxed as he knew he was supposed to be.

"Smokin' a cigar. Drinkin' a beer." Calvin's chair creaked as he rocked forward and back. "What time was his release?"

"Three o'clock." Landon had looked it up on the Internet. Had become obsessed with the goings-on of the day. He was responsible, after all. Responsible for putting Cyrus in prison.

He wondered where Cyrus would spend the night. How soon he'd get to see his son. How the two of them would create the beginnings of a relationship. What the first meal he'd eat would be.

Beside him, Calvin seemed to understand he needed time to be alone with his thoughts. They sat silently for several minutes. In the distance, an owl hooted.

"You know," Calvin finally said, "you need to get over all this as soon as you can. Quit blaming yourself for everything that happened."

Landon stood to rummage through the cooler for another beer. "You don't think I should feel bad about sending a man to prison?" He'd already slipped into an endless sea of blame and culpability. He'd been nine years old at the time of the trial. Old enough to understand—at least vaguely—what was going on. Old enough to be at least partially responsible for the outcome of the proceedings. "How can I not be responsible for that?"

Calvin stood and walked toward Landon, pressing him against the railing. Landon wasn't sure if he was doing it on purpose or not.

"Just because one life is ruined doesn't mean you have to ruin yours," Calvin said.

Landon tensed with surprise and placed both hands on Calvin's massive chest, pressing him backward. "You need to back off." He glanced downward to the forest floor two stories below.

"God gave you a million things to be thankful for. You're a good-looking boy—a *white* boy—with a killer arm. You didn't pay a dime for college. You've got a good job. Do you know how lucky you are?" Calvin pushed closer to him. "Do you?"

The weathered wood of the railing creaked from Landon's weight pressing against it. "Why have you gone apeshit all of a sudden?" He tried to push Calvin away, but the big man was built like a sequoia.

"Do you know how stupid it would be to let this guilt ruin your life?"

"Do you know how stupid it would be if this railing broke?"

Calvin stared at him with eyes more intense than Landon had ever seen them, even during their biggest games. Their whites glowed against the setting sun while the dark centers burned the color of onyx. Finally, he backed away and bent to get another beer.

Landon skittered away from the edge and wiped his mouth with the back of his hand. "You're a crazy son of a bitch."

"You'd better not let this ruin your life."

Landon's breath came in short bursts. His body hummed with the flow of adrenaline. He grabbed his bottle of beer and took a big swig, mainly to kill time while he decided whether to try and throw the big guy over the edge of the balcony. Calvin stood with his back to Landon, looking out into the woods.

"It's not going to be easy to get over this," Landon said into the darkness.

"But that's my point. If anyone's up for it, you are." Calvin spun around, stomped to the sliding glass door, and threw aside the vertical blinds. He stalked inside.

Landon stayed on the darkened porch by himself. The smell of his cigar in the ashtray sickened him now. Now that the camaraderie of friendship had disappeared, the cigar no longer held its appeal.

What if Cyrus couldn't find work? Even with his murder conviction erased, he was still a man who'd spent almost two decades in prison. What kind of marketable skills did a person like that have? Not to mention the burglary conviction he'd had before Mama had died.

What if Cyrus didn't fit in well with his family? Maybe it would be like Christmas—when the buildup was sometimes better than the actual event. What if they didn't get along, and he ended up out on the streets?

He felt himself spiraling downward. Someplace he didn't want to be. He turned and looked inside. Maybe Calvin could say something to convince him this situation sucked a little bit less than he thought it did right now.

Through the slit in the vertical blinds, he saw Calvin in the tiny kitchen, washing the dishes they'd used for dinner.

Landon walked inside and grabbed a dish towel. Calvin glanced at him, but didn't say anything. They worked side by side for a couple of minutes.

Finally, Landon spoke. "So how do I keep from feeling guilty? I mean, other than being such a good-looking white guy?" He grinned at his friend.

Calvin jammed the pan he'd just washed into Landon's gut. "Fuck you."

Landon took the pan to dry. Damn Calvin, for getting the front of his shirt all wet. "You don't think I should feel guilty." It was a challenge more than a question.

His coach pulled the stopper from the drain and turned to face him. "I think there's nothing you can do to change the past. You can mope around feeling sorry for yourself—which doesn't do anybody any good—or you can admit how bad it sucks that it happened and then get on with your life." He grabbed the dish towel from Landon and dried his hands. "Your life. Your choice."

"You're a regular Dr. Phil." He appreciated Calvin's concern, but the guy code didn't allow him to say that out loud.

"You can sit around feeling sorry for yourself. Or you can start building a life with Gina." Calvin tossed the towel back at him and leaned against the counter. "And, believe me—I know which choice I'd make."

Landon scoffed. "There isn't going to be a life with Gina."

"Then you're even more screwed up than I thought."

"The last thing I need is something else complicating my life."

"Then I feel sorry for you, man." Calvin walked toward his bedroom.

"Why's that?"

"Because you didn't just ruin Cyrus Alexander's life that day. You ruined yours, too."

~

Gina paced her living room, waiting for Landon's arrival. It had been two days since Cyrus Alexander had been released from prison, but she'd only spoken to Landon via text since that time. During their last exchange, from this morning, he'd asked if he could see her tonight.

What did she say to a man whose life she had changed so much? How did she find out if they had a future together? If their feelings for each other were free to explore now that the case was resolved?

She peeked out the front window again and then went to the kitchen to check on the lasagna. The heat from the oven blasted into her face when she opened the door. Cheese and tomato sauce bubbled perfectly near the edge of the glass dish. The garlic bread heated on the shelf above it.

She wished she could be as certain of the outcome of this evening as she was about the taste of her dinner.

A knock pounded on the door. She jumped so hard the oven door slammed shut. She rushed to the apartment door and opened it.

Outside, Landon stood on the stoop looking disheveled. And sexy as hell. He looked like someone who could use a confidante, and she hoped that she was the one he turned to.

"Come in," she said, stepping aside to give him room.

He came inside just enough for her to close the door behind him. They stood in awkward silence.

"So," she finally said. "You're back in town."

"How was it?"

She knew he was talking about Cyrus Alexander's release. "Happy. Sad. Kind of nerve-racking hoping the media didn't ask about you."

He shoved his hands in his pockets. "Did they?"

"Yes, but Suzanne did a good job of steering them away from the topic."

He nodded and the awkward silence returned. God, she hoped this wasn't what it had come to between them.

She motioned toward the kitchen. "I made lasagna."

His gaze rose to hers and held there for several seconds. "'Second best in the country.'"

Her chest warmed inside. He was quoting their conversation from that first night they'd met.

He made quotation marks in the air as he continued. "'My mom makes the best, but I use her recipe.'"

She smiled. "You remember."

He took a deep breath, as if he was thinking about what he'd say next. "I wish I'd known that night what kind of trouble I was jumping into."

"That trouble would have come along whether you'd met me or not." She took his arm and guided him into the kitchen so she could check on the bread.

"Maybe I'm not talking about Cyrus Alexander."

She looked at him with a "we're not going to do this now" expression, then nodded toward the fridge. "Will you get the salads and dressing out? There's a bottle of ranch in the door." She switched off the oven, then leaned down to get the bread and lasagna out while he set the rest of the food on the table. "Go ahead and sit down," she said. "We'll let the lasagna cool off while we eat our salads."

She didn't have a basket in the apartment, so she put the bread in a mixing bowl and covered it with a napkin to keep it warm. She noticed that he remained standing.

"So where did you and Calvin go?" she asked as she joined him near the table, which she'd already set.

He pulled her chair out, just as he'd done before. "Some state park up in the Georgia mountains. It was nice."

She handed him the salad dressing to use first. "So what's he think about all this?" She wasn't sure she knew what "this" was, but she'd see how Landon answered.

"We're guys. We don't really talk about stuff." He reached into the bowl and took out a piece of bread.

"You just sat there and stared at each other the entire time?"

"Well, he did try to throw me off a porch that was about three stories up . . ." He took a bite of his salad.

"Why?"

"I think he was trying to prove a point."

"Which was . . . ?"

Landon shrugged. "I don't remember."

"Guys are so weird." She got up to cut the lasagna.

They fell into a friendly conversation that—thank God—didn't have a lot of tension to it: when he'd be traveling next, what the records were in their volleyball league, what classes she had when she returned to Nashville in the fall.

They'd been finished with their meal for almost an hour when she finally stood and started clearing the table. He got up to help her. They worked side by side until the kitchen was clean.

"I think we're done," she said as she bent to place the plastic-covered pasta onto the bottom shelf of the refrigerator. She stood as she closed the door. He was right beside her in the tiny galley kitchen, wiping his hands on the dish towel. He turned. His green eyes seemed darker, filled with emotion.

He reached up and slid his hand gently down her arm. "I'm not sure . . ." He didn't finish his sentence. His other hand rose and caressed her cheek.

Her heart raced. There was so much uncertainty between them. So much that had been unexplored and unspoken. So many possibilities now that the Cyrus Alexander case was no longer between them.

She took a step toward him and raised her hands to his shoulders. His arms wrapped around her waist as he pulled her toward him. Their lips met, tentative at first, then with more certainty. He pressed her back against the narrow wall at the end of the kitchen until she could feel the solidness of his body up and down her own.

He dropped his head to trail kisses along her jawline. "I don't know what's gonna happen after tonight." He nipped at her earlobe. "But I don't want to think about that right now."

Her body yearned for him, but she needed to protect her heart. To protect it from the one person who could hurt it. "I'm okay with that." She leaned her head to the side, giving him access to the most sensitive part of her neck.

His breath warmed her skin as he chuckled. "I'd hoped for a little more enthusiasm."

Her breathing was quick and shallow. All she wanted was to feel his skin on hers. She pulled the bottom of his shirt from his shorts and feathered her fingers across his abdomen. "I have . . . lots of enthusiasm." Her voice was low and husky.

"Oh, yeah?"

She dropped her hand so she could stroke his erection with her fingers on the outside of his pants. A low moan escaped his chest.

She smiled. She was pretty sure she'd gotten her point across.

CHAPTER THIRTY-ONE

Landon had to slow this down. He wasn't sure if he'd ever get to make love to Gina again after tonight, and he sure as hell wasn't going to rush through it. But God, he loved the way she writhed between him and the wall. Soaking up his touch. Touching him in all the right places.

Her hands moved to the placket of his shirt. Her lips followed her fingers, licking and nibbling at each inch of newly exposed flesh as she unbuttoned it. It was slow, agonizing torture as his body ached to plunge inside her.

A lot of nights, he'd lain in bed wondering if he'd have the chance to even just touch her again, be touched by her. Knowing that the touch of any other woman wouldn't feel the same. This was Gina. The one he'd remember forever.

She peeled his shirt off his shoulders and tossed it onto the cabinet. She was breathing as quickly as he was, and the way she looked at his naked chest made him want her even more. She ran her hands over his shoulders and down his biceps like she wouldn't ever be able to touch them enough.

But he wanted to touch her, too. He grasped the bottom of her shirt and pulled it over her head, then reveled at the beautiful mounds of flesh that spilled out over the top of her black, lacy bra. As he took in the sight of her, she reached up and—with a mischievous look that was sexy as hell—unfastened her bra in the front, then arched away from the wall as she let it fall to the floor behind her. The action pressed her breasts closer to him. He coddled them in his hands, running his thumbs over her hardened nipples.

Her eyelids drifted closed as she offered her breasts to him. God, she was beautiful. He'd hoped coming over here tonight that this would happen. That he'd get to hold her and make love to her and hold her some more.

What he didn't know was what might happen after tonight. But for now he wasn't going to think about it.

He didn't want to think at all.

~

Gina shivered at the feel of Landon's tongue on the side of her neck. His thumbs drew tiny circles with her nipples. Her breath came out in short, shallow bursts. Her hands instinctively went to his rear end, pressing his body toward her as she ached to feel him inside her.

His lips returned to her mouth, and he kissed her again—a long, passionate kiss that left her wanting more—then he took her hand and led her to the bedroom. A stream of evening light filtered in around the edge of the curtains, creating a dusky room that let them see each other's bodies in the light shadow. He drew her toward him, unbuttoning her shorts as he feathered kisses along her mouth, her jaw, her neck.

When her pants and underwear were gone, he gently guided her to the edge of the bed, where he sat and pulled her toward him, laving one of her nipples with his tongue, then the other, as she stood before him. His hands caressed her breasts, then her rib cage, then her hips, as if he couldn't get enough of her. His appreciation for her body made her feel like a priceless treasure. A goddess.

One of his hands slid to the inside of her knee and glided upward—his touch tender on the sensitive skin on the inside of her leg. His mouth returned to her breast as his fingers glided toward their destination. She marveled at his touch.

"Lay beside me," he said as he gently pulled her toward him. He guided her next to him and pulled himself up until they were side by side. Those olive-green eyes held her gaze as if nothing else in the world mattered. As if this was the moment she'd been working toward all her life. She tried to read his thoughts—to understand what those distinctive eyes conveyed—but all she saw was passion.

Slowly, he lowered his face to hers. His lips caressed hers as his hand continued its exquisite exploration of her body. His hand parted her legs and softly touched the most tender part of her body. He massaged her nub, moving his finger in tiny circles as her hips pressed into his touch, wanting more.

His mouth left hers as he trailed kisses down her neck, along her collarbone, and onto one breast. His finger never left her middle, gently massaging her as the rhythm of her hips met his touch. His mouth left her breast, and he slid himself off the bed and over her as his lips traveled down her rib cage. His teeth nipped at her hip bone. His tongue glided along the inside of her thigh, beckoning her to open her legs to him even more.

When the soft firmness of his tongue first touched her most sensitive part, she sucked in a breath. She'd known what he was about to do, but that first gentle-but-firm touch almost undid her. She wanted that feeling to last forever.

His tongue moved rhythmically across her nub. He stretched his long fingers around each of her hips, pulling her toward him, positioning himself at her core, focusing all his attentions on making her feel good. Her hips rose to meet him, her body involuntarily responding to the exquisite feeling with a thrust-and-retreat pattern as the pressure inside her built. She ran her fingers through that dark, curly hair. His eyes were closed as his tongue continued to pleasure her.

The pressure mounted inside her—building and building until it crashed in one final explosion, like an ocean wave building momentum before crashing against a seawall. Short gasps of pleasurable relief escaped her, but she was lost in the feeling. The sounds seemed to come from someone else. She was lost in what he'd done for her.

His tongue stayed with her until she'd quieted, then he pulled himself up to lie beside her, kissing her body as he traveled upward.

"I want to make you feel that good," she whispered as soon as his face was even with hers. Her hands traveled to the zipper of his shorts and unzipped them.

One corner of his mouth tipped up. "I think you're about to."

Her hands dipped inside his underwear and her fingers wrapped around him. So hard. So manly. So . . . Landon.

He rolled away from her and slid his wallet from his back pocket, took out a condom, and removed his shorts and plaid boxers. She took the wrapper from him and opened it, then watched his face as she slid the sheath onto him. His eyes drifted closed and he sucked in a long breath as her fingers encircled him. She knew she would treasure this moment—these intimate moments with him—for the rest of her life.

He rolled over and positioned himself on top of her, protecting her from his weight with his arms anchored beside her head. She opened for him, eager to have the feel of him inside her. The lubrication of the condom allowed him to slide in with one smooth motion, filling her up. Making her whole. In this moment, everything seemed right in the world. Everything and everybody was exactly where it was meant to be. Her entire body responded to him—aching for him, welcoming him—as he thrust inside her.

The pressure at her core built again. Her hands traveled first to the muscles on his back, then to his straining biceps on either side of her head. She lifted her knees toward the ceiling, offering him more. Wanting him to take anything from her he wanted to take.

He lowered his head next to hers and thrust into her with one final push as he came inside her. Her own body reacted to the fullness of him. She shattered at the feel of his final thrust inside her, as he shared his most intimate moment. Her breathy gasps filled the air around them as his hips ground into her.

When their bodies had stilled, he raised his head and looked into her eyes. His thumb trailed down her cheekbone as he studied her face. His chest heaved in deep, quick bursts.

He pulled her toward him, wrapping his arm around her. She rested her head on his chest, never wanting the cocoon of Landon's scent and touch to be disturbed. They lay like that for several silent minutes before either of them spoke.

He stroked her shoulder with his fingertips. "So you're leaving in a week." His voice rumbled in his chest beneath her ear.

Gina held her breath. She had no idea what he might be thinking. No idea whether what she felt toward him was mutual. "Yes."

"You know, I'm always going to remember you."

Her eyes shot open.

He was going to remember her?

Remember her?

A steel door inside her chest snapped shut, encasing her heart. Protecting it from whatever he might say next.

She'd hoped he would talk about them seeing each other after she left. How they might get together on long weekends. But instead, he would always *remember* her.

She was something from his past.

And she hadn't even left yet.

CHAPTER THIRTY-TWO

Gina lay there, stunned at Landon's words. They were close physically—his arm tucking her against his bare body, her smoothly shaved leg draped over his hairy ones—but they couldn't be further apart emotionally.

He cupped her shoulder in his hand and shook it gently as he nuzzled her hair. "So why aren't you saying anything?"

Because if she spoke, her voice would crack.

Because she wasn't sure what would come out.

Because she might cry.

He seemed to understand that he needed to fill the silence. "I mean, I didn't even know you a couple of months ago and now . . . a lot has changed."

She nodded, hoping that would suffice as a response.

"And I guarantee Cyrus Alexander is going to remember you."

She closed her eyes and nodded again.

He kissed the top of her head. "I wish you were in town for longer than just the summer."

Well, at least he'd given her that. At least he'd acknowledged—in some minute little way—that there was something between them.

They lay in silence for another couple of minutes—long enough for her to at least pretend to get over the sting of his words.

"So now that you've gotten Cyrus out of prison," he said. "Don't you think it's time you got on with your own life?"

She lifted her head to look at him. "What do you mean it's time to get on with my own life?" Her life was all planned. Finish law school, then a career of work to get innocent people out of prison.

"Your . . . entire life revolves around this stuff. Like every step you're ever going to take is because of the fact that you sent a kid to juvi. Like you don't have a choice."

Her mouth fell open. "It's not like I stole some kid's lunch money or dented in someone's car. I sent a kid to *prison*."

He tossed her a no-shit kind of look. Of course, he knew how she felt. He'd sent a man to prison for much longer than she had.

"And he's never going to be the same because of it." She felt like she was stating the obvious. It sounded stupid as soon as it had left her mouth.

"That doesn't mean every decision you ever make has to be shaped by it. Is there going to be a day when you just don't think about it?"

She charged out of bed, her anger flaring. "This isn't something you just *get over*. I mean, have you already gotten over what you did to Cyrus Alexander?" She yanked on her underwear. "He hasn't even been out of prison for a week."

He rolled up on his elbow in her bed. "I will never be able to make up for what I did to that man. We both know that."

"Then why are you giving me so much shit about this?"

"Because it's like you're punishing yourself. Like you want to remind yourself of the mistake you made. Every time you walk into a prison. Every time you consider taking on the case of some guy who may be innocent. Like some little self-imposed punishment that you somehow enjoy."

"It's called paying penitence." She yanked on her shorts and glared at him. "It's called being responsible for the things you've done."

"And how about forgiveness? Or did they not teach that in Sunday school, too?"

She stilled. It was like she'd been slapped in the face. Her eyes narrowed. Something in her body clicked. A switch turned from defense to offense as her fight mechanism kicked in. "How can you be so sure about what I need in my life?" Her voice shook, but she knew she had to get this out. "When your own life is such a screwed-up mess?"

He rolled on his back and stared at the ceiling. "I will have to work every day for the rest of my life to forgive myself for what I did to Cyrus Alexander. And to Tim. And to the whole family. I want to figure out a way I can help them." He paused. "But at least I'm going to try to forgive myself. That seems like a much healthier place to be than"—he motioned toward her—"than whatever you've got going on in that head of yours."

"You think I'm messed up? Me?" She bent down, retrieved her bra, and put it on as she spoke. "You stay in a town that worships you, yet all you want is to be left alone." She pulled her shirt over her head. "And as much as you hate it, you won't open your life up to any more possibilities than living in Tallahassee." She stopped, knowing if she continued, she would hurt Landon far worse than any lineman ever had, but she couldn't help herself. "Waiting around for your dad to love you."

CHAPTER THIRTY-THREE

Landon hurdled out of Gina's bed and stood toe-to-toe with her. No one had ever challenged him about wanting his father's love. Not Boomer. Not Ricardo. Not even Calvin.

His jaw tightened. "And who the hell are you to be telling me how to run my life?"

"Other than the woman you just made love to?"

He glared at her, wishing he could tell her that what they'd had between them was just sex, but that wouldn't be true. Of course, their lovemaking had meant something. It had meant everything. But she was talking about his dad here. All tactics were fair game. "Just because I have sex with you doesn't mean you get to pass judgment on my relationship with my father."

Her facial expression changed in slow motion, as if her natural reaction gradually won out over her desire to cover it up. Her eyes glistened. Her cheeks flushed. She was a fighter, and he'd dealt a damaging blow.

"You can't wait around for your father for the rest of your life." Her voice cracked.

He knew he'd hurt her, but she'd chosen to ignore his statement about their relationship. "I don't want to talk about my father."

"And maybe that's why you've lived with this for so long. Because you're the almighty Landon Vista." She waved her hands in the air. "No one is going to challenge you. No one is going to question your motives.

And you don't have the balls to look in the mirror and tell yourself what you're really doing with your life."

Landon searched the floor for his underwear and pants and pulled them on. "I don't have to take this from you."

She threw her hands in the air. "Yes, because nobody ever dares to challenge Landon Vista."

Except for her. She challenged him with just about everything she did. "And what is it you think I need to be challenged about?"

Gina stood and faced him, like a worthy opponent preparing for the final attack. "If your father was going to love you back, don't you think he would have done it by now?"

He bent down slowly and picked up his shirt, using it as an excuse to regain his composure. He would not let her get to him like this.

He pulled the shirt on and buttoned it without looking at her. Finally, he raised his eyes to meet her gaze. "Good-bye, Gina. Good luck back in Nashville."

~

Gina's bottom lip trembled—more in anger than in sadness—but she would not cry in front of him. She marched toward her front door, eager to get him out of her apartment before she broke down in tears.

But if this was the last time she was going to see Landon, she wanted to at least get everything out in the open. To at least show him what he'd lost. To make him understand what might have happened between them.

She stopped and turned as her hand rested on the doorknob. "I thought I was in love with you." Her jaw tightened. "Past tense."

Sadness and surprise seemed to swirl together in his eyes. But she didn't want to be at the mercy of those eyes. Not those damn eyes.

She opened the door and stepped aside to let him pass. "Good-bye, Landon."

CHAPTER THIRTY-FOUR

Landon slid down in the seat of his truck to wait for the few people milling around the freshly dug grave to get in their cars. He hadn't been to Horseshoe Lake Cemetery in seven years. Not after his last visit had caused such a ruckus and ended up as a feature story on Florida Sports TV.

But now, with everything that had changed over the last few weeks, he'd felt a need to come here. To have some quiet time to himself in the spot that had cradled Mama's body for the last fifteen years.

Finally, the funeral on the other side of the cemetery ended. The distant mourners got in their cars and drove away. He opened the door of his truck and walked toward his mother's grave.

Like the people who'd just left, he knew how it felt to leave a loved one here. He'd done that same thing, years ago, as a scared little boy not sure of where he'd live.

He'd felt different as a teen, when he'd come here on his own, once he was old enough to drive and had access to a car. By then he'd realized the depths of his father's disinterest in raising a child. He'd learned to recognize the looks of pity from his classmates. And that hard lump of anger in his gut had started to grow.

Come to think of it, since the funeral, he'd never come here with anyone else. Yes, that reporter had snapped pictures of him visiting Mama's grave on her birthday his senior year in high school. That was before he'd learned what kind of damage the media could do. When he'd been a sought-after high school recruit, but still an ignorant kid. But it wasn't like he'd brought the reporter here with him. No, he'd never shared this place with anyone. He'd never felt like anyone would understand what he felt when he was here.

But now there was Gina. And the hard lump of anger in his gut had started to chip away on the edges.

He reached Mama's grave and ran his fingers over the top of the humble marker. It felt hot in the Florida sun. He traced the first letter of her name with his finger, remembering how proud he'd been when he'd first learned to write both their names.

What would his mother have thought of everything that had happened the last couple of months? She'd have been angry, for sure, that Cyrus Alexander had spent so many years in prison. But she would have forgiven Landon for what he'd done to help send Cyrus there. She was that kind of woman. Kind. Forgiving. Loving.

So if she could forgive Landon for what he'd done to Cyrus, could he forgive himself? He tossed the thought around in his head like a couple of kids playing catch. He'd have to think about that one awhile.

She had never let him understand, when she was alive, that his father could have helped support them instead of ignoring his obligation to pay child support. That they didn't have to live in squalor in the back of the country store. She'd protected him from that knowledge as fiercely as a mother bear protects her young.

If his mother could muscle through life—loving and determined and kind as she was—while knowing that Martin had tossed them away, could Landon do the same? Could he, like his mother, accept what life had handed him and go on without the big lump of anger in his gut?

He thought about Gina and how she'd started him down the path of looking at things differently. How she'd forced him to examine the question that had lurked in his subconscious for years: Did he stay in Tallahassee waiting for his father's love? Yes, he'd been mad as hell when she made him face the truth. But after a few days of thinking about it, he knew she was right. He did need to move on with his life.

A slight smile crept across his face as he looked at the tombstone. "You would like her, Mama," he said out loud.

The breeze, almost nonexistent in this part of Florida in the summer, kicked up, tousling his hair, just as his mother had done when he was a kid. Like a message from her, it cooled his scalp and comforted him.

Something shifted in the world. Or maybe it was in his heart. Either way, it felt like his mother was releasing him. Like she'd watched him with Gina and she approved. There was now another woman to care for him. Another woman for him to love. Another woman who would be the most important person in his life. He looked around at the trees, thickly draped with Spanish moss, and wondered if he'd ever felt so much at peace as he did right now, in this place. He took a deep, contented breath and knew that the smell of confederate jasmine would always be the scent of peace for him.

But what would his mother think of his relationship with Martin? Would she want him to keep fighting for his father's love? Had *she* accepted the fact that Martin wasn't ever going to be there for her or the child they'd created together? She had to have accepted that fact. Otherwise, wouldn't Landon have picked up on her bitterness? She was the kindest, most loving person he knew. She couldn't have faked that.

He drew in a deep breath, the smell of the jasmine filling his lungs, then exhaled. If his mother had accepted the way his father had treated them, then maybe he could, too.

He turned as another car rumbled down the gravel drive into the cemetery. He would have liked to have spent more time here with her, but he didn't want anyone to see him. He knew he stood out. Not many men were his size.

He rushed toward his truck and got in, hoping the newcomers didn't recognize him. Maybe he'd come back again soon. Maybe he'd bring Gina.

But for now, there was someone else in Pascaloosa County he needed to see.

CHAPTER THIRTY-FIVE

Cyrus Alexander looked much older than Landon had expected, but then, he guessed prison could do that to a man.

"Tim." Landon nodded to the teen as he walked up the steps of their porch. His heart pounded, but he found some comfort in the fact that at least he'd met Tim before. Had thought maybe there was a connection between them.

Landon stood tall. Of all the times he needed to take responsibility for his own actions, this was one of the most important. He held out his hand to the older man. "Mr. Alexander." As often as he'd thought about this moment in recent days, he still wasn't sure what he should say.

Cyrus eyed him warily, but eventually stuck his hand out to meet Landon's. It was rough and calloused. Landon wondered how he'd spent his time in prison. Lifting weights? Working a job?

"I"—Landon cleared his throat—"I don't know what to say." His hands crossed over his heart—not a planned motion, but one that might at least show Cyrus how sincere he was. "I'm sorry, man. I know that'll never be enough for what I did." His gaze dropped to the weathered floorboards of the porch and his hands fell to his sides. There was nothing he could say that could make up for the time Cyrus had lost. "I'm sorry."

Cyrus was silent for several seconds. Tim shuffled his feet nervously. Landon looked up, wanting to see the expression on Cyrus's face, but it told him nothing.

Finally, Cyrus spoke. His Southern drawl was more pronounced—even for someone from Pascaloosa County—than Landon had expected. "I don't think it's your fault, son."

"But I testified—"

Cyrus held his hand up. Landon immediately stilled.

"I hold the police responsible." Cyrus's accent elongated each word. "And Maggie Buchanan. She's the one who never told 'em her boyfriend was in town that weekend. She was more concerned with her Daddy not finding out"—his voice cracked—"than with an innocent man going to prison."

"We saw a picture of her boyfriend," Tim said. "He looked just like the pictures we have from when Dad was that age."

Dad.

Landon was glad Tim could say that word with his father standing right beside him. "I'm still so sorry." Both of their lives would have been so much different . . .

"You were nine years old." Cyrus walked to the edge of the porch, his back to Landon and Tim. "What's done is done."

Landon was grateful for Cyrus's graciousness. This could have been a scene that was a helluva lot uglier than this one had been. "Can I loan you some money?" He didn't want to insult the guy, but he'd been in prison for fifteen years. What kind of money could he make in there? "Until you get on your feet?" He'd sure as hell rather give any extra he had to Cyrus than invest it in one of his own father's crazy schemes.

Cyrus shook his head and turned to face Landon. "I appreciate what you done, coming by to see Tim and all. That means a lot."

"Tim has my cell number." Landon motioned to the boy. "Please.

Call me if I can ever help with anything. If you just want to talk . . . or yell at me or something."

"This is all so new." Cyrus scrubbed a hand down his face. "I don't know what to do. What to say. How to feel." He stuck his hands in his pockets. "For now, I just want to put that whole part of my life behind me."

"I understand." Landon patted Tim on the shoulder. "I'll always be there for you." He looked at Cyrus as he headed to the stairs of the porch. "For both of you."

Cyrus gave a single nod in reply.

Landon let out a gusty breath as he walked toward his truck. He knew how Cyrus felt. How there was no precedent here. No road map to tell him how to feel or what to think.

All he knew was that he was glad he'd looked the guy in the eyes.

Glad he'd said he was sorry.

Glad that Tim had his father back.

~

Gina followed her dad down the stairs of her apartment, lugging the last of the boxes they had to load into the back of his SUV.

Her mother followed behind, carrying the pot of ivy she'd given Gina the first day she'd moved into her dorm freshman year. "You're sure you don't need to say good-bye to Landon before you leave town?"

Gina tried to ignore the worried-mom look cast her way. "We've pretty much said everything we need to say to each other."

"Suzanne seemed to think there might be some"—her mom glanced at her dad—"loose ends between the two of you."

"Yeah, well. I don't discuss my personal life with my boss." *Liar.* "Isn't that what you always told me, Daddy? Work is work and your personal life is personal?"

Her father held his hands up. "I'm staying out of this one."

Gina rolled her eyes and changed the subject. "So I'll leave first thing Saturday morning." Her parents had made a trip down to take a carload of her belongings home.

"You sure you'll have room for the rest of your stuff?" her mom asked.

"Yes, Mama."

"And you'll get your oil changed before you leave?" Her mom's voice pitched a little higher.

"Dad . . ." Both she and her father knew it was a plea to get his wife to stop mothering her so much.

Her mother took her hand. "I just don't want you to get hurt, honey."

Oh, great. They were back to talking about Landon again. She didn't want to talk about him. Not after she'd lain in bed every night this week thinking about their final conversation the other night after they'd made love. "I need to get going." She motioned toward her car. "I told Suzanne I'd be in by ten."

Her mother hugged her as if she wouldn't ever see her again.

Her father walked around the car and hugged her, too. "You've done good work here, you know that?"

"Yes, Daddy." She would always be her father's little girl.

She waved as they exited the driveway and then got in her car to head to work. Though she'd been here only a couple of months, she was going to miss this place. Its sprawling live oaks and rolling hills would always be a part of her.

She still needed to think of a way to thank Suzanne for the experiences she'd given her. And to tell her that she'd decided not to pursue a career in this line of work. She'd done a lot of thinking about what Landon had said. She'd always known that her guilt over sending Nick Varnadore to prison had colored everything she did, but until Landon, it had never seemed like it was wrong. It had been her penitence. Her payback to the world.

At least until Landon had shown her that she needed to learn to forgive herself. That it couldn't color every decision she made.

The forgiveness would take a while, but at least she could make different choices, starting today. She'd always be grateful that Landon had changed that trajectory of her life.

Suzanne's Audi pulled into the small parking lot right in front of Gina's SUV.

"You're getting here late," Gina said as the two got out of their cars next to each other. Her boss was normally here by seven in the morning.

"I was over at the prosecutor's office." Suzanne opened her car's back door and took out the leather messenger bag. Gina wondered if the pistol was still in there.

"They said they're done with this." Suzanne pulled a clear plastic bag from her satchel and held it out in front of her. "I think you'll know what to do with it."

CHAPTER THIRTY-SIX

Landon's body thrummed with energy, like it knew he was about to have the two most important conversations of his life. First with his father. And then with Gina.

But his father had arrived late, and now here was Gina, standing on his doorstep like a life preserver tossed to a drowning man. Chaos and emotion swirled inside his apartment, but there she was—the hurricane who'd become his safe haven, his rock—standing on his front porch, at precisely the time he'd invited her to be here. Tendrils of hair, typically swept back into a tidy ponytail, fringed her face. Her normally strong body seemed ready to collapse. He'd never seen her look so tired.

"I'm so sorry about this," he said as she stood on his doorstep. "I really want to talk to you. But it needs to be . . . after." He motioned with his head to where his father stood behind him, inside his condo. "This needs to be a father/son thing. So can you come back? Maybe in five minutes?"

She peered around him until she could see who was in the living room. Her eyebrows rose. "I've . . . got something to give you." She held a clear plastic bag in her hand, but he couldn't tell what was in it. "I was going to mail it from Nashville, but when you called me, I figured I'd bring it with me." She paused, as if making sure she understood the situation inside his condo. "I can give it to you after you talk to your dad."

He knew she was the one person who might comprehend what was about to take place. Hell, she'd been a catalyst for it. And most of all, she'd said she loved him. Or at least she *had* loved him at one time. He wanted to believe that whole business about how people in love were there for each other.

Because she looked like she needed him. And he sure as hell needed her.

"You can come back in a few minutes?" He hoped she saw the pleading look in his eyes.

She jabbed a thumb toward the street. "I'll go get a Starbucks. You want anything?"

He shook his head.

"Bye, Mr. Vista." She leaned to look around Landon. "Good to see you again."

Landon closed the door as soon as she'd gone and turned to face his father.

"If you're still not sleeping with her, you sure as hell ought to be." Martin chuckled. "Cute thing like that comes to your condo, she's looking for one thing." His fist pumped the air in a crude gesture. "A smart man would give her exactly what she wants."

Landon took a deep breath. He was *not* going to let his dad change the subject. And the disgusting way he talked about Gina fueled his courage to go on with what he'd planned to say. He ran his fingers through his hair, not sure where to start.

Finally, he decided to let everything inside him pour out without worrying about how manly he sounded or how needy he might appear. "I have waited my whole life"—he paused for a second, trying to stop the quavering in his voice—"for you to love me. For you to decide that a relationship with me was more important than whatever's in the bottle you happen to be drinking from at the time. But you know what? I'm done." He slashed his arm through the air. "I'm tired of waiting for that to happen."

"Is this all because of that damn Cyrus Alexander business? Why you still all over me when they know who done it now?"

"We're not talking about that here."

"Then what are we talking about?"

Landon's entire body shook with emotion. His whole life had been a series of events all headed toward this moment. And his father still didn't get it. "We're talking about me, Dad. The son who's waited . . . for years . . . to hear you say that you loved me. That you cared about me. That you made sure my homework was done and that I wore sunscreen in the summer and that when I looked up in the stands during a Little League, you were there."

"Didn't your aunt and uncle do all those things?"

"Some of them, yeah. Because they had to."

"So you had help with homework and sunscreen." The nonchalant way his dad shrugged made Landon want to punch him. "Why'd you need me?"

"Because it's the little things that count, Dad." He ran his fingers through his hair. "It's the little things that tell somebody . . . every day . . . that you love them."

"I know you think I should have been around more when you were a kid." His dad sat on the couch. "But I wasn't, okay? There ain't nothin' I can do about that now. Can we just see it for what it is, man-to-man?"

Landon nodded. "I've been hanging around Tallahassee since I graduated, thinking maybe our relationship would change. Maybe we would talk about things, *man-to-man*. Telling myself I had to stay here, when there's a whole world out there." He swept his arm in a wide gesture. "I didn't even look at other options, because deep down, I thought staying close would mean I would be here when you came around. When you showed up on my doorstep one day to tell me you wanted to be a part of my life."

Martin's eyes narrowed. "It's her, isn't it? She wants you to move somewhere."

Landon gave a humorless laugh. "We haven't even talked about that. I don't know for sure that she even wants me. But at least she's taught me . . ."

"To dump your old man?"

"She's taught me what it's like to be loved. What people do when they care about each other." These were thoughts he'd never had before Gina came along. Words he might never say again. But then, leaving your dad required extraordinary measures, beyond the everyday. "For the first time since Mama died I feel . . . worth something."

Gina had come to town to help wrongly convicted prisoners, but she'd also helped Landon climb to freedom.

His dad smirked. "You want in her pants so bad, you can't even think straight."

Landon's mind went to the curves of Gina's naked body, but that was none of his dad's business. He wanted to tell the old man to shut the fuck up about her. "We're talking about you and me, Dad. Not her."

"So you're moving? Is that what you're trying to tell me?"

"I'm saying I would love to have you in my life. I would love for my kids to one day have a grandfather. But it's not going to be one with liquor on his breath. And it's not going to be one who only comes around when he needs something. I'm not putting my life on hold for you anymore."

Martin sat for several minutes with his elbows on his knees, staring at the floor. Landon wanted to fill the silence, to jump in and add more, but he made himself remain quiet. He'd said what he'd wanted to say, and now it was his dad's turn. He'd been waiting on his father his whole life. Surely he could wait another minute or two.

Finally, Martin took a deep sigh and stood. "I may have been a total screwup as a dad, but at least I did one thing," he said as he walked to the door.

"Gave me my size?" Like everyone else, his dad saw him first as a football player. "Or my throwing arm?"

"All the crap I put you through"—his dad laid a hand on his shoulder—"gave you strength. Made you man enough. To have this conversation." His eyes misted. "I'm proud of you, son."

The older man walked slowly toward the door and walked out. Walked away from Landon's life.

Maybe for a while.

Maybe forever.

Landon stood in the middle of his living room for several minutes after the door had shut.

I'm proud of you, son.

Okay, so it wasn't "I love you," but it was the most recognition he'd ever gotten from his dad.

The fact that the conversation was over made Landon feel freer. Lighter. Every day since he was nine years old, he'd wondered why his dad hadn't come to get him. What he'd done to make his dad so mad that he didn't love him.

But now that burden had been lifted. Yeah, it sucked that he'd lived through it, but now he was done. He *was* worthy of someone's love. Gina had taught him that he was good enough for her and anyone else. She'd given him a sense of worthiness he'd never had before.

He was ready to move on with the rest of his life.

And he hoped like hell that Gina would agree to come along.

∾

Gina held the iced Frappuccino to the side of her face as she waited for Landon to answer the door. The five-minute walk to the coffee shop had done nothing but make her hot and increase her anxiety. She was worried about what had been going on between Landon and his father.

He jerked the door open and stopped. She studied him, waiting for some hint of what might happen between them. How this conversation might end. Finally, he rushed toward her and wrapped his arms around her in a hug so tight her drink squished between them, its coldness like a shard of ice between their warm bodies. She inhaled his scent, wondering if this would be the last time they'd be this close.

"God, am I glad to see you." His breath tickled her ear as he spoke.

Her rib cage shuddered with emotion. "I didn't know your dad would be here."

Landon released her and took the now-squished cup from her hands. He dropped it onto the sidewalk outside his condo and pulled her through the door behind him.

He stopped in the entry hallway and faced her. "He was supposed to be here two hours ago, but he's the most unreliable person I know." His hand cupped her chin. His fingers stroked her cheek. "I told him I was done. Finished with him."

A sudden fear sliced through her. What if she'd been wrong? What if Martin Vista was about to be the kind of man his son needed and now Landon had dumped him? "You did *what?*"

Landon ran his fingers through his hair, leaving the curls a jumbled mess. "I'm not going to wait around for him to want to see me anymore. If he wants to be a part of my life, it's his doing. His choice."

"And this is . . . okay with you?" Was he glad to have come to the decision? Or upset that it came to this? She tried to read his expression.

"It makes me feel better. Yeah." He moved closer, pinning her against the wall in the hallway. His arms framed her head. "Like I've been in a bad movie, but now it's over and I can move on to the next part of my life."

She swallowed. The next part of Landon's life. The part beyond this summer and beyond her internship at Morgan's Ladder. The part of his life without her. Like he'd said the other night, the part where he'd always *remember* her.

She looked down at their feet. She couldn't watch his face while she asked the next question. "So what are you going to do?"

"I hear Nashville's not a bad place to live." He nuzzled her ear. "At least until some hot volleyball player figures out where her first lawyer gig is going to be."

Her head shot up. "You . . . want to move to Nashville?"

"Who else is going to make sure you don't live the rest of your life in the shadow of Nick Varnadore?"

Yes. Nick Varnadore. For a few brief seconds, she'd forgotten the guilt and grief of it all, but now it was back. "You really think I need to deal with that, don't you?"

His green eyes bored into hers. "Yeah, I do. But I'm going to be there for you. For as long as it takes."

"I told you I loved you and you . . ." She couldn't finish. It hurt her too much to know that he'd said nothing in response to that.

"I'm a guy. We do really stupid things sometimes."

But he hadn't said he loved her. She nodded and pressed her lips together, determined not to let him see her disappointment. "I've thought a lot about what you said. And you were right. I need to decide what I want to do with my life."

"And have a career that *you* want to have? Not because your guilt is driving you to it?"

She nodded. "Will you help me get through it?"

He wrapped his arms around her. His fingers threaded through her hair as she rested her head on his shoulder.

"I didn't mean to hurt you," she whispered. "What I said about your dad."

His chest vibrated as he chuckled. "No. I'm pretty sure at the time you were going in for the kill."

She looked up and grinned. "So I'm a better fighter than you are. We established that on the volleyball court that first night we met."

One side of his mouth quirked up, but his demeanor was serious. He took a deep breath. She stilled, waiting to see what he'd say next.

"I've never come close to falling in love with anyone." He twined his fingers through hers on either side of them. "But with you . . . I'm not even sure when it happened." His voice was thick with emotion. "God, I love you so much."

Her body wanted to fly and collapse, all at the same time. Like a great weight had been lifted from her, she felt relieved and set free, all because of his words. "You don't know how badly I've wanted to hear you say that."

"We've got a lot to talk about. I really do want to move to Nashville with you. I'll quit my job and break my lease and—"

She placed a hand on his forearm. She'd come here on a mission and she needed to complete it. "I need to give you something."

He backed away, a puzzled look on his face, as she reached into her pocket.

"The prosecutor's office was done with this. They said you could have it."

She hated that such an important item was in a crumpled plastic bag, but she'd wanted to give it to him as soon as Suzanne had given it to her.

"What is it?" he asked.

She nodded toward the baggie. "Look at it."

His questioning eyes finally left hers as he dumped the item into the palm of his hand. "My mother's bracelet." He turned over the charm and touched his engraved name with his fingertip. His eyes glistened with unshed tears. "I . . . didn't think I'd ever see this again."

"Suzanne had told them she wanted to get it to you as soon as she could." She reached up and touched it. "She wanted you to have it."

He smiled. "She's brought a lot of good to me this summer."

Gina grinned. "Maybe you should apologize for yelling at her that first day you met her."

"I think we're going to have to name our first child after her."

Gina's eyes widened. He laughed.

"You're already thinking about having babies?" she asked. A warm feeling blossomed through her chest. He really did want to spend his life with her.

He nipped at the end of her nose. "I think the Seminoles are going to need a good quarterback in another eighteen or nineteen years."

"But what if *she* wants to go to Tennessee instead?"

"Let's argue about this later," he said as his lips settled on hers. His tongue explored her mouth. Though their previous kisses had been hot, this one was different. This one had the certainty of love. It held more promise of the future.

With her back against the wall, she could feel every hard ridge of his body as he pressed against her. He raised her hands above her head and held them there with one of his while his other hand glided down her rib cage and her hip.

"We need to get this slushie off our chests," he whispered as he nibbled at her earlobe.

She reveled in the tenderness of his mouth against her neck. "It's a Frappuccino."

"Whatever." He flicked the sensitive spot behind her ear with his tongue. "We need to get it off."

"Did you have something in mind?"

"Come with me." He took her hand and led her toward his bedroom. "I'll show you."

ACKNOWLEDGMENTS

Though writing is a solitary venture, no author travels this path alone. Special thanks to the following people:

- Thriller writer Steve Berry (www.SteveBerry.org), whose down-to-earth presentation at my first writers' conference convinced me that I could do this. Also, because he led me to Frank Green.

- Frank Green, whose weekly writing workshop has produced forty-five-plus published novels; thanks also to the various writers who populate Frank's living room every Wednesday night and who helped me learn the craft.

- Jill Marsal for her ability to show me how to make this story stronger.

- Maria Gomez for taking a chance on an unpublished writer.

- The First Coast Romance Writers, the Lucky 13s, and Romance Writers of America.

- The many accomplished romance writers who have shared their wisdom along the way, including Lena Diaz, Valerie Bowman, Alyssa Day, Renee Ryan, Mary Buckham, Vanessa Kelly, Terri Ridgell, Madeline Martin, Ava Milone, Lisa McKinney, Eileen Ann Brennan, and many others.

ABOUT THE AUTHOR

Photo by Michael Straley, 2014

As a child growing up in the Ozarks, Sheila Athens developed a love for the natural beauty of the outdoors and the quiet reflection involved in writing. Her earliest pieces included character sketches for her dolls and theatrical works for the neighborhood children. After many years—which included marriage, a couple of careers, and earning a master's degree—she bought her first romance novel in a hotel gift shop and her new dream was born. Now she writes stories that celebrate the power of love. In 2013 she became a finalist in the Romance Writers of America's Golden Heart contest. She currently resides in the South with her husband of twenty-five years and their two teenage sons.